Adrian Clarke

Rachel Cusk is the Whitbread Award–winning author of two memoirs and seven novels. In 2003, she was chosen as one of *Granta*'s Best of Young British Novelists. She lives in Brighton, England.

## ALSO BY RACHEL CUSK

# The Bradshaw Variations

RACHEL CUSK

PICADOR

FARRAR, STRAUS AND GIROUX

NEW YORK

The Library of Congress has cataloged the Farrar, Straus and Giroux edition as follows:

Cusk, Rachel, 1967–
    The Bradshaw variations / Rachel Cusk.—1st American ed.
    p. cm.
    ISBN 978-0-374-10081-0
    1. Families—Fiction. 2. Domestic fiction. I. Title.
    PR6053.U825B73 2010
    823'.914—dc22

                                                                2009031888

Picador ISBN 978-0-312-68067-1

Originally published in Great Britain by Faber and Faber Limited

First published in the United States by Farrar, Straus and Giroux

First Picador Edition: March 2011

P1

There's nothing remarkable about it. All one has to do is hit the right keys at the right time and the instrument plays itself.

J. S. BACH

[Bach] taught us how to find originality within an established discipline; actually – how to live.

JEAN-PAUL SARTRE

# The Bradshaw Variations

# I

What is art? Thomas Bradshaw asks himself this question frequently. He does not yet know the answer. He used to believe art was a kind of pretending, but he doesn't think that any more. He uses the word *authenticity* to describe what he thinks now. Some things are artificial and some are authentic. It is easy to tell when something is artificial. The other is harder.

In the mornings he listens to music, to Bach or Schubert. He stands in the kitchen in his dressing gown. He waits for his wife and daughter to come downstairs. He is forty-one, the age when a life comes out of its own past like something out of a mould; and either it is solid, all of a piece, or it fails to hold its shape and disintegrates. The disintegration is not difficult to imagine. It is the solidity, the concrete form, that is mystifying. Disintegration does not involve questions of authenticity, but of a solid form the questions must be asked.

Mostly, in fact, it is the lodger Olga who comes down first. He hears her tread on the stairs and doesn't recognise it: that is how, every day, he identifies her, by hearing her quiet, slightly plodding step and wondering who on earth it belongs to. She ducks her peroxided head at him, flashes her uncertain train-track smile. For six months now Olga has been embroiled in protracted dentistry. Beneath the metal braces her teeth are grey and disorderly. As a child her mother apparently never took her to the dentist. This was not out of neglect, Olga has told him. It was because Olga was frightened of going, and her mother couldn't bear her to be frightened, or to feel pain. She has told Thomas that she is saving up for a bridge and a set of caps. She has three different jobs and all the money goes on her teeth. She complains of the expense: in Poland the cost of dentistry is much lower. There, she could have all the work done – 'All!' Olga repeats, making a chopping motion with her hand – for what she pays here for just one monthly visit.

These conversations do not entirely engage Thomas. When he talks to Olga he is both there and not there. He is waiting for Tonie to come down, as the platform guard waits for the London train to come through. Tonie's appearances in the kitchen are brief. Like the train she stops, disgorging activity, and then departs again. It is a matter of minutes, but he needs to be ready. He hears Olga – in some ways he even identifies himself with her, both of them platform dwellers – but when she speaks he cannot reciprocate. He is as though sealed behind glass. He wonders if she realises this, realises that she can see but not touch him. She drinks tea from a giant Garfield mug and eats cereal, topping up the milk frequently from the plastic container that stands beside her bowl. He glimpses her bare, mushroom-coloured legs beneath the table, her feet clad in large soft slippers. He turns the music up a little: it is an offering, a form of explanation. He wants her to know that he is aware of his own limitations, of his failure to make anything of their conversations in the morning. Sometimes this failure appears to him as something intrinsic to time itself, as an inner force, like decay. They pass and are forgotten, these interludes in the kitchen. And yet they are always the same: he could stand here for a hundred years and still have much the same conversation with Olga. There are, it seems, limitless copies of this conversation, but it never goes anywhere or develops. By the same token, it never dies. It has no relationship to time. This may be because it lacks authenticity.

At seven-thirty Tonie comes down and Olga goes up. Olga has a cleaning job at the hospital: her shift starts at eight. Tonie gets the seven-fifty train. It interests Thomas to see that while Olga's priority is food, Tonie gives precedence to her appearance. She stays upstairs until the last possible minute, while Olga sits at the table for half an hour or more in her dressing gown, working at her mug and bowl. Upstairs doors bang, taps run, Tonie's footsteps stalk to and fro. Olga gets up and slowly carries her dishes to the sink, her slippers dragging and hissing across the floor, and reties her dressing-gown cord before beginning her unhurried ascent to her room. Sometimes she and Tonie pass on the stairs and Tonie says, 'Hi, Olga,' in a voice that is half whisper, very deep and throaty, very exotic and *distrait*, as though she has just disentangled herself from a situation that is too complex and passionate to explain. 'Hello!' Olga replies, cheerful as a trumpet.

The stairs run through the core of the tall, narrow house and the treads are uncarpeted. The footsteps go up and down them like arpeggios up and down a keyboard. To Thomas the rooms at the top have a sweet, tinkling atmosphere, light-filled and harmonious. The kitchen, where he stands in his dressing gown, is in the basement. It is deep and sonorous: it underpins the melody of the house with its static, structural confirmations. Tonie does not like being in the kitchen. She is always carrying things on trays up to the higher regions. She has taken down the curtains to let in more light. Sometimes she cleans it, thoroughly and punitively, but her feelings do not change. Thomas, however, is happy down here. He likes the atmosphere of the bass clef, its fundamentality, its insistence on necessities. It is in the basement that he has begun to consider time, and its relationship to authenticity. It is here that he has discovered an underlying structure, a plan. Often he doesn't change out of his dressing gown until eleven or twelve o'clock. By then he is finished with the revelations of the bass clef. He turns off his music. He is ready to read. Reading, he admits, has to be done on a sofa, upstairs.

Tonie eats, drinks coffee, standing up at the counter. She wears bracelets that rattle when she lifts her cup to her lips and glances at her watch. She has, he thinks, an atmosphere of quest about her, of honour. She will join the seven-fifty as the soldier joins his departing regiment. She will not think about him all day; she will not think about Alexa, nor about the sun moving in golden panels across the floorboards of their room, the clock ticking in the hall, the sounds of cars and voices that drift in from the street and then vanish, the day passing through the house, passing irretrievably through its core, its very fibres. She will be valiant not to think about these things, but she will derive, he knows, a rudimentary pleasure from it too. It is the pleasure of self: Thomas knows because he has felt it himself. Once it was he who stood there, clean, bright-eyed, dressed for departure, and Tonie who remained behind to witness the day's passage. Did she wear a dressing gown? He isn't sure. He can't recall what she looked like when he was leaving her. She was part of a pattern, like a figure in a tapestry, woven into her setting.

She puts things into her bag. She says something, but the music is so loud that she has to repeat it, raising her voice. It is Schubert's *Fantasiestücke*. She says,

'I've got a meeting. I won't be back before eight.'

'Okay,' he says loudly. 'Fine.'

He goes to turn the music down but it is too late. She has

swung her bag over her shoulder and is moving towards the stairs.

Alexa is still asleep. She lies in her bed like a girl in a fairy tale. In sleep she is very soft. She exudes something, a kind of mist, as though when she sleeps she sets aside her solidity and takes on the transmutable properties of light and liquid and air. Thomas doesn't want to dwell too much on his daughter's beauty. He looks at her but he can give no name to his looking, no motive. He would like an artist to paint her. It would be easier to look at a painting of Alexa than at Alexa herself.

Later, downstairs, she sits at the table, neat in her uniform. She wears her hair precisely parted and brushed into a ponytail. She is so orderly: every day it is the same.

'Are you going to the shops today?'

Thomas muses, rubbing his chin.

'I don't know,' he says. 'Why, what do you want?'

'I need batteries.'

He stands at the window, looking out at the garden. It is September. The year has always been fixed at this point, pinned to its backing of time like a butterfly in an exhibition case: September is the skewering place, the heart, where the pin of routine is thrust in. But this year it is different. For almost the first time in his life he has not gone back into harness at the summer's end. He has not returned to work: the pin has not been driven home. He is free or he is cast out, one or the other. Alexa is speaking to him.

'– size for my clock,' she says.

'What? What are you talking about?'

'You need to get the right size for my clock.'

'What clock?'

'My alarm clock. It's stopped.'

7

He sighs. A little thread of headache is inching across his brow. Why does an eight-year-old child need an alarm clock? It is the pin of routine again, searching for its mark. She is standing in front of him now.

'I'll try to remember,' he says.

She has something in her hand. She places it on the counter in front of him.

'That's the size of battery you need,' she says.

'Where did you get that?'

'I took it out of the clock. It doesn't work any more. I need two. Please don't forget.'

'I might forget. I said I'll try.'

She is frustrated. She wants to impose her will on him, to exact his promise. It is artificial, this conversation. He sometimes has conversations with Tonie that are like this, that are showcases for the determination of one or the other of them.

'Please,' she says.

'I'll do my best.'

The doorbell rings. It is her friend Georgina, tall and strong-limbed and responsible, reassuringly earnest. They walk to school together in the mornings, Georgina gripping Alexa's arm when they go over at the crossing and looking wildly about her for cars, as though they might at any moment find themselves under enemy fire. He kisses Alexa goodbye. Later, when she comes back, she doesn't ask about the batteries. He has forgotten all about them. It is only when he is putting her to bed that he remembers.

'I'll get them tomorrow,' he says.

She nods unhappily. Then she says:

'Can I borrow your clock for tonight?'

He is almost angry with her, but instead he feels sorrowful. He pities her for the inanity of her persistence. He is disappointed in her.

'All right,' he says.

'I want to wake up early,' she says.

'I can wake you up.'

She looks at him. She doesn't trust him.

'I'd rather have the clock.'

'All right.'

'Will you set it for seven?'

He laughs. 'All right.'

She sits back in her pillows, contented.

'From now on I'm going to get up early and have breakfast with Mummy,' she says. 'I've decided.'

His heart clenches, just as it does when the music gains its highest note, grasping and grasping out of its own confusion until it reaches its mark and the screw of emotion is turned. The confusion, he sees, is necessary, for it is what the resolution is born from. It was necessary, in other words, for him to misunderstand Alexa in order that he might understand her. He is satisfied by this perception. He opens a book and begins to read to her. Every night he does this, sometimes for as long as an hour. At first he was self-conscious reading aloud, but he isn't any more. When he reads he feels as though he is flying through darkness, lit by the single bulb of Alexa's bedside lamp; he is unbodied, a soaring arrow, a force of pure narration. In her books he finds explanations for everything, for love and survival, struggle and pleasure, happiness and grief, for belief, for the shape and arc of life itself. The only thing that is never explained is reality. He sprawls on her bed while she sits neatly beneath the covers. Her eyes are brown, tawny: in the half-light they seem rich with age, like mahogany. Their beauty is at once his and not his. He does not own them, yet they are within his possession. She does not look at him while he reads. She looks into empty space – she is visualising. This is one of the causes of his lack of inhibition. Were she to look at him, he would instantly regain the formality of personality. As it is, he can forget himself. At some point, usually, he begins to weep. Unlike most of the people he knows, Thomas has never mislaid his ability to cry. They are clear, abundant tears that roll soundlessly down his cheeks as he reads. It is the stories that release them. Freed from reality, he weeps over the image of life.

Afterwards he wipes his cheeks and kisses her goodnight, and goes downstairs to wait for Tonie to come home.

# II

On the train, Tonie thinks about sex. It's like some old friend she hasn't seen in years and then bumped into on the platform. She rides with it in the carriage, her old friend sex, who one way and another she lost touch with, somewhere around the time when Alexa was born, when love seemed like a mathematical problem to which, all of a sudden, she had found the answer.

The other passengers, daylight chorusing in their faces, the mood transitive, a shedding of properties: the train flies through the September morning and Tonie feels it, an element that is all surface, all publicity. She is a little suspicious, almost resentful. It is as though she has blundered uninvited into some event and discovered that everyone she knows is there. So! This is what people are up to, while women care for babies in wholesome rooms, while they push strollers through the slow afternoon, satisfied that they have solved the problem of love. The rest of the world doesn't care about love at all. The rest of the world is pure self, present tense, neither bad nor good, just flying free through the morning's instant. And it comes over her in a rush, the memory of what it used to feel like, being alive.

On the way home she bumps into it again.

A month into her new job, the evening train, the mood reflective. There is a rushing darkness at the windows and yellow portraits on the glass, like the steady images a light makes from a black river of film. What has she been doing all this time? This is the question, after an eight-year absence. At intervals, her husband has turned to her in their bed and posed questions with his body: do you still love me? Is everything all right? And she has acceded, as often as she has been able to, not wanting to trouble him with her strange numbness, her indifference. What else? Giving, caring, watching, remembering, feeling, but not – not truly – participating. It's been like reading a great book, life represented as fully and beautifully as it could be but the commodity itself suspended. All her sympathies have been engaged, and left her body motionless, inert.

At the station she gets a taxi.

Thomas, in the kitchen, slightly tired-looking, the crow's feet standing in bright starbursts around his eyes. It is nine-fifteen. He has made food for her, something heaped on a plate in the oven, keeping warm. He is wearing an apron. She laughs. She reaches around his waist, trying to untie the strings. He looks bashful, a little foolish. He looks shy, embarrassed, like a young girl with someone trying to undo her bra strap.

'I'll do it,' he says.

When they kiss it is fumbling, slightly awkward, and Tonie laughs again, against his teeth. There seem to be folds and folds of blankness between them. She struggles to break through it. He is like a well-packaged object she is trying to get to, tearing away the blank wrapping. It is as though he is resisting her, as though he doesn't want to be found. Her determination begins to drain away. There is too much reality, too much light in the kitchen, too much visual detail of ordinary things. And she has a sudden fraternal sense of Thomas that is like a bucket of cold water poured over her head. He is over-familiar. They have stood together in this kitchen too many times.

The kissing peters out. They hug, comrades.

'What's in there?' Tonie says, still in his arms but looking out, down, at the humming oven. Usually it is Alexa they look out and down at, the view from themselves, the distraction that has become a necessity. But the oven will do.

'Fish pie. Do you want some?'

So Tonie eats it, the pale mound of fodder, the creamy potato that sticks to the roof of her mouth, and it is hard to reconcile this filling of herself with the wanting feeling she had earlier. The potato stops her tongue, sits like a boulder in her stomach. It is a kind of imprisonment, to feel so full, when it was something else that she was asking for.

But the next night it's different.

She comes back even later, ten o'clock, and this time there's no food and Thomas is more alert, more mysterious. They sit in the sitting room on opposite chairs.

'It won't always be like this,' Tonie says. 'I'll get quicker. I have to read everything four times. I have to suck up to everyone.'

'We're all right. Do what you need to do.'

He's wearing a dark blue shirt that makes him look sharper, clearer, less fuzzily familiar. Seen objectively Thomas is good-looking, pale fine-grained skin, fine black hair that falls over his face, something light and boyish about him though he is tall and broad-shouldered. Tonie's female friends make envious jokes about Thomas. They see him objectively, but Tonie doesn't. She sees him in pieces, from particular angles. Sometimes, when they are away from the house, she is amazed to see him walking down the street towards her, whole.

In the bedroom she turns away while he undresses. She waits until he switches out the light. She is determined to hang on to this gossamer inspiration, desire. She knows that if her eye falls on the alarm clock with the big ear-like bells, on the toys Alexa has left on the floor of their room, even on Thomas himself, it will break. She needs Thomas to become a stranger again. She needs to reinvent him. Is that wrong? He might think it was, if she told him. But not telling is what will make a stranger of herself.

And it is exactly as she had hoped, in the way that a performance of a play might be, the feeling of a structure, an event, passing through time unharmed. The form was honoured: nobody made a mistake or fluffed a line. It is strange, that transcendence should occur not by abandoning structure but by adhering to it exactly. Thomas turns to her, strokes her hair. In the darkness he is a shape, autonomous. It is a long time since she has felt him to be so distinct from herself. It is from the distinctness that the closeness, the harmony, has arisen.

In the middle of the night she wakes up and he is still there, the shape, draped in shadow. He is as beautifully turned as a musical instrument, as finished, as mute and solitary lying on his side in the darkness. The desire is this: to find him, to use him, to make him respond. It is the only way that she can possess him, as the musician possesses the instrument, and though it feels like youth again it is not, not at all. As a young woman she did not possess the bodies of men. They possessed her. She was the instrument, in those days. And the time in between has been a blank, a silence, because after Alexa was born she was neither instrument nor performer but creator, alone suddenly, her body a slump of giving, all untouchable aftermath. It did not recognise the discipline of performance. It wanted only to be left alone.

She puts out her hand and touches the skin of Thomas's neck, his back, his taut rounded shoulder. He wakes up. She feels it, the vibration of life under her hand. He turns to her, mouth slightly open, eyes shut. He obeys her.

Montague Street runs straight downhill towards the city. It is steep, so that the bottom looks remote from the top, the hazy geometric spill of buildings levelling out below with its light-inflected blocks and angles, its wreath of pollution, its drone of traffic and sense of life as something inalienable and general rather than fragile and particular, though close up this illusion is successively unmasked as the moderate scale of the reality becomes clearer. The town is just a picturesque, convenient, middle-sized town an hour from London. But from the top, where the Bradshaws live, it has an appearance of grandeur and ruination.

Theirs is a region of parks and churches – the former small and crowded, the latter large and empty – and of row after row of red-brick two-storey Victorian terraces that rise and fall across the undulating townscape, and that again conjure up an atmosphere of generality, the image of a contented and solidly unexceptionable bourgeoisie, as opposed to the fretful-looking, badly paid liberal professionals who for the most part live in them: academics like Tonie, teachers, social workers.

In Tonie's experience, these are people whose capacity for deep, undisclosed suffering and worldly indifference, for extreme feats of virtue or nihilism, for the repression of passions and staunchness in the face of reality, is so violent that it ought to leave some visible mark on their surroundings; and yet the surface of their lives is so bare as to suggest a reluctance to impose themselves on the world that runs deeper still. Time and again she has visited her neighbours' houses and found them to be lacking both luxuries and necessities, found rooms empty of furniture or ornament, stained walls with no pictures on them, cardboard boxes that have never been unpacked, desolate shelves, and in the face of it all a kind of impregnable vagueness, a dreaminess, that acquaints Tonie with her own alertness, her fathomless determination, and suggests these qualities are not, after all, entirely normal. Take her friend Elsa, for instance: entering Elsa's house for the first time, Tonie assumed they had only just moved into it, so powerful was its atmosphere of unoccupation, when in fact Elsa and her husband had lived there for years. In the hall there was a strip of wallpaper hanging loose, which Elsa admitted having torn off one day to see what was underneath – blood-coloured flowers and creeping foliage, better not to have known – and which hangs there still. Tonie would have had the whole lot off in an evening, would not have rested until it was all gone and something new and good put in its place; and yet Elsa is a virtuous woman, a woman who teaches disabled children, who would drop everything to help if Tonie was ill or in trouble, who has welcomed time into her face unprotestingly, though it has been brutal to her. When Tonie sees Elsa, sees the torn tongue of paper still lolling from the wall and the sitting room still full of boxes, she wonders what the meaning, what the moral value of her own competence is. She sees that she herself is not virtuous, in spite of the fact that she is driven by what feels like guilt or compunction. She would not rest until the imperfect was excised and the good accomplished, and it would feel like rightness itself was thrashing her and egging her on. But in Elsa's tattered hall she acknowledges that it is not rightness: it is the desire for success.

The houses in Montague Street are different from the rest, narrow and tall and white, Georgian, impractical. The world always offers a small opportunity for difference, among a large majority of things that are all the same; and equally unfailingly Tonie takes it, only remembering afterwards that being different is not the same as being right. She was besotted with the house at first, so that rationality, calm consideration, common sense could get no hold on her. They manifested themselves as purely hostile, as things that had only and ever sought to frustrate her, which made it right – rightness again – to defy them and cast them off for good.

It's true that the house is unusual. There is something fantastical about its narrowness and height, its overhanging windows, its quivering appearance of unfeasibility. It is more like a drawing – a sketch – than a building. It takes only a few paces to go from the front of it to the back: you walk through the door and the tiny garden is staring you in the face. When people come in there is always a moment of startled hesitation, a sense of spatial misjudgement, as though they were about to lose their footing on the edge of a cliff. They exclaim, half in wonder, but just as much out of consternation. Tonie does not like it when this happens. For seven years she and Thomas have lived in this house, and the steady disclosure of its shortcomings, its particular flaws, has had something almost sermonising about it. The rooms downstairs are dark; the windows are draughty and the garden too small; the sloping doorframes and uneven boards, most of all the ceaseless going up and down, up and down like a tune in search of a resolution – these things fray Tonie's nerves and exhaust her. Stuck with her choice, Tonie is being taught a lesson, which is that desire is dangerous, because it is magnetised by its antithesis, actuality. And actuality, no less automatically, is drawn to desire. What are you meant to do with a desire if not act on it? Living in her thin and

fantastical house Tonie has been haunted by new desires –
for the anonymous, the spacious, the frankly horizontal. She
has imagined large suburban lawns and garages, broad avenues, a house low and wide. It appears to her now that
it would be easier to distinguish yourself in such a house;
that time would stand more still; that the human subject
would be picked out, highlighted against the neutrality, so
that the glamour of being alive – so ineluctable, so hope-
lessly entrenched in the province of desire – could finally be
actualised.

What happened was that all those years ago, she fell in
love with the house: she fell in love with it, and then as she
came to know more and more about it the love was divided
and subdivided until each piece of knowledge was larger than
its allotted share of affection. This is the lesson, the sermon:
that facts outlive emotions, and that knowledge is therefore
more powerful than love. There are infinite things to know,
but the capacity for love is just that, a capacity, a space that
can hold so much and no more.

Six months ago, the head of the university English department where Tonie teaches retired. It was a strange time, no
one rushing forward to replace her, a feeling everywhere of
indifference bordering on decline, until someone asked Tonie
whether she would consider applying for it. It was out of the
question, a big administrative job a whole world away from
the part-time lecturing she was used to, a job for someone
like Angela Deacon, who had done it for years; an older
woman with a wardrobe full of cashmere and earth-tones, a
woman with grown-up children and an interest in Etruscan
art, a still-married woman who nonetheless wanted to keep
the little flame of her wickedness alive, who wanted her well-

preserved body out in the world, safe in its armour of bureaucratic procedure. Tonie couldn't do a job like that, that needed funds of time brought to it like a dowry. Tonie's time did not seem to belong to her any more. Her work had been shaped around Alexa's presences and Thomas's absences for so long that she forgot it had a form and force of its own, a power of its own.

There was a conversation in the kitchen, late at night. Thomas's eyes were watering. He said he had hay fever. Every few minutes he would produce a handkerchief and sneeze into it, and Tonie couldn't keep her fingers still. Sitting at the table she shredded stray bits of paper, orange peel, pieces of wax from the candle on the table, prising off the rivulets that had run down its sides. They looked so soft, so liquid, but they came away as stiff as branches, beaded with hard drops. She and Thomas talked about their life the way they might have talked about a film they had just seen, or a book they'd both read. They analysed it, their situation; they discussed it, and by discussing it seemed to emerge from it and set off somewhere, the two of them heading out over dark waters in the vessel of their companionship. It was as though all this time they'd been acting, playing parts, and now could finally be themselves again. In this atmosphere careers seemed trivial, interchangeable, to be picked up and put down again at will. Tonie snapped the petrified branches of wax into smaller and smaller pieces: they lay on the table like a heap of little bones. Every time she looked at Thomas he had water running from the corners of his eyes, like a saint in a religious painting. She remembers noticing that he was talking about his job in the past tense. He got a bottle of whisky out of the cupboard and poured an enormous measure for each of them. He said,

'I seem to have experienced a revelation.'

But it is true that Thomas has never been quite that sure again, that he became more doubtful as Tonie's promotion became more of a certainty, that even now he appears to be going through a process, an adjustment, as though life has simply hardened around him again in its new forms and the revelation that set it in motion is nowhere to be found. It has no concrete existence, this revelation. It has no reality. It merely changed, for an instant, reality's properties, as the flame changed the candle and sent it running over the edge of itself, running and running into new paths as though it sought to be free of what it was, of what it became once more as soon as it reached the air and stiffened in its tracks.

On the train, she looks at men. Some of them are wholesome-looking, attractive, but most of them aren't. She sits opposite a large, sandy-coloured man with thick white freckled arms protruding from the sleeves of his T-shirt. His hair is flattened in places and shock-straight in others, like a patch of long grass an animal has lain down in. He is fat, thighs melting over the serge seat, stomach lying in pleats over his trousers, white fingers as thick as sausages. It is eight o'clock in the morning. He has tiny speakers in his ears. He sits opposite her and eats an Aero. He stands a can of Coke on the table between them and cracks it open, his finger squeezed through the metal ring.

Compared with him Tonie is disciplined, almost professionally physical. She has entered the phase of atemporality that lies between childbearing and visible decay. And yet she feels taut with expectation, as though now that it has finished its biological work the real life of her body is about to begin. In three months' time she will turn forty, but she was more frightened of getting older when she was younger, when she was thirty-five and seemed all husk, Alexa at three or four the eager unripe kernel, shedding Tonie by degrees. But now it is Alexa who grows older: Tonie stays the same. And she roams around this sameness, excited and anxious, as though there is something in it she fears she won't find.

It is raining when she gets off the train. She takes the bus the rest of the way, pressed up against the other passengers, the windows blank with condensation. The wet smells of skin and hair and cosmetics and shoe leather make a pattern in the silence, an extension into non-language, as though everyone here is trying to describe themselves in a way that words have never accounted for and never will. The bus sways. A grey view of wet pavements and shopfronts flows and stops and flows again past the fogged-up windows. The university buildings – low, concrete, municipal-looking – make their sluggish approach through the middle distance. It is surprising, how many people are picking up their bags and coats and umbrellas, preparing to get off. It's like religion, people rising out of their anonymity, thronging and moving, all in the name of higher education. She sees Janine, shuffling in the crowd towards the doors.

'Hey,' Tonie says.

Janine makes a face, strangulation. 'I'm starting to feel antipathy towards certain social groups,' she says when she's close enough. 'It's the weak I can't stand. Old people, mothers, children in prams.'

Tonie laughs. They get off, go together over the road and through the big glass doors.

'You want coffee?' Janine hesitates by the entrance to the staff cafeteria and they go in, join the queue. She scans the room obliquely, out of the sides of her fronded eyes. She puts a warning hand on Tonie's arm. 'Martin Carson at three o'clock,' she says.

Tonie turns, sees Martin hunched at one of the far-off

Formica tables, spectacled and waistcoated like a character out of *The Wind in the Willows*. He has a slim volume open in front of him, on which his eyes are fixed. His eyebrows are raised. He wears an expression of faint surprise.

'He's *reading*,' Janine hisses.

'Hey Martin, this is, like, the twenty-first century.'

Janine guffaws, bats her eyelashes at the boy behind the serving hatch, orders black no sugar. 'I've realised that I actually find the sight of a man reading effeminate,' she says to Tonie. 'Do you know what I mean?'

Janine looks breathless, blowsy: she looks as though she's been out until dawn, and then rushed straight from the party here. She's wearing old-fashioned film-star clothes, a mauve chiffon dress and high-heeled silver sandals with pointed toes. Her long brown fraying hair looks windblown. She is big-boned and bosomy, frail around the wrists and ankles, the skin of her face and clavicle riven with friendly creases. She is motherly, in a way: Tonie can imagine a male desire that takes this form. Though in fact she has only one child, like Tonie, whom she brings up alone. They sit at a table with their cups.

'God, I feel like shit,' she says, half-closing her eyes. The lids are bruised with make-up. She opens them again. 'Greg and I had a fight last night.'

'What about?'

She swats the air, shakes her head.

'I don't know what exactly. We were just – fighting.'

Tonie wonders how this occurs: Janine's small flat, her daughter there, two adults trying to kindle something in the ashes of everything that has been, and either failing or succeeding in full view of it all. In certain lights she has considered Janine's life and envied it, envied its open-endedness, its lack of structure. She imagines possibilities for Janine that she cannot imagine for herself: the possibility of changing, moving, experiencing the unknown.

'Francesca was at the Bastard's,' Janine says, reading her thoughts. 'Greg came over to spend the night.'

'Is that how it works? She goes and he comes.'

Janine nods. 'Right,' she says. 'Like a French farce.'

'I imagine it less – scheduled.'

'Darling,' Janine says jadedly, 'it's a bloody rota. There's Greg's three from marriage one at the weekends, one from marriage two twice a month, a stepchild who has to fit in somewhere, a dog that needs walking, a cat that has to go to the vet. I'm off-peak nights only.'

'And you spent it fighting. Your night.'

Janine yawns, stretches her mottled arms, shows a crumpled glimpse of speckled armpit. Tonie feels it again, the mother, the taxed body, lapsing into imperfection.

'Well, you're sort of asking for it, aren't you?' Janine says. 'You get home, stash the child, clean up, light the candles, shave your legs, open the wine – you're really asking for your poor plans to be undone. Though in fact, that part was fine. It was later.' She yawns again. 'Three o'clock in the morning, I wake up and he's standing there by the bed.'

'Getting in?'

'Getting out. Apparently I said something in my sleep.'

'What sort of thing?'

'Apparently I said –' Janine laughs '– *Roger.*'

Tonie snorts, slaps the table top.

'So he puts all his clothes back on and he storms out of the room. I thought he'd gone home, and I was so sleepy I thought, you know, fine. I didn't care. I just wanted to go back to sleep. Has that ever happened to you?'

Tonie half-assents, silently.

'I think this is the real disenchantment of later life,' Janine says, pushing away her coffee cup. 'The inability to care. Having cared so much.'

Tonie shudders. 'Stop it.'

'Anyway, after a while I hear noises and I realise he's still here. So I drag myself out of bed and I go into the kitchen and there he is, sitting at the table with all the lights on and his laptop out. Working.'

They laugh: the apparent ridiculousness of male behaviour.

'How are you, anyway?' Janine says. She puts her spoon in the sugar bowl, takes it out and carefully licks it.

'All right.'

Tonie doesn't want to explain: language takes her further away from it, the mystery of her expectation. She remembers travelling somewhere with Thomas once, driving through miles and miles of empty wilderness, the map open on her knees; she remembers the way it looked on the page, the road threading through the emptiness, specifying itself while everything else remained unknown and untouched. They would have to stop, get out, walk. To know what was there they would have to enter it physically.

'I'm just – here,' she says, meaning this place, this concrete building on the roadside.

'Is it what you wanted?' Janine says, bright, matter-of-fact, as though they were discussing a present Tonie had received, both knowing that at their age there was no point masking your disappointment.

'I don't *not* want it. It depends. It depends how it works out.'

She can tell Janine doesn't understand: in Janine's eyes Tonie has done something irrational, has strayed from their particular female church with its ceaseless interpolations of the personal and the practical, its reverence for emotion, its believers-only humour where the punchline is always that you get away with whatever you can. Janine would not understand Tonie's desire for the harsh, the literal, the coldly imposing. She would not understand her decision to set down the sack of emotion.

'I'd miss the teaching,' is all she says, looking over Tonie's shoulder.

She is not the first person to say this to Tonie: here, teaching is equivalent to emotion. The women Tonie knows at home say they would miss the children, in exactly the same way.

'You can't teach if you're sick of books,' Tonie says softly.

She sees it in Janine's eyes, a flash of fear, a spark of genuine teacher's disapproval. There's a second of hesitation, then Janine laughs. She has decided that Tonie is being iconoclastic.

'Books make you sick,' she agrees. 'Literature. A virus.' She screws up her eyes, looks at Tonie through the lashes. 'Though spreadsheets can't be all that interesting.'

Tonie shrugs. She isn't going to defend herself.

'I hope it works out,' Janine says, all at once slightly formal, as though Tonie is going away somewhere and never coming back. Tonie looks up. Martin Carson is standing by their table.

'Oops –' Janine looks at her watch '– I've got to go and teach Hart Crane.'

'Really?' he says, significantly, as though Hart Crane were an opinion, not a poet. He turns to Tonie, bores into her through his thick pebbly lenses. 'How are *you*?' he says.

'Okay,' she says. She looks at her watch too. 'Late.'

'I like what you've done with your hair,' Martin says. He has a transatlantic accent, difficult to place. It makes everything he says sound ironic. Tonie has seen him lash out at his students, has seen him mortify big ropey-limbed boys in baseball caps, silent overweight girls with round cheeks encrusted with make-up and acne. He strikes at them with this ironic-sounding drawl: he makes them seem unfortunate and stupid.

'Thanks.'

'I'll walk with you,' he says.

Janine rolls her eyes, waves her hand, makes a run for it in her silver shoes.

'I have the feeling I interrupted something important there,' Martin says, with professorial satisfaction. 'I was watching your face. You looked – wistful. Sort of sad, but thoughtful.'

He does an imitation of it, there in the crowded corridor. He rests his fingers under his chin and gazes into the middle distance.

'Thanks,' she says again.

They go left and right and left along the grey-walled passages with their littered noticeboards and chipped paint, and Martin sticks to her as they push through the field of bodies, saying, 'Hello,' and, 'How are *you?*' to those students who raise their eyes to him. Instantly they look troubled, slightly guilty, as though their individuality was something they were meant to be concealing. She sees no blaze of youth in these faces, these bodies: they have bad skin, piercings, stiff, artificial-looking hair. They look pensive, irresolute, like people who have got off a train in the wrong town. They look like people to whom nothing has ever been explained.

'Hello, *Jamie,*' Martin says in the lift, to a chalk-white boy with a petrified fan of hair like a cockatoo's. 'I'm glad that you found the time to come *in* today. Really, I'm glad.'

They get out, leave Jamie gaping and solitary in the steel cubicle, pass through the double doors to their offices. ·

'We should have coffee some time,' Martin says, leaning against the door frame where Tonie turns off.

Tonie wants to be in her office, tucked up alone in the grey rectangle with its view of the car park, but instead she says: 'Do you think they're enjoying themselves?'

Martin looks nonplussed. 'Who?'

'The students. Do you think they're having a good time?'

Martin looks at the floor, focuses hard, as though he were being asked to guess at the feelings of a domestic pet.

'You're meaning in the mythological sense, right? Are they self-consciously inhabiting the myth of their own life? Does it mean to them what it meant to you? Right?' He adjusts his glasses, rubs his pale chin. 'The answer's no.'

Tonie can hear her phone ringing inside the room. She rests her fingers on the door handle.

'Oh look,' Martin says. 'They've put up your tombstone.'

She looks. There's a new plaque fixed to the door: DR A. SWANN, HEAD OF DEPARTMENT. Martin shakes his head.

'You seem much too young for that,' he says.

She laughs. 'Well, I'm not.'

He looks, shakes his head again. 'I just can't see it,' he says. 'It isn't you at all. I had you down as the faculty rebel. Obviously,' he fixes her, microscope-eyed, 'I was wrong.'

She smiles, unlocks the door, closes it gently behind her. The phone has stopped ringing. The room is silent. She sees the black swivel chair, the ledger diary, the stacks of files. She sees the car park with its grid of cars, three floors below. People are coming and going there, heads down, staring at the ground. The phone starts to ring again.

Martin Carson is unperceptive. This is the most rebellious thing she has ever done, by far.

27

# III

The other Bradshaws – Thomas's brother Howard, his wife, Claudia, their three children – live a mile or so away, on Laurier Drive, in the suburb of Laurier Park. Howard is a person whose jesting nature, which seemed when he was young to connote a disregard for convention in all its forms, has suffused his adult life with an atmosphere of irony in which his more-than-average conservatism wears the vague disguise of a joke. Thomas sometimes wonders whether his belief that Howard is different from other people is nourished solely by the backgrounds against which he sees him; whether, in a different setting, he might perceive that Howard is, after all, ordinary, and not just pretending to be. The snaking suburban avenues of Laurier Park, with their electronic security gates and floodlit gravel driveways, their smart cars and suggestive topiary and strange atmosphere of cluttered desertion, are the metaphor for Howard's placement of himself in the world. Howard and Claudia like to regale their visitors with stories of the new heights of tastelessness – the outdoor jacuzzis, the obscene statuary, the Hawaiian-themed cocktail bar that has recently been erected in next-door's garden – to which each month their neighbourhood ascends, but Howard's BMW stays parked on his front drive like the others. There are horse chestnut trees there, with big, rustling skirts that shed their cargo of leaves and rinds and nuts inconveniently over the tidy pavements. Occasionally a petition is circulated to have them cut down, and Howard and Claudia are outraged, genuinely so, for it is in the nature of irony to cherish something unironic at its core.

'I *must* paint them,' Claudia says, as though this activity, if she could ever get around to it, would guarantee once and for all their immortality.

Thomas has always regarded Howard as the most successful member of the family. At twenty-five Howard was already rich and losing his hair, two things that seemed to go together, though he has never become as rich as Thomas expected him to be, nor as bald either. It is just that Howard's successes are more real to Thomas than his failures; whereas the opposite is true of his younger brother Leo, whose perfectly comfortable life Thomas perceives through a mist of doubt, so that nothing Leo does ever seems entirely convincing. He understands that these are prejudices and therefore not rational, but sometimes they seem to be more than that, to have come from outside of himself: to be actual forces that govern behaviour and have governed it from the start, as the key signature governs the terms of the melody. From the beginning, it seems to Thomas, Howard was set in a major key and Leo in a minor, and though their lives are their own, to Thomas they will always seem to be resolving their harmonic destiny, as he himself, he supposes, will to them.

Howard has done things over the years that Thomas cannot reconcile with his version of his character, has taken up golf, Christianity, windsurfing, men's groups; has experienced doubt, depression, fanaticism, indifference, and whole seasons of opinion and belief; yet in all these inconsistencies he has demonstrated a fundamental consistency, has passed through discord back to harmony, to himself. Watching Howard live, Thomas has come to realise that it is impossible to fully understand another human being. But there is something else that enables him to anticipate Howard, a profounder divination that tells him what his brother is. Howard's phases intermittently fill him, like passengers filling a train. His behaviour is descriptive: whenever he takes something up, Thomas begins to notice that other people have taken it up too. It is as though Howard is describing the world he lives in. They pass through him, fads and fashions, general beliefs, emotional trends, yet his outward shape, his form, is not altered. It is this, the form, that constitutes Thomas's deeper knowledge of Howard. He does not have this knowledge of other people. Other people he has to learn. They are pure content, information. It is, in a way, a talent, the faculty he has in relation to Howard. He can see the stream and story of life pass through the vessel of his brother: some mysterious gift enables him to.

But sometimes, equally, it is Howard who teaches Thomas, by maintaining a relationship with reality that is more surprising, less predictable, than the life Thomas would have imagined for him. His wealth, for instance: in his early twenties, when he was still a student, Howard went to America and returned with a container-load of strange-looking bicycles, which he had bought with a whole term's grant money and claimed he intended to sell. Thomas remembers his own consternation, his dismay, the headachey feeling it gave him to think of these burdensome, ineradicable bicycles and their shocking impoverishment of Howard, who was forced to borrow money from their father; money he repaid, with interest, before the term was out, having sold every last bicycle and taken orders for more. These days, everyone has bicycles like the ones Howard brought over: Thomas has one himself. The same is true of the skateboards and scooters that, a few years ago, Howard remortgaged the house on Laurier Drive to import. Howard owns his own company: he is successful enough by most standards. It is just that the pattern he established early on has never changed. He risks everything and he profits, but the scale has not, fundamentally, enlarged. This is Howard's tutelary function: his enduring reality provides what Thomas thinks of as structure. The episode with the bicycles gave rise to a fantasy-Howard, a person who does not exist outside Thomas's imagination. Thomas can see him still, an unstoppable entrepreneur rolling in wealth and excess, a man with yachts and investments and a taste for esoteric luxuries, but the real Howard isn't like that at all.

Often, on Sundays, Thomas and Tonie find themselves on their way to Laurier Drive, for in spite of the topiary and the Union Jacks drooping on their polished flagpoles, Howard and Claudia's domain has the magnetism of cultural centrality. Usually, in the car, Tonie complains: she would like their own house to draw and pull the world to itself, or so she thinks. But she is often uneasy and out of sorts when they have visitors. It is this, Thomas supposes, that she is complaining about. She would like to be different, while not understanding precisely what the difference is.

Today, though, she is quiet in the passenger seat. It is late September, a brilliant, brittle day. He glances at her frequently: she seems to revolve in banks of sunlight that fall across her through the windscreen. She puts on her dark glasses, stares out of the window. Since she started her new job, he has noticed that she is more self-contained. The change has revealed her, as a room is revealed by things being tidied up and put away. But her new air of completion is enigmatic in itself: now that he can see her, he finds himself wondering what she truly is.

'All right?' he says.

'Ecstatic,' she replies, huskily.

When they arrive Alexa leaps from the car and vanishes around the side of the house to the garden, from where they can hear the sound of children's voices. Thomas and Tonie go the other way, to the front door, and ring the bell.

'Those are nice,' Tonie says. She touches the chipped stone urn brimming with geraniums that is standing on the doorstep in the autumn sun. She fingers their brash crimson heads. 'Those are so typical.'

She is reflecting on Claudia, on her knack of careless homemaking that pleases Tonie in the same instant that it seems to make her mysteriously unhappy. Tonie's methods are more purgative: she has fits of ruthless cleanliness in which the whole familiar surface of domestic life disappears, as though she were hoping to arrive at beauty by the route of annihilation. In Claudia's house beauty is approached – no less assiduously, Thomas thinks – along the path of randomness. When Tonie comes here she wishes she could be more like Claudia, could be released from her own driving sense of order, could remember certain things and forget others, as Claudia has remembered to plant the geraniums and then forgotten them sufficiently to let them grow. Tonie fingers the geraniums as though they were things she in her madness would have been compelled to tidy away. Howard opens the door. He engulfs Tonie in his slab-like arms and his face appears over her shoulder, round and grinning like a Halloween pumpkin.

'Come and see what we've got,' he says.

He beckons them through the dark core of the house, towards the big open glass doors and the bright garden that stands beyond them. Thomas observes the sweat-stain on the back of his brother's shirt, the redness of his balding scalp.

In middle age Howard has become all surface. His emotions sweep over his large body like weather systems over a prairie. Outside, the children are running across the grass. There is a buzzing noise, incessant, like the sound of a lawnmower. As Thomas comes out, Howard's son Lewis bursts from the greenery at the bottom of the garden, astride a tiny motorbike. He races the others up the lawn and when he reaches the end he turns and drives in a crazy circle around them, before collapsing on his side in the grass, wheels spinning, while they shriek with laughter.

Claudia is standing on the veranda, shielding her eyes from the sun.

'Isn't it *awful*?' she says. 'Howard just imported them from Japan.'

'I've got five thousand of them sitting in a warehouse off the M25,' Howard confirms, delightedly.

Thomas looks at the thing. He tries not to seem aloof, though it disgusts him, disappoints him, this latest proof of Howard's indiscriminateness. By Christmas, a miniature electric motorbike will have made its inevitable way into the province of childhood desire. He feels, suddenly, that it is Howard's fault, that he could stop it, if he chose to.

'What does it run off?'

'You charge them from a unit that feeds straight out of a domestic plug,' Howard says. 'They do twenty miles an hour on the flat.'

'Can you imagine anything more repulsive?' Claudia says. 'The noise alone is enough to drive you out of your senses. And you won't believe what they cost –'

'Five hundred, online price,' Howard says, nudging Thomas in the ribs.

'You'd have to be *sick*,' Claudia says. 'Don't you think?'

Tonie is standing with her hands on the rail, looking down at the lawn. She has put her dark glasses on again. Today she is dressed all in black, black trousers and shirt, a black leather jacket.

'Oh, come on,' she says, smiling. 'It looks fun.'

Claudia draws to Tonie's side, fingers the lapel of her jacket. She does not, Thomas thinks, like to be thought of as anti-fun.

'Darling, you're *très rock* today,' she says, admiringly. 'I felt sure you were a disapproving liberal, but now I can see how wrong I was.'

She herself wears old clogs, a poncho, flared corduroy trousers. When Howard met Claudia she was still a student at art college. It is part of the mythology of Claudia and Howard's life that he carried her off before she could finish her degree. The myth makes it difficult to remember exactly what happened. Claudia has a painting studio at the bottom of the garden, a kind of memorial to her forsaken career. To Thomas her clothes are symbolic too, commemorative, like the uniforms veterans wear on Remembrance Day to remind people of their sacrifices.

'I approve of everything now,' Tonie says.

'What a pleasing thought,' Claudia says brightly. 'I grow increasingly bitter. I'm turning to vinegar, like corked wine.'

'Oh, *darling*,' Howard says.

'The thing is,' she continues, 'I just don't want to believe people will buy them. I don't want to believe they're that stupid.'

Howard puts his arm around her, red-faced, smiling beatifically.

'Let's bloody hope they are,' he says.

'You see?' Claudia says triumphantly, though it is unclear what they are meant to be seeing.

'Well,' Howard says reproachfully, 'we've got to pay the mortgage somehow.'

'If it were up to me,' Claudia announces, 'there wouldn't *be* any mortgage.'

Howard looks bemused, as though, unlike everyone else, he has never heard Claudia say such things before. 'Claude, it *is* up to you.'

Claudia sighs. 'Why do we *need* all this? All this – establishment. Other people don't need so much. Personally I'd be happy to make do with far less.' Her gaze wanders over the bulky brick-coloured house, the expansive lawn, the trees in their autumn foliage, the numerous children. She appears to be deciding which parts of it she could dispense with. 'All *I* really need is my studio. The way things are, I hardly go in there from one month to the next. I don't have time.'

Howard looks stricken. 'We'll make more time,' he says. 'You should have all the time you need. We'll sort it out.'

'The problem is,' Claudia says to the others, 'that you don't make any money out of painting. Other people would have to make sacrifices. And they simply wouldn't do it.'

She disappears into the house. Howard's eyes follow her beseechingly.

'Poor Claude,' he says. 'She's too unselfish. All you women are too unselfish.' He goes after her to the door and puts his head in. 'Darling!' he calls. 'Is there a drop of wine we could offer our guests? And is there any of that avocado gunk left from last night?'

He sits, pulls up a chair for Tonie and rubs his hands together, happy again.

'These are good times,' he says. 'These are beautiful days, all of us together. Aren't we lucky to have this?'

Tonie smiles. She likes Howard in this mood. 'We are,' she says.

'And the children – look at them! Look at the lucky little sods. Think what their lives could have been like somewhere else. I was at our factory in Bombay last week. I saw little children, no more than two years old, picking food out of the gutter. Little girls, half the size of Martha.'

His brow abruptly darkens. He reaches for Tonie's hand and clutches it between his own.

'They're probably working in your factory,' Thomas says drily. 'You should pay them more.'

'I've told Howard I'll leave him if I find out he's been using child labour,' Claudia says, re-emerging with a tray. 'I'll just pack a bag and go.'

'We're not allowed to use child labour in our own house,' Howard says. 'Ours don't even make their own beds.'

'They're spoilt,' Claudia says. 'Selfish and spoilt.'

Down on the lawn Lewis has got the bike upright again, and is holding it at the front so that Alexa can get on. He turns and looks enquiringly at the adults. Alexa sits herself on the saddle, white-faced and uncertain. Thomas waits for Tonie to intervene, but she does not. Instead she picks up one of Claudia's antique glass goblets from the tray and revolves it carefully in her hands.

'Where did you get these?' she says.

Howard is rising, moving down the steps towards the lawn. Thomas hears him say,

'Actually, it's got a surprising kick on it, for a toy.'

He is still saying it as the bike bolts from Lewis's grasp. Alexa is carried jolting over the grass. Her eyes are screwed shut. She makes no attempt to steer. Almost immediately the bike hits the trunk of Howard's apple tree, head-on. Alexa is thrown forward. Thomas sees the impact from behind, then her face full of blood on the grass. Howard gets there first, running and wobbling like a bear. He picks Alexa up in his arms. When Thomas comes he surrenders her silently, and then turns to excoriate Lewis, who stands there with downcast eyes, nodding dolefully at every accusation.

'– bloody idiot! Totally irresponsible to let her –'

Alexa does not cry. Her eyes are wide with shock and blood trickles around the rims. Claudia comes running out with water in a bowl and a cloth. While Thomas holds her she carefully mops away the blood. The other children stand round silently.

'Get ice!' Claudia commands, pointing towards the house.

It is Tonie who obeys the order. Thomas glimpses her beside the apple tree, her face startled, aghast, as though Claudia's pointing finger were accusing her of something. Then she runs inside. The blood is coming from a single cut; presently it stops. In the same way that he wonders how Claudia could have got the water so quickly, so he ruminates blindly, disjointedly, on Tonie's absence. finally she comes. She gives the ice to Claudia. Then she stands beside Howard. He hears her say,

'I thought she was dead.'

He sees Howard put his arm around her. He sees her cover her eyes with her hand.

In the kitchen Claudia serves out roast lamb. Alexa is lying under a blanket on the sofa, with a glass of lemonade and a plaster on her forehead. There is Lego all over the kitchen floor and piles of paper everywhere. Lottie, the eldest, is at the table, eating an enormous mound of ice cream slathered with chocolate sauce.

'Lottie, put that away now,' Claudia says. 'We're about to have lunch.'

'I don't want lunch.'

Lottie is thirteen, sullen and thickset. She has narrow light blue eyes which she looks out of uneasily, uncomfortably, as though they were chinks in the prison of her pale, plump body.

'– gorging yourself on ice cream and then refusing to eat the healthy lunch I've provided,' Claudia is saying, banging the oven door. 'Howard, will you speak to her?'

Howard isn't there: he is in the hall, talking loudly on his phone.

'Anyway, I'm vegetarian. I told you.'

'Vegetarians eat vegetables,' Lewis says. 'You're not a vegetarian. You just eat cake and stuff.'

'She's a cake-arian,' Martha says.

'Fatarian,' Lewis says, laughing. 'Just some fat for lunch, please, with a side order of, um, fat.'

Lottie shrieks. She picks up a book from the table and flings it across the room at Lewis.

'Stop it!' Claudia bellows, enveloped in clouds of steam from the cooker.

Tonie is getting knives and forks out of a drawer. She gets plates from the wooden dresser. She is reserved, acquiescent, efficient, as she is in the mornings when she goes to work. Thomas sees that she has returned to this mode as a way of managing the day's disorder.

'I feel we're completely out of control,' Claudia says to Howard, when he comes in. She stops what she is doing, leaves the lamb steaming in its dish of fat, the vegetables cooling in their saucepans. She leans against the cooker and folds her arms.

Howard looks concerned. He puts his hand on her shoulder. 'We're all right, aren't we Claude?'

'How can you say we're all right!' Claudia exclaims fiercely. 'We've got one child with a head injury, the rest are fighting like wild animals, and we can't even get lunch on the table by half past three! It's bloody selfishness – just utter bloody selfishness!'

She is tearful. She rubs her eyes with her fists. Howard looks miserable.

'A child only has to come into this house,' Claudia resumes, 'and she's concussed in the first half-hour!'

'I'm so sorry,' Howard says, to Tonie. 'It was my fault, I gave them the bloody thing. I should never have let her go near it.'

'It was an accident,' Tonie says.

'It should never have happened. Please forgive me.'

Tonie, in black, is suddenly the priest, the confessor, and Howard and Claudia – red-faced, dishevelled – her penitents. Claudia embraces her, wiping her eyes. Howard, absolved, ranges around the kitchen bellowing orders at the children. Thomas senses that Tonie is relieved: her own conduct has been lost in the general commotion. But in the car on the way home it seems to return to her. She turns around often in her seat to look at Alexa, who is silently gazing through the window. She reaches back for Alexa's hand and holds it.

'It felt like it was my fault,' she says.

'It was nobody's fault,' Thomas replies, though secretly he agrees with her.

'It felt like it was because I'd lost control of her.'

Thomas is silent. He thinks they shouldn't discuss such things, with Alexa there. It used to be Tonie who had the finer sense of what was appropriate, and now, all at once, it is him. It is as though Alexa has become less real to Tonie and more real to himself.

'Claudia seemed on edge,' she says.

Thomas smiles coldly, unsympathetic. 'She's always like that. All that fuss about lunch – the truth is that she doesn't want lunch to be on the table by one o'clock,' he says. 'She wouldn't know what to do next.'

He wonders whether Claudia is good: he has always wondered it. On another day he might have said this to Tonie, but today he does not. He doesn't want her to think that he is judgemental. In spite of everything, he has a dark sense of advantage over her.

Tonie laughs. 'She might have to go to her studio,' she says.

At the sound of her laugh, he laughs too. It is the sense of form that makes them laugh, the feeling that in family life they are at once confined and eternal; like music, Thomas thinks, which could be anything and at the same time cannot be other than what it is. He puts his hand on her knee. For the rest of the journey he says nothing more.

# IV

In Little Wickham people are mowing their lawns. It is a clear Sunday afternoon and the village buzzes like a nest of hornets. Mr Bradshaw pushes his mower around his garden along with the rest. The lawn at the back of the house is undulating: it rises like a woman's body into two mounds with a soft sloping space between them. The mower moves firmly over its contours, up and down, with Mr Bradshaw's hands on the bar. His feet tread rhythmically in a shorn passage that is always renewing itself. He has a feeling of domination as he goes over the tender flanks and creases. Afterwards the grass is smooth. He cleans the mower and returns it to its shed.

It is four o'clock and his wife has not returned from the hospice committee lunch. The sky is flushed with pink; the swallows swoop around the telegraph poles. The rooks are already calling across the fields, above the sound of the last mower. It is Gus Robertson's, outlasting the rest as though to advertise the size of his domain. Mr Bradshaw can see him through the screen of trees, sitting on his ride-on. It is brilliantly new, as big as a small tractor. He rides it passionlessly, staring straight ahead. Mr Bradshaw has not seen this mower before: it causes him a pang of betrayal to see it, as though he has witnessed Gus in an act of disloyalty. Sometimes it seems that Mr Bradshaw has only to hear of a new gimmick for the Robertsons to own it. It is unsettling, to be among people who are always interfering with what they have, who seem to proclaim their indifference to others by changing what is familiar about themselves.

Recently the Robertsons installed a pump and waterway feeding into their pond: when you switch the pump on, the waterway becomes a running stream. The Bradshaws were invited to observe this ceremony, and stood on the lawn while Gus dashed about checking the supply and drainage, his white, well-styled eave of hair flopping up and down. He is a handsome man for his age, tall and trim, suntanned, perfectly groomed; and yet watching the electronic stream trickling down into the plastic-lined lily pond, Mr Bradshaw gave birth to the perception that Gus is tragic, not because of his vanity or ostentation but because of his poor taste. It is something Gus will perhaps never know about himself, but it has been an important and liberating realisation for Mr Bradshaw. The new mower, however, is a blow. Brash and ugly though it is, he nonetheless feels, lover-like, that Gus has been unfaithful.

At a quarter to five she comes, with Flossie at her heels. She comes around the path at the side of the house, where Mr Bradshaw is pulling weeds out of the gravel.

'Oh!' she cries. 'I thought I'd never get away! They simply wouldn't stop talking – have you had tea?'

'No,' he says, without looking up. 'You said you'd be back by three, so I waited.'

'Charles, you didn't!'

'Tea is at four,' he says. 'It didn't seem unreasonable to expect you to be back by then.'

'Oh dear – oh, I *am* sorry. You must be parched!'

'I started mowing at three in order to be finished by four.'

'And in the hot sun too!' she wails. 'I don't understand why you didn't just get yourself a cup.'

'You said you'd be here. It seemed sensible to wait.'

He *is* parched, and when he straightens up from stooping over the gravel he is slightly dizzy. She stands there with flushed cheeks, her mouth drooping at the corners. Sometimes he forgets that he and she are old, and then the sight of her reminds him.

'Never mind,' she says. 'I'll make it now.'

'I don't want it now. I don't like to have tea later than four. It spoils my supper.'

'But you can't just go without!'

'I'd rather go without now. As I said, it spoils my supper.'

He bends down again with his trowel. He can see her feet beside him on the gravel path, the ropes of blue veins, the calloused toes bunched in her sandals. He wonders what she will do. The air between them seems to tremble; the atmosphere is a dark bud straining to burst into flower. He wants its offering, of love or violence. He wants to be located in the maze of his own rigidity and offered something. That is the test, as it has always been.

'I don't see why we can't just have supper later,' she says.

He does not reply. This is not what she ought to have said. It leaves him in the maze; it asks him to find his own way out.

'Well,' she says presently, 'well, I suppose I shall have to have mine on my own.'

He hears her crunch away. She is gone. He feels the presence of a terrible void, advancing on him, coldly enveloping him. It is silence: Gus has turned his mower off. Later he hears her return through the dusk to where he still bends over the gravel, weeding. She places a cup of tea at his feet with two bourbon biscuits in the saucer, and then swiftly she is gone again. The biscuits are his favourite kind. He watches them out of the corner of his eye as he works; he meditates on them darkly. They have, he decides, been spoilt. He has been separated forever from their sweetness. He lets the tea go cold. When it grows dark he returns to the house and pours it down the sink, and places the biscuits back in their tin.

# V

It was Howard who got the dog. He came back from his mother's with it tucked into his jacket.

'Flossie had her puppies,' he said.

Howard specialises in this sort of thing. He is never more sure-footed than when embarking on what is easy to do and difficult to undo. He specialises in commitment. The dog is a Jack Russell. He is small and firm and vigorous, with a coarse white coat and bright, staring eyes. They call him Skittle.

Claudia likes having a new life in the house. The puppy has to be fed at night, like a baby, and he leaves little pools of golden urine all over the floor. Her sister Juliet tells her to keep Skittle close to her at this early stage. Claudia carries him around in her arms when the children are at school.

One day, sitting stroking him on her lap while she reads the paper, Claudia looks down at Skittle's body. He is prone with pleasure: his hairy muzzle is flung back and his sinuous loins are quivering. Suddenly Claudia is repelled. There is something unsavoury in the dog's excitement, in his pink trembling groin. She puts him on the floor. He frets at her legs, raking her calves with his sharp little claws.

'No!' she says, grasping him firmly around the middle. 'Don't scratch – no!'

She places him a few feet away. He writhes in her hands. When she lets him go he scrabbles frantically towards her and gets up on his hind legs again, putting his claws in her flesh. She spanks him with the flat of her hand. He cowers, contorting his narrow body, gazing at her with his orb-like, fanatical eyes.

It is October, and the garden is gilded with yellow light. The grass is sodden in the mornings. Claudia puts the covers on the outdoor furniture. She gathers the apples where they lie rotting around the tree. Everything is poised between readiness and decay. She watches the children playing after school in the crisp late afternoon. Their bodies have lost the fluidity of summer, though the weather is fine. They move around the rectangle of lawn in their uniforms, laughing and jostling, throwing sticks for Skittle and crying out when he bounces up to catch them smartly between his jaws. Later, when they have come in and the garden is wrapped in its blue-grey pall of evening, Claudia looks through the window and sees Skittle cavorting alone in the indistinct light. He leaps in the air, his jaws snapping at invisible sticks. She watches his white twisted form, suspended. She can hear the murmur of television from the other room.

Howard gets home at half past seven. He wears an air of expectation, of excitement, though for him the day is nearing its conclusion – Howard is usually asleep by half past ten. Claudia sometimes wonders what his excitement signifies. He is like someone eagerly awaiting dessert, the main courses behind him. Sweet though they are, these are the rituals of conclusion. He discards his coat and briefcase in the hall, finds the children and roughhouses them with his big bear's body, drinks two glasses of wine one after the other standing by the kitchen counters; after which he is red-faced, blissful-looking, rubbing his eyes with his shirt tails hanging out.

'It's been the loveliest weather,' Claudia says wistfully. 'I was thinking what a shame it is we can't go away this weekend.'

Howard blinks. 'What are you saying, Claude? You're telling me something but I don't know what it is.'

'Just that we could have gone to Scotland, or to that place in Derbyshire your brother told us about. There hasn't been such a lovely autumn for years.'

Howard leafs through the letters on the kitchen table, looking at them over the tops of his glasses. 'Well, *I'm* going to Scotland,' he says, abstractedly. 'I don't know what you're doing. I'll be back last thing Sunday.'

'But we can't!'

'Why not?'

'We can't take the dog.'

Claudia notices the smallest hesitation before Howard replies.

'Of course we can take the dog. We just chuck him in the back of the car with a bowl of water.'

'We're not *driving* all the way to Scotland, just for the weekend. We'd have to fly, or go by train.'

'We'll do the other one, then. Derbyshire. Where's Derbyshire? It can't be that bloody far away. What's the name of this place? Let's phone Tom and ask him. They can come too – we'll all go together.' Howard is now standing by the telephone with the receiver in his hand. 'What's his number?'

Claudia finds the number. It is Howard's speciality – commitment. She has grown accustomed to it, going with Howard into the future like a boat breasting choppy waters, the sensation of uplift just ahead, the momentary resistance and the breaking through. She is dependent on it – she was from the start. Years ago they stood on the beach at Mothecombe, watching a family play cricket on the sand at the end of the summer's day. Howard was enchanted by the sight, the children calling and laughing in the pink light.

'Let's get on with it Claude,' he said, rubbing his hands together, sunset on his face. 'I don't want to fuck about. I want
the lot. I want a cricket team of our own.'

They had only known each other three weeks.

Thomas and Tonie can't come to Derbyshire. Howard
tries Leo, who agrees to meet them there with Susie and the
children.

'What about those people in Bath – the Mattisons?'

'The Morrisons,' Claudia says.

'We haven't seen them for bloody years.'

He rings the Morrisons. They too agree to come to Derbyshire. It is nearly ten o'clock. Howard, bleary-eyed, eats
his dinner on the phone, shovelling it up with his fork. He
rings the hotel. Claudia remembers that she hasn't put Martha to bed. She hurries upstairs. Lottie and Lewis are watching television. Martha is reading in her room. She looks very
small, sitting cross-legged on the floor. Claudia wonders if
her growth is being stunted. Someone told her this could happen if a child didn't get enough sleep.

Downstairs Howard is still on the phone. He puts his hand
over the receiver when he sees Claudia.

'They don't take dogs,' he says.


Skittle gets into the bedroom and savages Claudia's shoes,
her silk dressing gown, the old Gucci handbag she had as
an art student in London, before Howard took possession
of her with his plans. It is this last piece of vandalism that
smites her heart. It is as though there were nothing else left
from that time, nothing to hold it off from extinction but the
once-familiarity of that object in worn rust-coloured suede.
Now it is mauled beyond recognition. She raises it above her
head, about to throw it at him. He is cringing beneath the

bed, a shred of silk trailing from his jaw. His crazy eyes stare at her out of the shadows. He is delinquent: he is, she sees, beyond the reach of punishment. She puts the bag in the dustbin.

All day Skittle whines and scratches at the door, begging to be let in or out. She takes him for walks, dragging him by the lead along Laurier Drive. He is maddened by the whirling piles of yellow leaves, by the springing birds, by plastic bags that occasionally swim like phantoms across the pavements in the breeze. He flinches whenever she speaks, emitting nervous squirts of urine. When he runs his body is so bowed and contorted that he goes diagonally, scuttling like a crab. He stands in the middle of the room, barking at nothing. Juliet gives Claudia the name of a pet psychiatrist.

'He hates me,' Claudia says. 'Also, I think there's something wrong with him. He isn't like a normal dog. I see other people with their dogs. He isn't like them.'

'A dog is like a child,' Juliet says. Juliet has no children.

'I just told you, this dog isn't even like a dog.'

'I did wonder at the wisdom of your taking on something else, when you've got so much already. I didn't like to say anything.'

'Howard brought him home. It wasn't up to me.'

'Why do you always say that? He wouldn't do it if you didn't let him. It's the same with your painting. It's always other people stopping you doing it. It's never you.'

Claudia has noticed the way a childless woman will defend the man. She will side against the mother, for her sympathies haven't yet been transformed. Claudia remembers, when Lottie was born, the prospect of self-sacrifice coming into view like a landscape seen from an approaching train; she remembers the steady unfolding of it, a place she had never seen before in her life, and herself inescapably bound for it; and then after a while the realisation, pieced together from numerous clues, that this was where her mother had lived all along.

The pet psychiatrist phones Claudia several times a day.

'Where is he now?'

'Outside. In the garden.'

There is a steady thumping at the back door. It is Skittle hurling himself against it. Claudia has watched him do it, watched him take a little run and then fling himself at the wood. It startles her, for she often has the impulse to pick Skittle up and throw him, dash him against an unyielding surface. The way he looks is exactly as she had imagined it.

'How would you describe his behaviour, Claudia?'

'Angry. He wants to come in.'

'Why don't you let him in? What would happen?'

Claudia sighs. 'He'd be just as desperate to be let out again.'

The psychiatrist suggests that she leave the door open. This improves things, though it makes the house cold. At the weekend Howard buys a catflap and fits it to the back door. The children sit there all afternoon, teaching Skittle to jump through it. He is small enough to fit, but his sense of its physical impossibility is difficult to overcome. He has proved the door is solid: how can it have changed its properties? Lewis and Martha sit one either side of the flap, passing and re-passing Skittle through the hole.

'I should think that's quite therapeutic,' Claudia says to Howard.

Later she hears a shriek from downstairs.

'Watch this,' Lewis says calmly, when Claudia appears.

'He did it! He did it!' Martha cries.

They put Skittle out in the garden and close the door. Lewis kneels by the flap and then claps his hands twice. There is a pause, before Skittle comes flying through like a torpedo.

'Extraordinary,' Claudia says, laughing, while Skittle tears wildly around the kitchen, making mad arabesques in the air.

The feeling of letting go, of surrender: it warms her veins like a tranquiliser, spreading its numb bliss. She has blunted the sharp end of life this way. She fades out, her doubt and pain and anxiety left hollow like a casing, like a shell on a beach. She is used to it, to leaving hollowed-out things behind her. They lie scattered in her past, questions to which the answers were never found. What is the right way to live? What is the value of success? And the most important, the most unanswerable: if love is selfish, can it still be considered to be love?

# VI

Leo is in the fast lane of the A23 when Susie tells him to pull over, right now. She has her hand over her mouth. In the lay-by she leans out of the car door and retches over the tarmac. Juggernauts thunder past, one after another. The Vauxhall rocks with the vibrations. In the back seat, Justin and Madeleine are silent.

'That's the worst,' Susie gasps, wiping her mouth with the back of her hand. Her long scarlet fingernails flash against her cheek, a blood-coloured bouquet. 'When nothing comes up.'

An uprush of air pressure slams into the side of the car and is sucked instantly back. They rock from side to side: for a few seconds they are in the lee of a monster, engulfed in the roaring, churning wheels, the crazily flapping tarpaulins.

'Let's get out of here,' Leo says nervously. 'Those things come so fucking close.'

Susie flips down the passenger mirror, reapplies her lipstick. She turns around in her seat, scanning the road through the back window.

'I'll tell you when,' she says.

They stop twice more before they get there. On the winding B-road Susie groans and clutches her stomach. The cows look up at them from the fields as they pass. A mile from Little Wickham there are crows hopping around a tattered carcass in the middle of the road. Leo stops, blares his horn. They are picking at the bloodied flesh and fur, unheeding. He blares again, revs the engine. He can see it was a rabbit. He can see a torn ear, a crushed fragment of skull.

'For Christ's sake,' he says. He realises he is trembling. 'Leave the bloody thing alone.'

Reluctantly they lift themselves away on their black wings and settle on the verge, their beaks engorged. Susie puts her hand on his knee. She is all right now. She keeps her hand there, firm.

'Nearly there,' she says.

It is a grey day, gusty, the bare trees twitching and irritable, the countryside lying in unconscious mounds of rough vegetation. Ma is on the front lawn when they pull up the drive. She is wearing a funny hat, a man's jacket, thick socks that she's tucked her trousers into.

'Oh, hello!' she says, through the car window.

She sounds surprised. Leo and Susie joke about it, the way his parents always seem surprised to see him, despite the fact the visit has been arranged: not a pleasant surprise and not a shock either, just a mild lack of expectation, like when you've forgotten something and it turns up again. There's an imitation Susie does, lifting one eyebrow very slightly, widening her eyes, the hint of a query in the voice. Oh, *hello*? She gets it exactly.

His mother's clothes say it all. She isn't putting herself out, put it that way.

'Leo,' she says, when he gets out of the car. She hugs him. He can feel her gnarled vigorous body through the clothes, her eternal unstoppable sufficiency. 'And Susie.' Susie gets a hug too. Her high heels are sinking into the grass.

'Get you, darling,' Susie says, fingering the man's jacket, the crumpled old hat. 'Get your fashionable androgynous look.'

Ma screeches with laughter, delighted. Susie knows how to handle her, has always known. Justin and Madeleine are banging at the car windows.

'Oh dear, shall we let them out?' Ma says.

'Let's leave them there,' Susie says. 'I could do with a day off. We can toss them in a bag of crisps at lunchtime.'

Ma screeches again. Susie hams it up, her bad mother act, and Ma soaks up every last drop of it. She wants to be in the club, the gang.

'Don't!' she says. 'I was *forever* locking mine in the car – I'd go off and forget about them for hours!'

At home Susie does an imitation of that too. *Once I didn't see Leo for seven years! I completely forgot about him!*

'Thomas here?' Leo says.

'Not yet. I can't think where they've got to – they phoned hours ago to say they were leaving. And the others aren't coming at all because Howard's unwell. I've got this great big joint of beef and at the moment only us to eat it.'

It's another thing, the way after fifteen years she doesn't seem to know that he and Susie are vegetarians.

'Oh well,' he says, because she makes it sound as though it isn't enough to have him there, as though without Howard and Thomas the day might as well be cancelled, because she has so many other things she needs to be getting on with. His father is coming out of the house, peering around like a policeman investigating a disturbance. He sees Leo and Susie, changes his expression to one of recognition. Leo wonders how long he waited inside before coming out. He imagines him pressed against the wall beside the curtains, his eyes screwed up, trying to see through the crack.

Susie is getting the children out of the car, fussing over them now, straightening their clothes. He shakes his father's hand.

'Nice to see you,' his father says.

Inside the house there is the old darkness, the old smells.

54

Flossie is in her basket. The clock in the hall ticks. The house is cold. The scarred wooden floor, the hunting prints with their unfunny antique humour, the faded William Morris wallpaper full of strange, devouring forms: it is more than familiar, it is thick with subconscious life, like a forest in a fairy tale. The house is haunted, Leo knows it is. Only once, when he was seventeen, he spent the night here alone. Something said his name, sat on the bed. He had been asleep and the feeling of a weight on the bed woke him. It made it worse, to have been asleep. It is worse to go into something unconscious. He shouted at it to go away, went all round the house turning the lights on and shouting. To shout at nothing is to break some contract with yourself, with reality. Thinking about it now, he sees that his life has been punctuated by such incidents. Reality is personal too. He's had to break it to advance himself, to go forward. It's the only way he can get to the place where he feels comfortable.

'Work going well?' his father says. 'Any new commissions recently?'

'It's all right,' Leo says. 'It's much the same.'

He doesn't know where Dads has got hold of this commissions idea. Leo is a copywriter. He writes copy for the same agency he has always written for. Yet every time he sees his father he starts talking about commissions. It sounds like an army word: it isn't a word Leo has ever applied to himself. He supposes it's his father's way of rationalising the troublesome fact that Leo is not an employee. He is freelance, a mercenary, a soldier of fortune. One day he'll receive his commission and off he'll go into the sunset.

'How about you?' he says. 'How is everything?'

'All right.'

There is a silence. Leo looks around for Susie, but she isn't there. He needs her. He doesn't know what to say. He feels the silence consuming him, swallowing him up.

'How's the garden?' he says.

His father looks mildly at him with his cold eyes. He wears a cravat at his throat. His snow-white hair is plastered into place.

'Not much happening in the garden at this time of year. Just some pruning, cutting back for winter. We're thinking about thinning out some of those trees over by the garage. The roots are starting to undermine the foundations.'

'Really?' Leo says.

'The problem is that your mother won't hear of any of them being cut down. The tree surgeon came out to explain it to her, but he couldn't seem to make her understand. We rather wasted his afternoon, I'm afraid. I wouldn't be surprised if he took us off his list, which would be a pity.'

Justin and Madeleine are petting Flossie in her basket. She snaps her jaws a little, rolls over. They tickle her coarse old belly and she lies back, stiff with pleasure on her filthy blanket. Leo looks at their soft hair, their new fresh skin, feels the tension of love for them, as though in this place his love were illicit.

'Oh well,' he says.

At last there is a commotion at the door; the others come in, Susie smelling of cigarettes, Thomas and Tonie close behind with the breath of the world on them, of blessed modernity. They look young and clean and slim. They look eminently, relievingly competent.

'Sorry,' Thomas says. He puts his arms around Leo, pats his back. 'We had to take a detour. We got here as quickly as we could.'

'I would have had to have eaten cow,' Leo says. Now that they are here, he can acknowledge how miserable he feels.

'We need a drink,' Thomas says. 'Dads, we could all do with a drink, don't you think?'

Madeleine looks up, startled.

'Don't give Mummy anything to drink,' she says. 'She had too much to drink last night. She was sick in the car.'

Susie rolls her eyes. She's wearing a lot of make-up and her skin is deathly-looking, grey. She has lipstick on her teeth. Her dress is all creased down the front. Leo feels guilty. He should have let her stay at home, let her sleep it off. He worries that he doesn't look after her properly. He worries that he's going to wear her out.

'Mummy had a tummy bug,' he says sternly, to Madeleine.

Madeleine creases her forehead, perplexed. 'No she didn't. *And* she was smoking just now. I saw her in the garden.'

'Isn't she sweet?' Susie says, through her teeth. 'Isn't she everything you'd want in a daughter?' She catches hold of Alexa, kisses the top of her shining head. 'Now *this* is a nice, discreet child. This child is house-trained.'

Tonie is in the doorway. Leo sees her, sees her watching everything. She looks like she is watching a play.

'Come outside,' he says in a low voice to Madeleine.

She opens her mouth in protest, but she doesn't say anything, just gets up and walks sullenly ahead of him, out into the garden. He lectures her there on the grass, in the windy grey day. When they go back in the others are sitting down, talking, drinking watery gin-and-tonics. Madeleine glances meaningfully at Susie, glass in hand, but Leo has silenced her. She goes and sits on the windowsill and stares out until Ma calls them for lunch.

Susie drinks a second gin-and-tonic, and then wine, and by three o'clock she is flushed, blowsy, her red hair cascading wildly over her shoulders. The children have left the table. Leo can hear them calling and laughing on the lawn.

'How's the new job?' he asks Tonie.

She smiles mysteriously, distantly. She nods.

'Yeah, it's good.'

'And the – what's it called? – the sabbatical. How's that going?' Susie says, to Thomas.

There is, Leo thinks, a hierarchy, an order to these conversations, and he and Susie are at the bottom of it. It is understood that they will ask questions, will find out about the others, as they might find out about somewhere interesting they were visiting, like Paris. He is the youngest, five years younger than Thomas, seven younger than Howard. He is also the biggest, the tallest, taller even than Howard, though he doesn't feel it, not in this house. Howard used to make him sit under the table at mealtimes, when their parents were out. He kicked him if he tried to come out. He used to give him his food on the floor, like a dog.

'I'm learning to play the piano,' Thomas says.

'Are you?' Susie says, perplexedly. 'What – professionally?'

Susie wouldn't understand about playing the piano. She doesn't understand any middle-class hobby. She's always worked, looked after other people, even as a child she worked, cooking and taking care of the house. Her mother was a cleaning lady. She couldn't read or write. Susie couldn't either until she was fourteen and someone at school noticed it.

'Not exactly,' Thomas says, laughing.

Leo wants to shield her, to defend her. He wants to hit and hit until she is safe. He loves Thomas, but with a passive love, a background love. It is something he never looks at straight on. He is used to seeing it there out of the corner of his eye. He didn't choose it, yet it's always been there. He doesn't really know what it is.

'You can't spend a whole year playing the piano,' he says.

He sounds more indignant than he wants to. It's always the same, the difficulty of being himself with these people, his family, the difficulty of locating his own authenticity. He says things he doesn't feel, and what he feels most keenly he doesn't say at all.

Thomas looks surprised. 'Why not?'

'It's – it's a waste, isn't it?'

'*I* don't think so,' Thomas says. 'Anyway, it might be more than a year.'

'You want to be careful,' Dads says. 'If you stay out too long, they might not take you back. Things move on, you know. Your experience becomes obsolete.'

'I don't want to go back,' Thomas says. 'I like being at home.'

Dads chuckles mirthlessly. 'That may be so,' he says, 'but no matter how much you like it the question has to be, is it sustainable?'

Leo hears it, that tone, the way it goes over everything and mechanically levels it, like a tank. It is benign, ruthless, unvarying. He has never heard his father raise his voice. There has been no need to raise it: it is in the levelling persistence that the violence is accomplished. His voice has talked constantly in Leo's head about the world and its ways since he can remember.

Thomas laughs too, slightly combative, shrugs his shoulders. 'Ask Tonie. Ask Tonie whether it's sustainable.'

'I've always tended to the view,' Dads continues, 'that work is life for a man, as children are for a woman.'

A ridge of silence which they all go over together, bump.

'But work wasn't life for me,' Thomas says carefully. 'As children aren't all of life for Tonie.'

Suddenly there is something new, an atmosphere. Leo feels it, a shift far down at the bottom of things, like a rumbling of plates on the ocean bed. He feels upheaval, change, far down below.

'Hey,' Tonie says, in her low, husky voice that always makes the hairs rise on the back of Leo's neck. 'Hey, let's change the subject.'

She puts her hand with its single silver band over Thomas's. Leo thinks there is something unreassuring about Tonie's ring. Susie wears a big emerald in a gold claw on that finger.

'Yes, for heaven's sake, do let's,' exclaims Ma. 'You're all sitting round with faces like a wet weekend.'

As though if it had been left up to her, life would have been different, would have been all frivolity.

Later, when it's time to go, Leo is searching around the house for the children and in his father's study finds a book of crossword puzzles on the desk, all completed and dated in his father's neat fountain-pen writing. He has to help Susie across the lawn. He holds her firmly by the elbow, but even so she staggers when her heels sink into the turf, and one of her shoes comes off. Ma is weeding the flowerbeds, kneeling on a mat she has laid in the earth. She looks up at them. Sometimes there is something so vague about her pale blue eyes that Leo wants to cry. She makes his existence seem more random than he can bear. When he was a child, she used to go around freely telling people that Leo was a mistake, until he was old enough to ask her to stop.

'Oh, are you going?' she says. 'I feel I've hardly seen you.'

'Oh well,' he says. It is all he can say, all he's been able to say today.

In the car on the way home, he tells Susie about the crossword puzzles.

'Well, he's got to fill his time somehow, hasn't he?' she says sleepily.

She's right, of course, but all the same it has upset him. He can't quite explain it but he doesn't have to, because Susie is now snoring lightly, slumped into the seat beside him. There's nothing particularly wrong with a crossword puzzle. It's just that it doesn't go anywhere. It is rigid within itself, but it has no force of extension. It is trivial. The flat motorway landscape is radial, infinite, extending and extending itself into nothingness. A kind of hollowness opens out in Leo's chest, a feeling of weightlessness.

A yellow Lamborghini is overtaking them in the fast lane. Leo has no interest in sports cars, but suddenly it cheers him, tickles him, the sight of this pointless banana-coloured contraption. He turns to Justin in the back seat.

'Look at that,' he says.

# VII

The plane pitches about in the grey air. People are quiet, strapped to their seats. They ride the cliffs and troughs, the mountains and the sudden dizzying voids. In their tailored clothes, with their books and briefcases and laptop computers, they are like a platoon going forward in the name of civilisation. They hold on to their newspapers, to their gin-and-tonics. Their onward motion seems rational, even when the storm forces them off their path. The plane is thrown this way and that. The engine drones, a wavering line of sound. Tonie is not afraid. She is glad to be on the side of rationality. It is far worse to be the storm, to be tormented and hysterical, to be uncontrolled.

Amsterdam airport appears, low grey buildings in drifting horizontal veils of rain. There are box-like vehicles parked on the asphalt among shapeless patches of water creased by wind. Its anonymity is almost arousing. It too is rational, impersonal. It seems to lift Tonie out of the brawl of relationships. It seems to relieve her of everything that is private and particular, of emotion itself. By the time she gets a taxi it is dark. The storm drives unchecked across the flat landscape, across the port with its black shapes of cranes and containers, across the choppy waters and concrete isthmuses of the city's outskirts. Scraps of litter bowl through the darkness; the wind warps the fragile vertical line of the alien streetscape, bending the skeletal trees, rocking the metal posts in their concrete moorings. It appears to come out of the infinity of the low horizon, out of black nothingness. For the first time, looking through the taxi's rain-streaked windows, Tonie is frightened. It is the force of the horizontal, pouring unrestrained over the lip of the black earth, that frightens her.

The taxi driver doesn't know where they are going. He too is from somewhere else. He is dark-skinned, vulnerable in his short-sleeved shirt. He pores over the address of the hotel where she has written it on the back of an envelope – he studies her handwriting, the cryptic, consonant-heavy words. He gets out of the car and shows the envelope to a passerby. They huddle over it in the rain, pointing and discussing. Tonie sits in the back seat, her hands folded in her lap. They are parked in the darkness of an empty street in an industrial-looking area, full of warehouses and unmarked modern buildings with their metal shutters down. The wind makes a plaintive sound as it comes off the sea. The rain spatters against the glass. The rough black water frets at the concrete esplanade. The driver comes back and they set off again slowly. They turn a corner and after a hundred yards or so they creep into the darkness at the side of the road and stop. The driver points. Tonie sees a big, gloomy factory building behind a wall. Suddenly she is exasperated.

'That isn't a hotel,' she says. 'That doesn't look like a hotel.'

'Yes, hotel!'

The driver points again. He is insistent. He is as full of certitude as a minute ago he was riven by doubt. He is capable, she sees, of leaving her here whether it is a hotel or not. A feeling of disenchantment passes over her, the feeling that she has been let down not by what she knows and trusts but by what is new and unfamiliar. She stays where she is on the back seat. She has always been susceptible to ill treatment: she becomes pliant, victimised. It is the driver's masculinity that paralyses her. She is unable to deliver herself from it. He must release her, as a fisherman roughly releases a fish from his hook. Suddenly she sees people, three or four figures pulling suitcases up the front steps through the gloom to the building's entrance. The big anonymous door opens and closes again behind them, showing a segment of orange light. The driver exclaims. He is happy. He springs from his seat and opens the car door for her. He gestures again towards the dimly lit entrance, lest she remain in any doubt. She gives him his money. She realises that he wouldn't have abandoned her after all.

In her room she sits on the bed and goes through her notes. The room is big and bare and brightly lit, white like a gallery. The wind moans at the windows. The tall white shutters move and knock. She peers through the slats and sees again the flat black distances streaming with rain, the shapes of cranes and beyond them the darkness boiling indistinctly on the low horizon. It seems to be advancing on her across the desolation, to be bent on prising her out. But the room has a force of its own, with its enormous immaculate bareness, its strange long clusters of pendant lights, its futuristic untouched furniture. On the table there is a giant block of glass – a vase – with a sheaf of orchids and blood-coloured gladioli in it. The flowers are odourless, three feet tall with thick, poison-green stalks. They look synthetic, but when she touches them she finds that they are real.

Tonie is here to speak at a conference. The conference is tomorrow at ten o'clock; after that she will fly home. She forgot, when she left the house this morning, that she would be returning so soon. It was the rift, the departure, that concerned her, as the hurdle concerns the jumper, not the same continuous earth that lies on the other side of it.

She remembers that Alexa was wearing a red dress when she stood at the door to say goodbye. Tonie had never seen the dress before: Thomas bought it for her. It made Alexa seem unreal, like a girl in a dream. In it, she seemed to have no further need of Tonie, except to be numbered among her accomplishments. Yet the mark of possession was Thomas's: in the red dress Alexa was hallmarked, like a silver figurine. This, it struck Tonie, was what someone looked like who was taken care of by Thomas. In a sense it was what Tonie herself ought to look like. When she looked at Alexa she was looking at a version of her relationship with Thomas, at one of several possibilities, in which she was his cherished object, decked out in a dress he had chosen himself.

There is a restaurant downstairs. Tonie prepares herself in front of the mirror, trying on a different shirt. Who is she? What is she doing here in this room, with its sinister flowers, with its white shutters the wind and darkness seem to be trying to prise open? Her own body, the unit of herself, so sealed and single: it is all she is, and yet she lives in it so little. Away from home, she is only this unit of flesh. What experience can she offer herself? What physical event will justify this form and bring it into knowledge? Alone, she eats a plate of fish and drinks a glass of cold yellow wine. The waiter is young, attentive, so formal that she becomes awkward and strange when he approaches. She has brought her notes down with her and she finds herself looking at them, looking at what she wrote down at the kitchen table last night in Montague Street, when she sat and thought of her trip, imagined the great inviting sea of the unknown and herself plunging bodily into it. Now she doesn't know what it was she thought she would find here. She notices a stain on one of the pages: it is gravy, from last night's chicken pie. She looks at other people talking, eating, in the fashionable room.

Upstairs she phones Thomas. He is distant-sounding, slightly curt. He doesn't know that there is anything in her plight he ought to be moved by. And she can never explain it to him, for as a story it revolves around the disclosure of a desire for something that has no name and is itself nameless, that she could arrive at only by a path of negatives that would somewhere along the line have to pass through Thomas himself. But he doesn't enquire. She is on a business trip, that's all: he used to go on them himself. Afterwards did he complain of loneliness, of disenchantment? She thinks that perhaps he did. He complained about them as the conscript complains about the discomfort of his standard-issue boots. Perhaps he didn't tell her everything either.

She sits on the bed. She both wants and doesn't want to go home. She remembers this feeling from childhood, when she would go to her room after some family dispute; and lying on her bed would experience the same division of desire, the same choice that now she sees was no choice at all, between returning downstairs and staying where she was. Downstairs was the ongoing story, plot-filled and relentless, of everything she knew; but in her room there was silence, daylight, an absence of structure. By stepping out of the story she had come upon the emptiness that lay all around it. It was so transparent and silent in that place: it seemed to presage the creation of something, though the moment of realisation never occurred. There was only solitude, beautiful but sterile, unpollinated. She never found anything there. In the end, she always went back.

She goes to bed and is woken all night by the knocking shutters, and by the wind moaning across the Zuider Zee.

# VIII

What is art?

It is the opposite of waste, of redundancy. Thomas goes through his cupboards and finds box after box of obsolete junk. Cables, computer parts, a whole case of grey plastic cartridges still sealed in their airtight transparent wrappers. The printer they were designed to fit no longer exists, and there is no other printer compatible with them. Yet they will last forever.

It comes to him, the physical feeling of his London office, the big steel and Perspex building with its wires and blinking screens and shrilling telephones, the bitter smell of plastic and electric light, the hushed grey spaces, the sealed windows muffling the world, the make-up smell of his secretary Samantha and her synthetic clothes, everyone so chemical-smelling and costumed, and the way people spoke, language itself made artificial, so that you found yourself looking at their teeth, their eyes, to remind yourself there was a human being in there. And most of all the feeling of being on board, of living in a never-resolving present, the feeling that all this artificiality could be sustained so long as it was never permitted to slip into the past. He remembers the way reality itself was made unreal. The last thing Thomas did before he left was to restructure a firm of dog food manufacturers. Three or four weeks in, someone produced a tin of dog food in a meeting. Until that moment, dog food had been theoretical. Now here it was, actual. After all that artificiality the actual had been uncovered. Thomas realised it had been there all along. Dog food had been there all along. Dogs, friendly and filthy and mortal, had been there all along.

He finds three tiny pairs of headsets, unopened, coiled in their little plastic sacks like embryos. They came with a mobile phone that has since been upgraded. The headsets don't fit the new phone. Yet they will last forever.

On the train, Thomas used to decide various things. He decided not to let himself fall asleep. He decided not to read newspapers. He decided to keep a diary. He decided to keep a sketchbook and make portraits of the other passengers. It was forty-five minutes each way, sometimes more. That was an hour and a half that he could reclaim from the wastage of every day. He wanted to sink an anchor down into that narrow channel of time. He wanted to stop himself drifting away.

In the cupboard he finds the diary, three notebooks, the book of watermarked paper where he meant to do his drawings. The diary is completely blank. In the other one there are two pencil sketches that he doesn't have any memory of making. For that reason they are slightly frightening. One of them is of a woman in glasses, with frazzled hair like a witch.

The image comes to him of a black dome-shaped thing made of plastic that used to sit on the desk in his office. He has no idea what it was. He looked at it every day. It had a kind of fissure in its casing, a scratch four or so inches long that travelled to the left and then straight, with a kink at the end. It seems possible he will not forget this strange and pointless object. It will survive in his mind forever, unchanging. It will, in a sense, outlive him. His recollection of the scratch is so exact that it might be a scar on his own body. Yet the woman whose face he drew, and the act of drawing it, have disappeared.

He finds a whole file full of instruction manuals for things that are broken or that he no longer owns. It is called progress, the replacing of one thing by another, the making of one thing meaningless by another. The meaningless things do not live, and nor do they die. Most of the people he knows think that progress is good.

Often, he would arrive at the station to see his train all packed and ready, the doors sealed, would see it begin to pull away from the platform without him. He has never felt more individual, more distinct than in those moments. Yet it was only that he had stopped going forward. For a second, he became the past. What was strange was that there seemed to be more possibilities there. He remembers the way he would automatically think of going to New Zealand, or South America. Never once did this idea occur to him at any other time. Only there, when he'd missed his train, the urge to take flight for distant lands, as though it were something about himself he'd dropped long ago on the platform at Waterloo and stumbled over again every once in a while.

Art, he thinks, is not progress.

# IX

Howard, fallen ill, lies and looks out of the window at the grey suburban midday. It is a view of bare forked trees against a blank, light-filled sky, of the gabled upper storey of number thirty-two. He never sees the world like this, in its weekday torpor. Mornings he is gone by eight o'clock and returns twelve hours later; he is always leaving or coming back, plunging in and out like a needle through the cloth. He does not ask how the cloth weaves itself, but here it is, knitting itself out of silence, out of stasis. Howard loves it, knitting itself round him like a cocoon. In this bedroom time has a certain thickness, an opacity: over the hours it seems to form a skin, like a cooling liquid. He hears cars passing outside, sometimes voices. There is a bird that makes a sound like a squeaking bicycle wheel. *Ree-ree-ree-ree-ree.* The voices come in jigsaw pieces which he fits together to make little broken-edged sections of life. Mother and child. Man walking dog. Postman delivering outsize item next door.

Claudia visits, sitting on the far edge of the bed. She, too, seems to feel the torpor, the heaviness in the atmosphere. He expects her to be familiar with it, but apparently she is not: she appears to believe it emanates from him.

'How are you feeling now?' she asks, brisk and enamel-eyed, scented, fully clothed. A little impatient, he senses, as though he were a piece of machinery that has broken down on her property and that she is keen to mend and move on its way.

He folds back the rumpled covers and pats the sheets.

'Do you want to come in?'

'Into bed?'

He touches her wrist. She looks alarmed.

'There's nobody here,' he says.

It is, he now sees, the problem with the day: it lacks the imposition of a human will. It is formless. It is a lump of clay which must be shaped by inspiration and desire. This, he recalls, is what freedom is. At forty-three freedom generally comes to him refined, in small quantities: decisions, directives, intricate opportunities for success. He has forgotten what the raw material feels like. Claudia fingers the silver pendant that hangs around her throat. He has seen it before but never noticed it, never noticed its cold compactness and the way it magnetises and draws her fingers to itself.

'I can't.'

'Come on, Claude. Just for a minute.'

He has irritated her. He has made her angry. The black shapes of birds pass silently across the dun-coloured sky. Claudia lies beside him, somewhat stiffly, on the bed. She does not take off her shoes. But she rests her head in the crook of his arm so that he can stroke her hair, which is dirty-looking today and held back by numerous little silver clips. This is what amazes him, the way people give themselves, the way they create, in the emptiness of the coming moment, another instant of life. He hears it rising from the blankness of the street: the woman so patient with her child, the man whistling for his dog. He thinks how virtuous they are, how good. The winter trees make stark, cross-hatched shapes beyond the window. He doesn't think people can ever be as good consciously as they are by instinct, on an empty street on a midweek morning in November. As his wife is, in this throwaway bit of the day, lying beside him on the bed.

'Do you want anything?' she says, when she is standing in the doorway again, straightening her clothes.

'Just a little soup,' he says weakly. 'Nothing much.'

'Soup,' she says. 'Any particular kind of soup?'

'Whatever there is. The one you make with leeks is very nice. And perhaps a roll, just one, with some butter.'

'Right,' she says.

He sees her look of resignation, of momentary oppression. Perhaps when he is at work she forgets all about him. What does she think about? What is he deflecting her from, stewing here in sheets that smell of himself, in their room that is becoming steeped in his own presence? She should air it, straighten the covers and open the windows, put flowers in a vase. Instead she straightens her own clothes, and looks slightly grim around the mouth when he asks for soup. In the window of the house opposite he can see a figure behind the dark glass. He sees a pale arm, lifting and moving, lifting and moving. He sees a dim fall of hair to a white shoulder. It is a woman ironing. He can see the metallic glint of the object, the pressure and repetition of her movement. Her face is in shadow. She is so steady, so industrious. He watches her, comforted. It is true that life lays a fetter on love: this, he thinks, may be Claudia's secret. There is virtue in industry, even as it sets its limitations on affection, even as it stints the hand of feeling. It is good that Claudia doesn't drop everything to lie beside him all day. He remembers the way his mother used to look after him when he was ill. There were always flowers in a glass by the bed, and a tray coming up the stairs. He remembers the feeling of paralysing love, the way she seemed to want to keep him there and he half-wanted to be kept, as though she had stolen him back from the world in order to perfect her care of him.

He sleeps for a while, and when he wakes he can smell the soup from downstairs. The day is unchanged. The bird is calling at the window. *Ree-ree-ree-ree-ree.* The telephone rings and he hears Claudia speaking. She speaks for a long time. Several times she laughs. Later she brings up a tray and puts it beside him on the covers. It is a quarter past two: his mouth is dry and bitter-tasting with hunger. The soup is pale green, thick, flecked with herbs, just as he had imagined it would be.

'Where's yours?' he says. 'Aren't you having any?'

She is moving around, picking things up, keeping out of his reach.

'I had mine earlier downstairs. I was hoping to get into the studio this afternoon. Have you got everything you need?'

He remembers this too, the feeling of his mother's secret life, and of himself as an interloper, eavesdropping on it; as though home were a trick, an artifice, and his illness the manifestation of his mother's guilt. After she goes he eats the soup, imagining her sitting alone at the table downstairs, eating hers.

# X

The house is empty. Olga moves through the rooms, looking at things. She is back early today, with a headache that sends big shivers all through her body. They let her go home. All the way on the bus the headache beat her, like a stick beating a drum. And then the driver shouted at her because she pressed the button too late, and he put the brakes on hard so that she was thrown against the rail. It hurt her: she has a red welt on her arm. Why did he do that to her? If she ever meets him again she will ask him. She has no friends here, no family, no language to express herself in. Why was it her he chose to hurt?

She stands in the room with the velvet sofa, where she is never invited, where they sit in the evenings and talk. There are chairs, a leather one and another one with an old-fashioned flowery cover. There is a table all piled up with newspapers and magazines and two dirty glasses. There is a piano, old, brown-coloured. The curtains in this room are green. She likes the material, raw silk, and she likes the gold mirror above the fireplace and the things that stand on the mantelpiece, a little gold clock with tiny engraved pillars like a temple, a paperweight with a blood-coloured peony engulfed in the glass, a sky-blue china vase with a narrow neck. There are little white figures engraved on its sides. They are dressed in tunic-like clothes, like gods and goddesses. They are dancing and talking and feasting all the way around. She looks at the books, leaning higgledy-piggledy on the shelves.

They are dusty, as the piano is. But the chairs and the sofa look friendly, like people talking, and the curtains make her think of the ball gowns actresses wear in old films. It is a good room, a warm room, but they never ask her to come in and sit down.

She goes upstairs to their bedroom, dusty too, clothes everywhere, the bed unmade. One night she heard them shouting in here. She does not like people who shout. But in the morning they were normal again, as though nothing had happened. The bed is like a rat's nest with the covers all tangled. It is strange, that two people would agree to leave it in that state. It is mysterious. She herself would refuse to get into that bed. She doesn't understand why they don't make their room nice. It is disgusting, to live like this. She opens a drawer, glances in. Men's underclothes, neatly folded. She is surprised. He is so untidy, so lazy, and yet in his own drawer where no one can see, everything is in order. She has come home at three or four in the afternoon and found him lying on the sofa, reading a book, while downstairs the kitchen is full of terrible sights and smells, flies buzzing around the dirty plates, the unswept floor crunching underfoot, pans with burnt food at the bottom left sitting there for days. She would never have guessed that he folded his underpants.

In her own room everything is clean and orderly. The white winter sun is coming through the window. There is a bluebottle swimming noisily at the glass. She swats it dead with a rolled-up magazine. The headache has left a hollow behind it. She touches the red mark on her arm with her fingertips. She feels lonely. She sits on her bed and dials her mother's number.

# XI

The piano teacher lives with his boyfriend in a basement flat on the other side of town. Ignatius is a pianist too: his grand is wedged into the cramped bedroom while Benjamin's upright occupies the living area, where brown damp stains spot the low, sagging ceiling, and the window looks out onto a small concrete courtyard and a flight of mildewed steps up to the street.

Even before he arrives, Thomas feels the atmosphere begin to act on his attitude to culture like astringent on a raw wound: the rows of run-down houses, the pavements piled with broken furniture and bloated sacks of rubbish, the rusted railings and bright venomous green of Benjamin's stairway, even the chipped front door, low like the door to a dungeon – it is all bracing, corrective, so that when the door opens and Benjamin appears, Thomas feels a confusing, lover-like rush of sensation towards him. Benjamin is not especially beautiful: it is just that in the squalor of his own hallway, his clean humanity is momentarily overwhelming. Thomas is slightly ashamed of the pleasure it gives him to look at Benjamin's milk-coloured skin, so restful to the eyes; at his hair, which is black and glossy, and at his pink mouth, with its choir-boy's expression of faint astonishment. His body suggests itself through his unexceptional cardigan and corduroys like a statue through a dust sheet. Lately Thomas has come to realise, as they face each other in the doorway, that Benjamin is pleased to see him too. A feeling of warmth, almost of excitement, is shed in the space between their irreconcilable bodies.

Thomas offers his hand – 'Hello again' – and after a brief hesitation Benjamin takes it, so that he wonders whether, in fact, Benjamin finds something awkward in the male handshake, something quaintly heterosexual. It occurs to him that gay men perhaps do not shake hands, that they hug or kiss each other's cheeks like women do. He wonders whether, next time, he will offer to hug Benjamin.

'Nice to see you,' Benjamin says, pressing his fingers and then releasing them.

They enter the hall, where torn pieces of brown vinyl skid underfoot and a single electric bulb hangs from a length of dirty flex. Benjamin has to duck his head to avoid hitting it. He rounds the corner, ducks again at the door to the lavishly untidy sitting room. Thomas follows him in, so closely that the pile of Benjamin's fawn cardigan is only inches from his eyes, for there is no possibility of distance in the cramped, warren-like flat and as a consequence the human form seems more significant, more textured, denser with association. Along with its squalor, it is this that causes Thomas to identify Benjamin's flat with youth. When he comes here he is reminded of a closer and more sensually vivid experience of the body that he did not realise, until now, he had forsaken. Sitting with Benjamin at the piano, their knees nearly touching, their hands crossing and recrossing as they explore the keys, Thomas is more physically proximate than he has been for years to anyone but his wife and child. Benjamin's chair is a wooden schoolroom chair that creaks whenever he leans forward to turn the pages or to demonstrate something on the keys. His limbs graze Thomas's field of vision, the legs and arms so rod-like and mathematical on their big knuckle-like hinges, the expert, spacious hands with their broad, clean nails, the firm male wrists and the vigorous brown hair of his forearm that is disclosed when he reaches up for the metronome: this is intimacy, this nearness that is always renewing itself through movement. It is hard to impress someone who is sitting so close. It has taken Thomas time to get used to the fact that it is through his hands and not his face that the impression must be produced.

Benjamin observes him unblinking behind his glasses.

'How has it been this week?'

'Good, I think. Fine.'

The first time, Thomas was flustered by this question, which seemed to press at some unexposed part of himself – to be somehow clinical, like a doctor's examination of hidden regions of the body. He sought to cover himself up; he tried to re-establish in words the sense of distance he could not accomplish physically. But now he is used to the exposure. He looks forward to the acknowledgement of it, this patch cleared of shame where now, week by week, he cultivates himself.

'You've kept on with the two-part invention.'

'Actually,' Thomas says nonchalantly, 'I've started looking at the *adagio*.'

Benjamin arches his narrow brows. 'The Beethoven?'

Thomas nods. He can see that Benjamin is surprised, a surprise that is faintly sceptical, so that Thomas's heart is made to thud against his breastbone. He knows what is coming next. The fact is that unlike nearly every other aspect of his adult life, there is no getting around a claim to have learnt to play the *adagio*. It cannot be explained, or deferred, or talked away. He has to show that he can do it.

'Do you have the music with you?'

'Yes.'

'All right, then.'

Benjamin rises, picks up his chair. He wades through the sheaves of manuscript paper that litter the filthy carpet and establishes himself three or four feet away, hands clasped attentively in his lap. His scepticism has evaporated: his brow is once more unclouded and eager. This is, after all, no place for scepticism. What would be the point of it? Thomas, when he watches Alexa carry her plate precariously to the sink, or observes Tonie reversing the car into a parking space, feels scepticism, doubt; he feels the world teetering just beyond his reach, like some toppling object he wants to grasp firmly and set squarely on its feet again. But Benjamin, apparently, will feel no such unease watching Thomas. Does he think it isn't important, how Thomas plays the *adagio*? Has he decided that since Thomas's performance represents no practical gain or loss to himself he may as well be indifferent to it? Benjamin inclines his head towards the piano. It is a courtly gesture: Thomas imagines himself inclining his head to Alexa, to Tonie, as they teeter on the brink of disaster. It signifies that Benjamin has left the field, the keyboard that sometimes seems to grin like a set of teeth and sometimes to glimmer like a far-off frozen landscape, a place as beautiful as it is inhuman, whose silence is occasionally interrupted by the sounds of struggle before swallowing them up again.

Benjamin clears his throat: 'When you're ready.'

The truth is that for the past week Thomas has worked on the *adagio* like a solitary prisoner tunnelling under the fortress walls. He is slightly ashamed of it, his secret determination, the rigidity of his methods, the insistent, repetitive labour he has put into it, for this is how he has always got the things he wanted in life, and how he has got the better of what he didn't want too. It has felt like cheating, just as it did when he studied all night to pass an exam, or got through the tedium of meetings by knowing more than anyone else, or planned down to the last detail his strategy for attracting the attention of a woman he liked. It has always seemed that work occupied the place where something more natural ought to have been, something instinctive and innate, something he associates with honesty, though he doesn't know exactly why. Sitting at the piano, he has felt sure that there is a more honest way of learning the *adagio* than to play each bar until its sanity has been broken down and become a rattling box of madness, but he has been unable to think of what it might be. He has felt a fleeting, bitter discouragement, even as his fingers were fumbling with and then tentatively mastering the music, for his decision to learn an instrument contains a nameless hope that seems to be being confounded before his eyes. He imagined, secretly, a kind of abandon awaiting him somewhere within its discipline; imagined himself freed, untethered by it to wander in great white fields of self-expression. But all that has happened is that ever-larger distances of method and minutiae have been disclosed that have turned the screws of his personality even tighter.

'As I say, I've barely even scratched the surface,' he says to Benjamin. 'It's hard to find the time. You know how it is.'

Benjamin inclines his head again, smiling.

'Well, here goes,' Thomas says.

For an instant his mind is filled with the white light of performance, the strange featureless lucidity left behind by the knowledge that he mustn't think, that his brain must be vacated, that instead he must act; and the next time he checks, he sees that he is already halfway down the first page, and the thinking makes him falter so he quickly vacates his brain again and returns to his hands. There is an awful passage that is like inching along a narrow ledge, and then a period when he seems to be safe in miles of firm level ground; then suddenly it is a cataract, a rushing to the edge, to disaster, and over he goes, swept down through the complexity and out the other side, where there is stillness and daylight and the untidy room with Benjamin sitting in his chair.

'Bravo!' Benjamin says, very flushed and astonished-looking.

The bedroom door flies open. It is Ignatius, as ruddy and squat and prodigiously hairy as Benjamin is slender and marmoreal. He stands in the doorway, applauding and exclaiming loudly, in his plush American that makes everything sound pleasanter and less sincere than usual. Then he advances into the room, cheerful and cocky-looking in his tight T-shirt, chest hair foaming at his throat, trousers straining around his haunches, a little reddish-blond tuft of beard sprouting from his chin. Benjamin is looking slightly pinched around the mouth.

'That *adagio* is just divine – I had no *idea* you'd got so important! I had my ear to the door, thinking who can that possibly be in there?'

'I can't play the other movements,' Thomas says apologetically, though his face is red with pleasure. Ignatius is a real pianist, not a teacher but a performer, whose name can be seen on flyers for lunchtime recitals at the Wigmore Hall. He is ashamed of his disloyalty to Benjamin: vaguely he understands that it is their intimacy that causes him to feel ashamed. Usually, only Tonie can constrain him in this way, web him finely with the knowledge of herself, so that he feels clumsy, tearing the gossamer threads.

'Well, it's hardly surprising,' Benjamin says. His voice is a little terse. 'It's only been a few months.'

Thomas turns the pages with their ferocious black peaks and chasms of semiquavers, their turbulent, chord-filled bass clefs. He doesn't fully understand why he can't play them. He has learned the *adagio*, yet the *allegro molto e con brio* and the *grave* remain as encrypted to his eyes as ancient Greek. Ignatius looks over his shoulder at the music.

'Lord, who can?' he says, sotto voce, as though this heresy were in danger of being overheard by the Bengali family who live upstairs and complain constantly to the Environmental Health department about the intolerable levels of noise in the basement. 'I say go for the big tunes, the big sensations, the highs. I just live for it – I live for that *adagio*! I'm all over gooseflesh.' He holds out his thick forearm. 'Am I flushing?' he asks Benjamin.

'Slightly,' Benjamin says stiffly. 'Your neck looks a bit red.'

Ignatius tugs at his collar, feeling around his neck. 'I have a weak skin,' he says. 'I am a litmus paper of emotion. Once it gets a hold, it's all over me. Rashing, blotches, hives – I can feel it spreading insidiously all through those defenceless cells and corpuscles. My mother used to say it was God's way of making sure I never told a lie.'

'When it was quite obviously a vitamin deficiency,' Benjamin says, apparently in spite of himself.

Ignatius tuts. 'Admittedly I am one hundred per cent trailer trash,' he says, to Thomas. 'In our house, the Pop-Tart was considered a health food. That darling faux-fruit centre – it makes my teeth ache just *thinking* about it.'

'It ought to be regarded as a form of cruelty,' Benjamin says. He stands and repositions his chair beside Thomas at the piano. Ignatius looks at him with fond vexation.

'Benjamin's just *marbled* with vitamins. Look at that hair!'

Benjamin blushes, touching his glossy dark hair. 'We ate a normal balanced diet, that's all. Just normal English food.'

'Shepherd's pie,' Ignatius says dreamily. 'I adore your mother's shepherd's pie. I would have followed her around all day like a puppy, hoping she'd drop some of that pie in my mouth. Or one of those tiny potatoes, all crunchy with goose fat.'

'It wasn't perfect, you know,' Benjamin says. 'There are other things children need besides food. I'm simply saying that it was normal.'

Thomas feels the current of the men's relationship flowing treacherously around him. It has never occurred to him that two men would make of love something that so resembles its heterosexual equivalent. He wonders whether love is a form, like music, that takes what has no name or being of its own and shapes it.

'I was perfectly well fed,' he says. 'But now I think I'd have preferred to have piano lessons.'

They both look at him inquisitively: a newcomer in their home town. All at once he feels his grasp of music ebbing inexorably away from him, as people forget whole languages in which once they were able to express their feelings. The *adagio* has become ancient Greek again. If they were to ask him to play it now, he wouldn't be able to.

'Was there no music in your house?' Benjamin asks, as though he considers this, too, to be a form of cruelty. 'That's quite unusual, I have to say.'

'Oh, my dear!' Ignatius flaps his hands in the air, distressed. 'That is just pure, pure fantasy! I hate to disabuse you, but in the world beyond that delicious place where you grew up, music is strictly, strictly for sissies.'

'East Sheen,' Benjamin says, with dignity. He folds his arms obstinately. 'I'm afraid I don't agree with you,' he adds, in a peevish, quavering voice, as though disagreeing with Ignatius was itself sissyish and hence something in which Benjamin compels himself to take a perverse kind of pride.

'Believe me,' Ignatius says, 'where I come from, any boy who asked for piano lessons was a certified fruit.'

Benjamin instantly reddens.

'That was a terrible place. That place ought to be destroyed.'

'How old were you when you learnt to play?' Thomas asks, a frail little hope fluttering in his chest.

'Eighteen before I played a note,' Ignatius says. 'Though I saw a piano once, in a friend's garage. It was so tragic and beautiful, sitting there among the power tools and the garbage cans. It was like a beautiful woman, all hemmed in by those ugly factual things. I just burned –' he wiggles his thick, hairy fingers '– burned to touch it, but it was not to be. I carried a torch for that old piano all through my dreary youth.' He shudders. 'It still makes me tingle all over to think of it.'

Benjamin is listening, though he must have heard the story countless times before. His expression is respectful, uncontrolledly interested, and Thomas glimpses it, the ferment of love, surging like a dark river around the roots of his being. But the next minute he seems irritable, officious, plucking back his cuff to look at his watch.

'We're falling very behind with our lesson,' he says. 'We really must get on.'

Ignatius puts his hand on Thomas's shoulder, and Thomas realises that he is kind, kinder even than Benjamin, for love has not undermined him as it has his lover; and Thomas feels himself yearning suddenly for the solidity and sincerity of this second man, for his unethereal pungency, so different from Benjamin's cleanly boyishness. It is as though their relationship has entered him and is enacting itself through his own senses.

'The *adagio* was divine,' he says, squeezing with his fingers. 'You played it well.'

Another time, a grey turbulent afternoon, shadows falling and rolling heavily through the dim window of Benjamin's room, the feet of passersby going past on the street above, litter whirling around their ankles. Ignatius is away, on tour in Germany. Benjamin has tidied up. He offers Thomas tea, and when it comes it is filmed with brown scum. Benjamin takes it away and brings back another in a clean cup. The door to the bedroom is ajar. Thomas can see the heavy flank of Ignatius's grand piano, the lid closed. The room is so small that the bed acts as a piano stool. He wonders, shocked, how they survive like this. With Ignatius away, Benjamin's atmosphere has already expanded, filling and marking the space. He imagines him tidying and putting things away. He imagines him closing the lid of the grand piano, satisfied.

'I've actually managed to get some of my own work done,' he says, like a housewife ritually oppressed by her husband's success.

Yet it is in this lesson that Benjamin changes things for Thomas. They sit together in front of the *adagio*.

'It's like a clock,' Benjamin says. 'Imagine you are inside a clock. The music is the mechanism.'

He plays a few bars, fingers going up and down like hammers, head swinging from side to side like a pendulum. He makes ticking noises with his tongue against his teeth. Thomas laughs. Benjamin rewards him by ticking even louder and wagging his head so violently that his whole body rocks in its chair.

'Tick tock tick tock –'

He pounds the *adagio* with his hammer-like fingers, and suddenly Thomas understands that what Benjamin is talking about is time.

When he gets home, he sits down at the piano and plays the *adagio* again. Alexa is there, standing in the doorway.

'It's like a clock,' he tells her, tick-tocking along with the music like Benjamin did, but she doesn't seem to understand, and when he tries to explain it to her he finds that he can't.

# XII

Claudia calls. There's a party she wants to go to but Howard is ill. She asks Tonie to go with her instead.

Tonie agrees – she likes the unexpected. And it's touching, sort of, that Claudia requires a chaperone, that after two decades of marriage she doesn't quietly seize the chance to experience something on her own. She picks Tonie up in her dog-smelling estate car. It is a black, penetrating night. Claudia is wearing something with a fur collar, like a Russian aristocrat. Her eyelids are bruised-looking, the mascaraed lashes tarred into spikes. Her hair is untidy, her nails bitten, her earrings expensive. In the yellow street lamps she has a pleasing look of degeneracy.

'They're *such* interesting people,' she says of their hosts.

'What's wrong with Howard?'

Claudia makes an exasperated sound, lifting her hands from the steering wheel.

'Don't even ask! I've been *beside* myself – he hasn't been to work for three weeks! He just doesn't seem to get better. He spends all day moping around the house in his dressing gown.'

Tonie has known Claudia for years, has caught her eye over countless family dinners, has stood beside her, their smart shoes chafing their feet, at christenings and funerals, has held her babies in her arms. She knows the forms her joy and resentment take; she has heard it for most of her adult life, Claudia's part, like the melody from another section of the orchestra.

'But what is it?' she says.

Claudia looks into the dark distances of the windscreen.

'Something to do with his lung, apparently. He finally went to the hospital two days ago and got it X-rayed. He thought it was flu, but flu doesn't just stay the same day after day, does it? I've been saying, you know, for heaven's sake go to the doctor and get a diagnosis! Get a diagnosis! Get a *diagnosis*!'

She thumps the steering wheel.

'So he did get one,' Tonie reminds her gently.

'Well, only after he'd laid waste to all my work plans and virtually barred my path to the studio, because he felt I should be looking after him, even though this was my first real chance to do some painting since the children went back to school after the summer –'

It is now December: the Christmas holidays start next week, as Tonie must suppose Claudia knows. They drive along in silence for a while.

'Anyway, it turns out he's got a patch,' Claudia resumes.

'What's a patch?'

'Just a sort of dark – *patch*, on the lung. They want to do a whatsit, a biopsy. I suppose sooner or later they'll tell us what it is.'

Tonie presses her palms flat against her thighs. The night is as fine as pitch. Outside the trees and railings are already rimed with frost. They are in a suburban area she doesn't recognise, big houses, their bulky forms dark, smart silvery cars in driveways with white frost on the windows. Everything looks perfected, abandoned. They pull into one of the driveways, ring the bell at a door lit by carriage lights. It is a big, rambling place. The bell sounds deep in the house. Tonie is afraid.

A large woman, robust and richly dressed as an opera

singer, opens the door. At the sight of them she flings out her arms.

'Darlings!' she exclaims.

They are in a room full of people. The woman makes a lot of noise. Tonie can't hear what she's saying, just the sound she makes saying it. Her name is Dana or Lana. The room is bright, busy, confusing. The walls are painted red. There are African sculptures, primitive masks, a tiger skin nailed above the fireplace. Tonie looks at the other people, middle-aged people with crumpled faces and thinning hair and soft shapeless bodies. They are depleted, exhausted-looking among the giant ebonised phalluses, the carved forms of pregnant savages. Claudia is talking to a documentary film-maker. She asks him questions about himself while Tonie watches. He is pale, moon-faced, with eyes like chips of vacant blue sky: Tonie notes the consideration with which he has dressed himself, his look of battered fashion. He has recently returned from filming in the Galapagos Islands.

'How *fascinating*,' Claudia says, so ingratiatingly that Tonie thinks she must be being ironic.

She asks him one thing after another, like a mother spooning food into a baby's mouth: when he comes to the end of one question she is ready with the next. They hear about the iguanas, about the turtles coming up the beach to lay their eggs, about the valour of his dedication to vulnerable beasts. Claudia nods and coaxes and smiles, and every time someone offers Tonie a drink she takes it.

'Why do those films always make the world look like it's perfect?' Tonie asks him.

He ponders her, the baby in his chair: is she friend or foe?

'Yes,' he says, 'I sort of see what you mean. We're editing

89

out all the mess, aren't we? People don't realise that just out of shot there's a car park and a big line of hotels – not to mention other film crews all going for the same thing and getting in each other's way. Sometimes it's a nightmare, getting what you want and keeping out what you don't.'

'*Terribly* difficult,' Claudia agrees.

'But why can't you show it as it really is?' Tonie says. 'What's the point?'

He frowns, puts his hands in his pockets. 'People don't want that sort of reality. And it isn't my job to give it to them.'

'Then you're just a liar,' Tonie says, but the room is noisy. She isn't sure he's heard her.

'Hasn't your wife had a baby?' Claudia asks him. She says the word 'baby' as though it's a big treat, something to reward him for having done so well. Tonie is surprised: she didn't think Claudia knew this man. She is certain he doesn't know Claudia's name. He has not asked them one question about themselves: she and Claudia do not exist for him, they are just lines of perspective, ways for him to measure his location in space.

'– six months old,' he is saying. 'I've barely seen her because of the filming. I think I've spent –' he calculates '– one fortnight at home in the whole six months, you know? But that's what it's like to have a vocation. It's hard, really hard. But that's how it is. You have to make sacrifices.'

Claudia looks almost tearful with sympathy, as though she were nothing to do with the person Tonie once witnessed screaming out of a top-floor window at Howard that she had bolted the door and wasn't going to let him into the house, because Howard had promised to be home that night by a certain time to help her with the children, and had either broken the promise or forgotten it. Tonie thinks about Howard, considers him. In her mind he is suddenly very small, like a doll. He is ringed by destiny: he has become representational. Everything he has done and been has been compacted into this tiny figure, emitting the squeak of life. She sees him being moved as though by an invisible hand around a toy kingdom. She sees he could be dashed away in an instant.

She leaves Claudia and pushes through the room. Later she finds herself talking to a man who makes coffins. He is threadbare, hippy-looking, with long grey hair. He makes the coffins by hand, out of wood from sustainable sources. He arranges natural funerals, in accordance with the wishes of the family. Tonie learns about the diversity of these wishes, their sources and outcomes. By now it is almost sexual, her desire to be penetrated by a question, but nobody asks her one. Instead she learns about the woodlands of Sussex and Kent, the tensile properties of the chestnut tree. There is African music playing, loud. Half of what the man says is blotted out. She watches his mouth moving. He glances at her frequently: he can tell she is untouched, disengaged.

Suddenly Claudia is at her elbow, listening. She nods her head as the man speaks; she asks questions. He becomes aware of her, turns the stream of information in her direction. She is a more gratifying audience than Tonie. She asks about the coffin made of English oak. She asks about the ultra-sustainable willow model. Her interest is genuine, the man can tell. Tonie watches in consternation. Has Claudia gone mad? She feels suddenly that she was brought here to witness Claudia in an act of betrayal. It is the ineradicable quality of her dependence – on Howard, on men – that is being exposed tonight. Claudia puts a hand on the man's arm. She is bright, transactional, faintly tragic in her fur collar.

'Do you have a card?' she asks him.

'As it happens I do,' the man says, producing one from his back pocket. 'Are you anticipating a – passing?'

For an instant Claudia looks both startled and mesmerised, like a snake being charmed out of its basket: her face is lit up, her mascaraed eyes unblinking. She takes the man's card and puts it in her handbag.

On the way home, there is a feeling of constraint between them. It is clear Tonie did not enjoy the party. And Tonie feels, suddenly, that she does not know Claudia at all. She is aware of Claudia's body, her hands with their rings on the steering wheel, her atmosphere coming at her across the dark. But her knowledge of this entity – Claudia – has been marginalised. They turn left and right through deserted roads. At Montague Street Tonie gets out, and Claudia drives away.

# XIII

'Do you ever hear anything about Clare?' Tonie asks Thomas.

'Who?'

'Clare. Clare Connelly.'

'No,' he says. 'Why do you ask?'

'No reason. I just think about her sometimes.'

'Do you?' He seems astonished. He seems to find it astonishing, not that he doesn't think about Clare but that she does. Yet once they talked about her all the time.

Tonie laughs. 'Don't you ever think about her?'

They are in the kitchen. It is late at night. Thomas is putting things away. She watches him, the way he holds each object – the pepper pot, the butter dish, the saucepan with the chipped enamel lid – while he establishes where it belongs. There is nothing automatic about it. It is as though male pride forbids him to acquiesce in the order of things. He has to consider the saucepan and then decide himself where it ought to go.

'The honest answer', he says, 'is that I haven't thought about her since the last time I saw her.'

She realises that he is pleased that he hasn't thought about Clare. It pleases him, to detect this shallowness in himself, this simplicity. In fact, she can't exactly say that she herself thinks about Clare. It is more than that: Clare is a place in her mind she touches in passing, sometimes intentionally, sometimes brushing against her by accident. Tonie feels a kind of nostalgia for her, as she might for a particular song that fits like a key into the lock of time and lets the past come rushing out. The intricate Clare-ness of Clare unlocks her memory of the first weeks with Thomas in just the same way. In those days Thomas talked about Clare constantly. He wrestled with the moral problem of her while Tonie watched in wonder and admiration. So it's strange – isn't it? – that now he doesn't think about her, can barely remember who she is.

'That's so – weird,' Tonie says.

During that winter he would meet Tonie clandestinely by the river in Putney, where he lived at the time, and they went for long walks in the dark. Camouflaged in shadow they walked and walked beside Richmond and Kew, beside the silent swift-running water, passing and re-passing the riverside bars and restaurants without ever going in, though secretly Tonie wanted to. She wanted to sit with Thomas in the warmth, at a candlelit table. She wanted his full attention, which on the muddy towpath in the dark she was not sure she ever got. But she never suggested it: she realised he would find it inappropriate. Instead they walked for miles in the cold, talking all the time. When they talked Tonie had the sense of something big and bounteous nearby, as the sea can be sensed when it is still just out of sight. Sometimes, overcome by excitement and emotion, she would turn to Thomas and try to kiss him, and her lips would bump against his chin or his ear as he averted his face. He would not kiss her, because of Clare. He would not be unfaithful. Tonie believed that she had never in her life seen someone behave honourably. She could barely breathe with the exacting thrill of it. She was electrified: she was driven out of her wits, as with other men she had been by passion. Except that to see passion subjugated to honour was a thousand times more tormenting. After three weeks of this, Thomas had a conversation with Clare and moved his possessions out of her flat. For a while she phoned, her voice high-pitched and distant-sounding in the receiver when Tonie answered it, and Thomas sometimes met her for lunch. Then one day he said that Clare had decided to put an end to the conversations and the lunches. She did not want to talk to Thomas any more. She found it too painful.

Tonie wasn't really concentrating, during Clare's final chapter. She saw Clare on the periphery of her vision: she registered her gradual disappearance as she might have registered a city passing and ebbing and falling behind through the windows of a train, without really looking. If the train had stopped, if the city had never given way to suburbs and green fields, she might have looked up and noticed, but as it was Clare's diminishing presence did nothing to alert Tonie or arouse her suspicions. By degrees she vanished, that was all, while Tonie and Thomas went forward into a future that seemed as full and fluid as the past was desiccated and fixed.

Clare came to the house once, with a parcel for Thomas that had been delivered to her address. She was just passing, she said; she left her car in the middle of the street, the engine running, the door wide open. She was tall and statuesque: Tonie was amazed by the solidity of her body, its grandeur, the clean healthy look of her, her breasts bouncing in a tight white jersey as she ran up the steps, her fair, well-shampooed hair in its ponytail bouncing too. Thomas always insisted that Clare's blondeness was natural. Tonie remembers the energy she expended disabusing him of this quaint notion, but now she wonders whether she was wrong, whether everything about Clare that at the time seemed so fictitious was in fact real. It is because she was real that Tonie has not forgotten her. Nor has she been able, though ten years have passed, to forget the way that Thomas, during those night-time walks by the river, averted his face and imposed something penitential, something almost punitive on his first encounters with Tonie. Increasingly, she feels that her life has been marked by a lack of pre-eminence. She feels that the only person who has ever loved her first-hand is Alexa. Perhaps it is this authentic love that has shown her how incomplete the others were.

It strikes her now that life is not linear, a journey, a passage, but a static process of irreversible accretion. It is perspective that moves, passing over it all like the sun, now illuminating, now casting into shadow. The angle changes, the relation of one thing to another, the proportion of dark to light; but experience itself is block-like, is cumulative and fixed. That is why it surprises her, troubles her, that Thomas does not think of Clare. For Clare has not vanished. On the contrary, ten years on she casts a longer shadow than she did before. And those nights by the river, when Tonie looked at the lit-up places and yearned to be inside one of them, sitting opposite Thomas, the object of his gaze and full attention: they, too, have grown more significant, not less. The more she thinks about them, the more symbolic they become. They symbolise the impossibility of perfection, of true and perfect love. She wanted to go in and yet she pretended for Thomas's sake that she did not. It is the extension of want and pretence into the sufficiency of love that is symbolic. While he gave unfettered expression to his guilt, his anxiety, his conception of honour, she suppressed the small, indignant voice that told her she was entitled, while taking the risk of love, to his full attention.

She thinks now about Clare's final act of renunciation: again, she barely noticed it at the time, but it reminds Tonie that she herself could have renounced Thomas, that she could have lived the other life, the non-Thomas life, as Clare even

96

now is presumably doing. She wonders which life has turned out to be better. She wonders why she wanted one so much more than the other, when in fact, in a way, they are the same. She realises that of the three of them, she, Tonie, is the only one who did not act decisively.

'It's so weird that you don't think about her,' she says.

He is still holding the saucepan. He is wondering what she means. She sees that for him, too, not thinking about Clare has become the same as thinking about her. All the same he is offering it to her, to Tonie, as a tribute, a gift; the latest incarnation of his sense of honour. But she wants to remind him of all that caution and concern he went in for by the river. She wants to draw his attention to the fact that once, when it mattered, he stinted Tonie's share. He ought to know that Tonie has felt hungry ever since, that she worries about this hunger, worries that she will be driven one day to placate it.

'I wouldn't like that, if it were me,' she says.

It's true, she wouldn't.

'But it isn't you,' he says.

'It could just as well be.'

He looks at her, puzzled. He sighs, shakes his head, puts the saucepan in the cupboard.

'Would it be better if I said I thought about her all the time?' he says.

# XIV

The house is such an odd little house, tall and thin and spindly as a doll's house. The Swanns joke to their friends that when they visit Antonia's house they have to breathe in.

Recently, their elder daughter Elizabeth moved with her family to an eighteenth-century manor house with five acres, a swimming pool and superb transport links to London for James: there can be no jokes about that. Mrs Swann has encountered unexpected difficulties in describing Elizabeth's house to her friends. She doesn't know what tone to strike. She has always ridden Elizabeth well, like an expert jockey rides a racehorse, but lately she has felt herself to be clinging on as the pace gets faster and faster. She finds that she has little to say on the subject: she is simply trying to maintain a foothold.

So there has, unusually, been some relief to be had in the contemplation of Antonia, whose affairs Mrs Swann can encompass in conversation without effort, in the way that a novelist encompasses a minor character. It is achieved by means of repetition: when Antonia appears, it is to enact the qualities of contradiction and eccentricity that already define her to her audience. She is never developed, merely confirmed. Currently, it is far easier for Mrs Swann to revert to stock than to consider how the story of Elizabeth's unstoppable rise, with all its dark tumult of jealousy and fear, could be told without publicly diminishing its narrator.

But as her husband turns the car up Montague Street, Mrs

Swann remembers that it isn't like that at all. Her sense of Antonia as a set of quirks, like a set of piano keys awaiting her touch, vanishes entirely. Instead there is a dense atmosphere of bitterness and failure that has not enveloped her since the last time she was here, and that tells her better than any road map that her youngest daughter's house is nearby.

Her husband feels it too. He eyes the street. They linger, not wanting to leave the safe harbour of their four-litre Mercedes.

'Will the car be safe out here, do you think?' he says.

It is Thomas who opens the door. Antonia is standing just behind, in the narrow hall. Mrs Swann sees her eyes, wide and unblinking, sees their expression of wonderment. From the street the hall looks dark, filled with shadows, and Antonia's eyes are floating among them, gazing at Mrs Swann as though they can see into her soul.

'Mind your head,' she says to her husband, as he passes ahead of her beneath the door frame.

He waits for her on the threshold.

'Be careful you don't trip,' he says. 'There's a loose board in the floor there.'

Once inside Mrs Swann immediately produces the bag of Christmas presents that is the occasion for their visit. They are lavishly wrapped, the paper glossy and unmarked, the gold ribbon twirled into perfect ringlets. Her husband wrapped them. He is generous with the paper, as only a man can be, for he barely knows what it is he is wrapping. Mrs Swann bought the presents, alone. She left it to her husband to be generous with the paper: her own involvement is with what is inside.

Thomas tries to take the presents, and Mrs Swann discovers that she is reluctant to part with them. Her hands will not let go of the bag.

'Where's little one?' she says, looking around her for Alexa.

'She's at a birthday party,' Thomas says.

'Oh no!' cries Mrs Swann. She is astonished. Not once has she imagined this scene occurring without the presence of a child. It is like Mass occurring without a priest at the altar. It casts a dreadful, civilian greyness over everything. 'Couldn't she have missed it, just this once?'

Her husband puts a cautionary hand on her arm.

'Selina,' he says, 'don't get involved. The child has her own life to lead.'

She understands him: he is speaking to her in a language that underlies even her own consciousness, that is the more private and profound for the fact that over the years it has blotted out her native tongue, solitude.

'Well,' Thomas says, 'only until four o'clock.' He looks at his watch. 'She should be back any minute.'

'Oh,' says Mrs Swann. She doesn't care when Alexa is coming back. What she wanted was to have her here when she arrived. 'Hello, Antonia,' she adds, so that it sounds like an afterthought.

Antonia steps forward, receives a cool kiss on the cheek.

'Hey, Mum,' she says.

Her daughter is wearing black trousers, a black T-shirt, black shoes – all negative, like those things in space that can swallow you whole while taking up no room at all. She wears no make-up or jewellery. Her full, flesh-coloured mouth is provocative in its nakedness. Even as a teenager Antonia wore black. The daughters of Mrs Swann's friends wore Laura Ashley prints with frilled collars, smart little pumps, mohair jerseys in pastel shades, while Antonia went around like a Greek widow in black. Someone once called her that to

Mrs Swann's face – your daughter, the Greek Widow – and there in the supermarket Mrs Swann felt the hot uprush of rage all fenced around with powerlessness, so that she went home bursting with it, with a boiling anger whose urgent need for discharge seemed to threaten a public indignity of the kind Mrs Swann had not experienced since childhood. She remembers it now, the feeling that she might be about to disgrace herself, a feeling so violent, so overpowering, that it led Mrs Swann to pity herself, to pity herself profoundly. And even afterwards, when she had found Antonia in her room and unleashed herself on her daughter's black-clad form, when she had said and done things that seemed to mirror the disgrace and even, in moments, to become it, she could not feel other than a victim, hitting out in whatever way she could at her attacker.

Such scenes have characterised her relations with Antonia from the beginning: even on her first day of life, Mrs Swann remembers feeling very distinctly that she had lost something, and that it was Antonia who had stolen it from her. She re-members a phrase – *codes of formality* – that haunted her during Antonia's babyhood, for the fact that she had already irrevocably violated them. The problem is that once broken, such boundaries are difficult to rebuild. She has tried, but they crumble at the slightest pressure. It would have been different if her husband had taken Antonia's side. But he did not: Mrs Swann wouldn't allow him to. Over the years she has often considered cutting free of this control and isolat-ing herself in her anger; she has sensed, instinctively, that if her anger could be isolated it could be cured. But there is something deeper than her anger, something pre-existing, something original and authentic that is only revealed when her husband allies himself with Antonia. Mrs Swann fears it more than anything else. She takes one look at it and knows that there is no alternative – has never been nor ever will be any alternative – to her and her husband standing united against their daughter.

Now Antonia embraces her father there in the hall, in front of Mrs Swann. Her arms encircle him for a second too long; her narrow hips and pert little buttocks stare at Mrs Swann insolently.

'Shall we go through?' Mrs Swann says, imperatively. 'I'd appreciate a cup of tea, if it isn't too much to ask, after all those hours in the car.'

In the cramped sitting room, Thomas goes around clearing old newspapers off the chairs and picking up dirty cups and glasses. It is like the absence of Alexa, the fact that they haven't tidied up or prepared for the Swanns' visit: it makes the world seem grey, random, devoid of belief. Mrs Swann sits with her husband on the velvet sofa, which creaks and shudders under their combined weight.

'Have you had this re-covered?' she says, fingering the mangy velvet arm.

Antonia shakes her head. 'It's the same as always.'

'Is it? Oh. But the curtains *are* new,' she says.

'I had them made.' Antonia is obviously pleased. 'Don't you think they're fabulous? They're antique silk.'

'Are they?' Mrs Swann is aggrieved by the curtains. There is something critical about them, something that smacks of personal rejection. 'Why didn't you say you wanted curtains? I've got *boxes* of old pairs I could have given you. You could have had them altered for next to nothing.'

Instantly she sees Antonia's face close, close shut like a door.

'I wanted green curtains,' she says. 'I wanted that particular colour.'

'What a waste!' says Mrs Swann. 'When I think of all those curtains in the attic, all beautifully lined, with proper pelmets, just sitting there gathering dust –'

She thinks of the attic, the twilit space, with its freight of wastage and accomplishment. She pictures it, finding the box and getting it down, unfolding the heavy musty cloth as though it were a section of the past that could be redeemed, relived. It would be good to redeem some of that wastage. She imagines the curtains, her curtains, at Antonia's window. On second thoughts, perhaps she wouldn't like it after all.

There is a sound at the door, and a moment later Alexa comes in. At the sight of the Swanns her face lights up, cautiously.

'Hello, Grandma,' she says, coming closer.

Mrs Swann grasps her, receives her, pulls her unresisting form on to her lap. She is like a doll, or a teddy bear. Mrs Swann feels that she could tell her everything.

'Silly Mummy,' she says. 'Silly Mummy getting curtains made, when Grandma has boxes of them at home.'

Alexa smiles anxiously, glances at her mother.

'What curtains?' she says.

'All the curtains I've got in my attic. You remember my attic, don't you? Well it's full to bursting with curtains, all going to waste.'

'Why don't *you* use them?' Alexa asks her.

'Grandma can't use them, darling. Grandma already has curtains in her house.'

Alexa considers it. 'Why don't you give them away to charity?'

Mrs Swann feels a faint vexation, a sense of entanglement. She remembers it from her own children, the feeling that a child who had come into the world pure and new, unmarked, had somehow become knotted up, full of snags and resistances. What she liked best was a baby, a clean sheet.

'Grandma believes that family comes first. If everyone took care of their own family, there wouldn't be any need for charity, would there?'

Thomas has come in with the tray. Mrs Swann wants to grab it from his hands, a steaming cup, a unit of nourishment. She wonders how she will drink her tea with Alexa on her lap. She sees Thomas wonder the same thing as he passes the cup to her. His hand hovers with it, just out of reach.

'Alexa, let Grandma drink her tea,' Antonia says, motioning her to get off.

Alexa tries to move, but Mrs Swann is holding on to her for dear life.

'Let her stay where she is,' she says. 'I won't hurt her, you know. I think I can be trusted to look after a child without scalding her.'

Antonia and Thomas exchange looks. Thomas places the cup on the table, just out of reach. Mrs Swann joggles Alexa up and down on her knee.

'We'll just let it cool down a bit, shall we?' she says. 'Mummy and Daddy are such terrible worriers. They think Grandma can't drink her tea without spilling it. But in fact Grandma's bigger than they are. That's funny, isn't it?'

'I hear you've gone freelance,' Mr Swann says to Thomas.

'In a manner of speaking,' Thomas says.

'They using you much? I did a couple of years of consulting myself. At the time it looked like that was where the real money was, but personally I couldn't stand it. I didn't like the lack of structure. I saw other people getting out, working for themselves, and some of them were making serious money, but it all comes unravelled sooner or later. A lot of them went under. Some of them good friends of ours. Meanwhile I'm drawing my share options and my pension. They all said I was too conservative, that I should take more risks, but look who's had the last laugh.'

There is a silence. The others drink their tea, but Mrs Swann has been separated from hers.

'The main difficulty,' she says, 'was that he hated being at home all day. What's a man doing, hanging around the house? That was the problem. A lot of those marriages,' she adds significantly, 'ended in divorce. The women simply couldn't stand it. They lost all respect for their husbands. I think marriage needs an element of mystery,' she continues, warming to the sound of her own voice. 'I told them, but they wouldn't listen. They thought it would all be long lunches and jumping into bed in the afternoon. I said to them, no, don't let them come home! A man isn't a man if he's in the house all day. You *need* a man, in a marriage. But they wouldn't listen. And then they're surprised when their –' she remembers Alexa is on her lap '– their intimate life goes to pot into the bargain!'

She laughs merrily. She is almost fond of them, these deluded souls she has created. She created them and then she sent them to their doom, for failing to heed her wisdom, her experience.

Thomas laughs too. 'Oh, Tonie's pretty mysterious,' he says.

'Is she?' Mrs Swann finds something distasteful in this remark.

'And she's hardly ever at home these days. So perhaps that proves your theory.'

Mrs Swann blinks. 'Why is she not at home?'

'I told you, Mum,' Antonia says. 'I've gone full-time. They made me Head of Department.'

Mrs Swann draws herself up. Do they think she suffers from senility? 'I knew they'd made you a head,' she says. 'But I thought it was some kind of – of certificate. I didn't realise it meant working extra hours. You didn't tell me that.'

'They're getting their money's worth out of you, are they?' says Mr Swann, with the laugh he uses to express disapproval.

Mrs Swann clutches Alexa closer. 'And who looks after little one?'

'Thomas does.'

'But I thought Thomas was working from home! How can he work and look after a child at the same time?'

Antonia sighs. 'I've told you all this already, Mum.'

Mrs Swann is trembling. It is the effort of bringing this scene to its just conclusion, of saying what needs to be said: it exhausts her and it invigorates her, both at the same time.

'So they've given you unpaid leave, have they?' Mr Swann asks Thomas.

'No,' Thomas says. 'I've resigned.'

'Have you now?' Mr Swann sits back, apparently stunned. 'You've resigned, have you?'

Thomas stands, begins collecting the teacups. Mrs Swann has always had a strong feeling for Thomas, as a thing of value that lies within her daughter's possession. Antonia's other boyfriends were mostly people who could either be pitied or despised, but Thomas has always made Mrs Swann feel strangely alert and aware of herself. It is as though it is she he is attracted to, not Antonia. He has a lean, muscular body she would like to touch, with something tough and tensile inside it like a length of rope. She would like to take him; she would like to have him for herself. And yet she is dimly aware that this desire involves Antonia. It is refracted, somehow, from the maternal root. He acts like a prism, receiving her ambivalence and separating it, separating her hatred from her love. She passes through Thomas and she is liberated of her burden of dark feeling.

But looking at him now, she feels the sheen coming off him. She feels the first disintegration of the surface. In the end, she wants him to be destroyed. The reality of the root, of its deep and primary confusion, requires it.

When it is time to go, Mrs Swann draws her daughter aside.

'You've got very thin,' she says. 'You look tired. I hope you're looking after yourself.'

Antonia's black trousers are tight-fitting, impossibly minute. Mrs Swann remembers, years ago, an afternoon spent in Antonia's room when she was out; remembers taking clothes from her daughter's drawers, shirts and trousers and dresses, and forcing her own mottled arms and legs into them. She was so very large, as she still is today. She remembers laughing, at the trousers that wouldn't go past her knee, at the shirtsleeves her hands could barely worm through.

Antonia looks surprised. 'I'm fine,' she says. 'I feel good.'

Suddenly Mr Swann is by her side. If she could have got him there by magic, he couldn't have appeared at a better time.

'You mustn't let the responsibility wear you out,' Mrs Swann says. 'I'm just saying, Richard, that Antonia looks very tired, very worn.'

Mr Swann looks stricken, in his rigid, metallic way. She makes a mental note, to encourage him to change his glasses. The steel frames have a touch of the robot about them. She envisages him in tortoiseshell, something more modern and forgiving.

'We should have a talk,' he says to Antonia. 'Your mother and I have – well, let's just call them concerns. We think you and Thomas may be making a serious error. We'll talk in a few days' time. Please just hear us out.'

Mrs Swann couldn't have put it better herself.

Antonia looks troubled. 'All right,' she says. 'But I'm fine, honestly.'

In the car on the way home, the Swanns talk everything over. They pick through every strand of the afternoon. By the time they arrive, they have analysed the situation so thoroughly that no further need to discuss it with Antonia herself remains. In bed, in the dark, Mrs Swann lies awake for a few minutes, putting together the story of their visit to Montague Street. There is a word she needs that is the key to it all, a word she has heard several times lately and not entirely understood. But she feels confident that this story will explain the word, or the other way around, when she comes to tell it. She grasps and grasps and finally lays her hand on it. *House-husband*. She is satisfied. She closes her eyes, and feels herself grow smaller and smaller until she disappears.

# XV

At first he doesn't miss Alexa. One minute she is there, standing at the door in her school uniform, and the next she is
gone, non-existent, just as she used to be when Thomas was
at work. He barely thinks of her when she is at school. There
are two realities, one where she exists and another, unrelated,
that he occupies alone. Then, at four o'clock, she reappears at
the door, slightly scuffed, estrangement filming her features,
and their life together resumes.

One day, in the middle of the morning, Thomas finds himself searching his mind for the moment of her departure.
At breakfast she had complained that her stomach hurt. He
dimly recalls her face, wan and drooping, but after that all he
can remember is his own determination to send her to school.
It is as though his will were a loud sound that has drowned
out everything else. Why did he want her to go so much? He
doesn't exactly know. He wonders now what the trouble was.
He wishes to reconstruct it, Alexa's stomach ache, her experience of the hour they spent together, her reluctant passage
out of the house, but there is only himself, crashing above
everything like a symphony. At half past three he doesn't wait
for Georgina to bring her home. He goes and collects her
himself.

Sometimes, standing in the tarmacked playground, he is
enveloped in vague feelings of beneficence and sympathy, almost of sadness. Usually he is early: the children have not
yet come out. The bright geometric climbing frames, the

empty sandpit, the neat, indestructible shrubs in the flower beds seem so familiar to him. He appears to be remembering them, and yet here they are before his eyes. It is as though he is observing them from a strange afterlife. This, he realises, is where Alexa spends the majority of her waking hours.

Other people arrive; he begins to hear the mutter of conversation, babies' cries, the shouts of small children. He has noticed that the levels of ambient noise in the playground make a virtually unimpeded ascent from *piano* to *fortissimo* in the half-hour that he is there. There is always a moment at which he is no longer able to distinguish one sound from another. It is this loss of the power of individuation that makes him feel unreal. He needs Alexa to come out; he needs something he can identify, in order to exist again. Little benches stand around the perimeter and he sits on one. He hums the *adagio*. He taps his fingers on his thighs.

# XVI

In a jug on the kitchen table there are yellow roses. Thomas put them there. They catch his eye every time he passes, a yellow sunburst in the shadowy depths of the downstairs room.

He tries to remember what month it is. The yellow colour of the roses makes him think of summer, but the surrounding light is grey and surrendered, as though it is ready at any moment to give in to darkness. He laughs aloud – it is funny, that he doesn't know what month it is. He says the names of the months to himself. No one name means more to him than any other. For a second he is not even sure which part of time he is in, whether the incipient darkness is rising or ebbing, whether it is day that is to come or night. He looks at his watch; he remembers that it is Thursday, that it is January. He feels better. He has accomplished a small but necessary task, something to make himself more comfortable. The year is an event he is observing, not participating in, like an audience watching a play. He has made himself comfortable in the audience, comfortable in its lack of ambition, but occasionally he is seized by anxiety, torn unexpectedly out of himself, like a small unwary creature suddenly gripped in the talons of a predator. There is something defenceless about his position. There is a vulnerability that comes with the lack of participation. Anxiety can swoop down on him at any time and bear him away.

He decides to go running. He sees Alexa to school and

then he runs away into the morning, running along the pavements, along the residential roads towards the park. He does this every day. At the end of a week his body feels prouder, more assertive. He is filled with a tension-like expectation that is never acknowledged or resolved, but passes into the expenditure of the next day's run. He feels the tension, and he feels the relief of its expenditure. The roses turn brown around their yellow hearts.

One day Tonie returns to the house in the middle of the afternoon. There has been a fire in the computer rooms and the university buildings have been evacuated. She comes in with her bag full of files, charged with a dangerous, unspent energy.

Thomas is sitting at the piano. He is learning the C major fugue of *The Well-Tempered Clavier*. The prelude is easy, but the fugue is defeating him. He can play the left hand and he can play the right hand, but when he tries to play them together he encounters an absolute deficiency in himself. The problem is that the hands are equal. In every other piece Thomas has played, the right hand has been dominant: he has come to depend on the leadership of the right hand, to identify with it, as he might identify with the hero of a novel. Usually, the left hand is purely supportive, making no particular sense on its own. But in the fugue the left hand is autonomous.

'What a sight,' Tonie says, standing at the sitting-room door, laughing. Her laugh is full of hard, concealed shapes, like the files in her bag.

Thomas looks up. 'I don't know,' he says. 'I just can't do it.'

She screws her face up, quizzical. 'You don't *have* to do it.'

'I want to. Other people can.'

Without taking her jacket off, she begins to tidy up the room. It is true that Thomas is increasingly preoccupied by the mystery of other people's abilities. He can hardly bring himself to listen any more to his Glenn Gould recordings, to his Clifford Curzon boxed set, to Feinstein's indistinct, primordial account of Bach, so swamped does he become in the knowledge that these men are vastly more capable than himself. And it isn't just music, either: the same feeling besieges him when he considers literature or painting, when he leafs through the photographs in his *Encyclopedia of World Art*, a feeling that is beyond jealousy, that is a sort of sulkiness. All these others, born just as he was, into the same world: they are all better, more capable, more exceptional than he is. Recently he took Alexa to the circus, and even the acrobat in his sordid spangled costume, even the hula-hoop girl in her greasepaint were more exceptional. The acrobat whirled around the half-empty tent on a rope, a force of pure plasticity. All his male stiffness was entirely subjugated: he could make his body do whatever he told it to. Yet Thomas cannot make his hands play the fugue. The gyrating hula-hoop girl spun twenty silver rings around her casually outstretched foot, grinning with her painted mouth. She was an artist, in her way. She has something Thomas does not have, an ability.

How has it eluded him, art, when all these others have grasped it? What has he done wrong? He remembers the afternoons of his childhood, his mother there, his own determination to secure her approval and love, to get to her ahead of his brothers. And he succeeded. He studied the situation and turned it to his own advantage. It wasn't particularly difficult. His brothers always seemed so distracted, so chaotic, their joys and satisfactions coming randomly, haphazardly, unplanned. Though all the same they came. When his mother cherished Howard or Leo it was for no reason that Thomas could identify. Thomas, thinking about his life, sees himself always grappling with a fixed creation, wrestling with it, turning it to his own advantage. Did he ever look at his mother, really look at her? Did he observe his brothers, people who were just as real as himself? He used to defend Leo against Howard, when they were children: he remembers deciding that this was the behaviour of a successful person, the defence of the weak against the strong, a kind of qualification, like a diploma. He remembers laying it at the feet of an unseen authority, his diploma. It didn't make him like Howard less, or Leo more. It didn't involve him personally. And his mother: the shape of her is all he remembers, the shape of what he wanted for himself. He would be unable to describe what she was like.

This is how art has eluded him, in the struggle to succeed at life. An artist, he supposes, dies to life, dies in that struggle, dies and is reborn. Tonie is moving around the room, bending and straightening. She too, he realises, knows what it is to create. She created Alexa: he remembers the way her old life died, went over the cliff and smashed itself on the rocks, unfinished; Alexa's birth also the old Tonie's death. And then something new struggling out of the wreckage, the new Tonie, this woman who stands here now in her work clothes, more alive than ever and full of dangerous energy.

'Don't do that,' he says, watching her.

'Someone has to do it,' she says. 'The place is a mess.'

It had occurred to him that they might go to bed, here in the afternoon. But it is clear that this is not a possibility. He sees that she is frustrated. She doesn't want to be back at home, washed up on the domestic shore before her day has run its course. Her existence relies on the separation of one thing from another. She can never be whole again, having smashed herself on the rocks of creativity. It would drive her mad to find herself in bed with her husband when she would normally be at work. It isn't that she thinks these things *ought* to be separate. It's that they *are* separate, as the two halves of a broken plate are separate, as his right hand is separate from his left. But neither half can be anything on its own.

'I was going to do it,' Thomas says. 'I was going to do it later.'

He looks at the room and sees its disorder. He sees that Tonie is wondering how he can live like this. She is looking at him as something totally separated from herself. It is possible that Tonie could betray him, betray him without conscience. The broken parts of her could neglect to correspond. They could go their different ways without a word.

'I know,' she says. She puts her hand to her forehead. 'It just suddenly seems important. I don't know why, but it does.'

He rises from the piano stool. He gathers up the music books that lie all around it on the floor and replaces them on their shelf. He collects the cups and plates – he has started having lunch up here, at the piano – and carries them down to the kitchen. There he finds more cups and plates and he gathers them, fetching and carrying, turning on the taps. Tonie appears: she has shed her jacket and rolled up her sleeves. She has an armful of things which she drops into the rubbish, one after another. Thomas finds dirty saucepans, roasting dishes, baking tins, and plunges them clanging into the foaming tumult of the sink. Tonie opens the cupboard and takes out the mop. Later he sees her washing down the shelves and doors. When he has finished the saucepans he cleans the cooker, involving himself more and more deeply in the intricacies of its plates and burners, losing himself in the black cavity of the oven. Presently, Olga returns. She comes down to the kitchen. She stands and stares.

'What are you doing?' she asks.

The next time Thomas looks, Olga has extracted the Hoover from the bowels of the understairs cupboard and is dismantling it with a screwdriver. She cleans the parts, reassembles it, revs it up. Thomas has moved on to the windows; Tonie is scrubbing the sills. The dishwasher is churning; the tap is dripping rhythmically into the polished sink. The thump and shriek of the Hoover recedes and comes back, recedes and comes back. Tonie dips and rinses her sponge in a bucket by her side, the water raw and slightly obscene-sounding, opening and closing around itself. His ears strain to order the noises. He hears the squeaking sound his cloth makes against the glass and he syncopates it, coming in on the Hoover's off-beat. He feels the imminence of chaos. He feels it poised on the brink of dispersal, his creation; soon it will atomise into nothingness. There are footsteps, the sifting noise of a broom. The water closes on itself; the Hoover dies into silence. The end is coming – oh, the tension, the spurious tension of control! He understands that to create is to lose control, to become purely receptive. Yet how can he save what he has lost control of? His fingers fumble with the cloth and it falls to the floor. He bends to retrieve it; and it is there, crouching, that he hears Tonie empty the bucket, the suds and dirty water cascading into the drain, a long, low sound, perfectly measured. It gushes in his ear, the torrent; his tension is resolved. And then, coming up from the floorboards, the final vibration, the sound of Olga approaching. She has the withered yellow roses in her hands. Her footsteps grow louder, a last siege on the encroaching silence. She pauses; she waits. Then she thrusts them triumphantly into the bin, and slams shut the lid.

He makes things for Alexa to eat, things that she likes. He washes her hair. He polishes her school shoes and sets them on newspaper beside the door. He knows which days she needs to take her gym kit to school. He sits with her while she does her homework, and makes sure she gives it in on time. At night, when she changes into her pyjamas, he observes with an artist's satisfaction the felicity of the white smocking against her skin, the exactitude of her inky brows and eyelashes, the sculptural rightness of her limbs. And the health of her hair and gums and fingernails, the acuity of her responses, even the sleep she takes, the restorative quality of its pause: it confirms him, reflects him, though she has her own existence. It is because she has her own existence that the confirmation comes. He is forming her out of the substance of what she already is. He is guiding her to her own perfection. It would be possible to ruin Alexa, to neglect or destroy her. There is no other person over whom he has this power.

The house is orderly and clean.

# XVII

At the beginning of February Tonie's boss glances up from his desk and says,

'The honeymoon period's over now.'

It is a grey lightless afternoon and the darker grey interior of the building is a grid of monochrome squares and rectangles that form strange block-like avenues of perspective leading nowhere. The whole place is a maze of corridors and staircases, of anonymous rooms jigsawed with desks and metal filing cabinets and identical black-upholstered chairs. This cluttered rectilinear gloom signifies thought, intellect, impersonal endeavour. Tonie has noticed how the human form is elided by its geometry: here she seems only to see people in parts, a pair of legs in a stairwell, a back disappearing through a doorway, a profile glimpsed through a shatterproof glass panel, bent over a desk.

'The honeymoon period's over now,' Christopher says, silhouetted by the grey light of the institutional window. 'At this point we need you to be functioning independently.'

'All right,' Tonie says, after a long pause.

Christopher's office is more home-like than the others. As Head of School he has a slightly larger version of the cubes the rest of them occupy. He has lamps on low tables, cushions, a rug on the floor. Since September she has come here several times each week, assuming herself to be entering the territory of an ally and friend. She likes to sit on Christopher's dovegrey sofa and consider the view, his orderly bookshelves, his framed Dutch prints. Now she wonders whether it is Christopher's house that is neutral, impersonal, or whether it exists at all; whether this office in fact is all he is, a man in a room which despite its atmosphere of comfort is still only ten feet wide.

'All right,' she says.

'I'm always available to answer questions,' he says, 'but my time is apportioned to favour the bottom end of the structure. I need to consider those younger, less experienced colleagues who have genuine reasons for requiring my help.'

Tonie is used to Christopher, used to his voice and appearance, to the reedy sound he makes, to the precision of his bachelor tastes, to the sight of his long, narrow form among other forms she knows. For years she has watched him go off to his lunchtime organ recitals at St John's, his medieval recorder evenings, his private views. Yet she has never, until now, put all those things together. She has never added him up.

'Fair enough,' she says.

'There simply isn't the infrastructure here for members of the department to be carried. We don't have the resources.'

'I get it,' she says.

Tonie has been associated with the English department for eight years. In that time she has seen people argue, flounce out of meetings, cry openly in corridors. She knows that emotion is a possibility here, as it is not elsewhere in the university or, indeed, the world. As a result the departmental discourse relies heavily on its bureaucratic origins. The grey walls pulse with rampant sensibility: only the rules stand in the way of a general outbreak of unconstrainable feeling. Now that Christopher has invoked this discourse, it would be perfectly acceptable for Tonie to shout at him, to weep, to storm back to her own cheerless office with its view of the car park; it is, perhaps, what Christopher expects and requires her to do.

She looks at his pleated silk lampshades, at his mohair cushion covers.

'Thanks,' she says. 'Thanks for the honeymoon. I enjoyed it.'

She laughs quietly, turns to go.

He stiffens in his chair, offended. 'As I say, I'm always reasonably available. And obviously, if any question is urgent I'll answer it.'

She laughs again. Once, she was Christopher's senior in the department, when he was a junior research fellow with a neck so slender his collars gaped around it. And he fawned on Tonie in those days, hungry for scraps of approval. It is this version of himself, she sees, that haunts him. He wants to exorcise it, to gouge it out of her recollection. He doesn't realise how many things have happened to her in the intervening years, how little she has considered him. He doesn't know how sad she suddenly finds it, that he should have spent his prime struggling to ascend through the ranks of a second-rate university, with only distracted mothers to impede him.

'I'll bear that in mind,' she says.

Outside, in the corridor, she realises that her arms are full of files. She looks down at them. They are hard, blank-faced, with metallic spines. She is holding them against her chest. For a moment she can't think what on earth they are.

# XVIII

Thomas wakes up. He has been dreaming. In the dream he and Tonie and Alexa were in some kind of shopping mall in a foreign city. It had long, grey, sinister concrete walkways as broad as motorways. There was layer after layer of them, travelling downwards into the earth.

Thomas and Tonie wanted to buy clothes for Alexa. They left her somewhere and found a small shop. The shop was full of light: its walls and ceiling were all glass. Thomas began to look at the clothes. They were very beautiful. He found a dress that was like a meadow of flowers, and another that was made of pieces of white cloud. There was a flowing garment like a Grecian tunic, composed of milk. Tonie had her own ideas, but every time Thomas found something she forgot them. She seemed to know that all of a sudden he had a special power of discovery. She waited to see what he would come up with next. From the rack he pulled a long-sleeved dress made from the original canvas of Botticelli's *The Birth of Venus*. At its cuffs and hem were flames that flickered palely in the daylight. They agreed that this was the supreme find. It was for Alexa: it seemed to contain something of her spirit, some essence of her they recognised but had forgotten, as though it had been present at the moment of her birth but had been obscured or diluted over the years by Thomas and Tonie themselves. Now that they had chosen, Tonie volunteered to go and retrieve Alexa. She left Thomas alone in the shop. She vanished into the vast grey intestine of the shopping mall. He wondered then why they had abandoned Alexa in this strange place. He had no idea where she was or what had become of her. What had he and Tonie been thinking of? The irrationality of it spoke to him through the dream. He strained and strained to understand why they had committed this irresponsible act. At last he realised that it was because this was a dream. The realisation immediately woke him up. It seems that it requires faith to dream. Once you have lost it the dream comes apart in your hands.

He lies awake in the darkness. It is so thin, so insubstantial: he feels as if he is falling through it, plummeting outwards or downwards. The universe yawns around him. He seems to see its infinite distances, its rashes of stars. The bed is like a tiny precipice on the edge of it. His contact with material things feels thread-like and minimal. It is the irrationality of the dream that has caused him to feel this. His own belief in his life seems in that moment incredible to him. Why doesn't he cling to the edge of the bed in terror? Why doesn't everybody? And Alexa, Tonie – what are these people to him? What are these relationships, these convictions, these codes of conduct? This forest of objects, dark now and indistinct – what is their significance? How can he have chosen them, the armchair, the chest of drawers, the dark ornaments on the mantelpiece in their darker ponds of shadow, when the universe was yawning just to the side of them?

The clock ticks steadily on the bedside table. After a while, Thomas goes back to sleep.

# XIX

For the forty-five minutes that the doctor is late for the appointment, Howard thinks he is going to die.

The nurse is there, moving around the room. The sky at the third-floor hospital window is blank. Her white form glimmers: it creases and unfolds as she bends and straightens, nodding in the light like a white flower.

'Would you like anything?' she says. 'Would you like a cup of tea?'

Her face comes near. It is painted: her youth is under the paint, as though some great sorrow has compelled her to inter it and don her painted death-mask.

'Yes, please,' he whispers. 'Tea would be very nice.'

She goes away. Then she is there again: he hears the teacup rattling in its saucer. When she puts it in front of him he sees her pale forearm. There is a mark on it the size and shape of a coin. It is dark red, livid, like the mark of a brand on her bland flawless skin.

'You've burnt yourself,' he says.

'I did it with the iron,' she says. 'That was silly, wasn't it?'

He imagines her ironing, piles of white sheets, her nurse's uniform. He sees the deadly steel tip nosing its way through the whiteness. It is terrible, the thought of her soft skin.

'Please be careful,' he says. 'You must take care of yourself. We should all take more care of ourselves.'

She moves about, tidying, her eyes gently lowered. There is paint on the lids.

'The doctor won't be long,' she says.

Howard watches the clock on the doctor's wall. The second hand lurches trembling around the face. Claudia is parking the car. She dropped him at the front, not knowing they would bring him up here. He sees now that they should have stayed together. He sees that it is a trap. He has been lured from his family, his house, his car, his wife, by a trickster who has waited all this time, who waited by his cot and by his childhood bed, waited through the years in doorways and stations and city streets, in fields and on foreign beaches, in hallways and hotels and the passenger seats of cars; and lately, waited in the darkness of the garden, beneath the apple tree, for Howard to be alone. Claudia waved through the glass as she drove away. He remembers how confusing it was to be standing by himself in the grey entrance area. He was born in this hospital. It was as though Claudia had returned him here to be reabsorbed; as though she had driven away with his name, his identity, his actual life, and left his casing, his body, here, from whence it had come, like an empty bottle being returned to the brewery.

The door opens.

'Mr Bradshaw?'

A man comes in. He is wearing a suit. There is a silvery sheen on the cloth that makes him seem not entirely real. Howard is afraid. The unreality of this man – he is young, brown-haired, has a harmless face – suddenly terrifies him. The man shakes his hand. He is like a game-show host shaking the hand of the winning contestant. Howard knows that anything could happen, anything at all.

'I've got the results of your biopsy here. There was a, ah, dark area on the right lung that was causing some concern, is that right?'

He frowns, wrinkles his brow. He scrutinises his notes.

'That's right,' Howard says.

'Well,' the man says, 'I have to say that I don't quite see what all the fuss was about.'

'Really?' Howard says.

'There's obviously been a touch of pneumonia on that side, but that's not the end of the world, is it?'

'No,' Howard says.

'Is it?' the man repeats, widening his eyes and laughing.

'No,' Howard says, laughing too.

'It's rather a case of using a sledgehammer to crack a nut. Isn't it?'

'I suppose it is,' Howard says.

'Bed rest, yes,' the man says, wagging his finger. 'But a biopsy – whoa there!'

He slaps his knees and laughs again, and Howard laughs too, though he feels a certain consternation at what he has discovered here at the milled edge of life, the lunatics and incompetents in charge of the machinery.

'Bed rest,' he says, rising unsteadily from his chair. 'That's all?'

'And plenty of fluids. Preferably non-alcoholic, Mr Bradshaw.'

'Whoa there,' Howard says weakly.

On the way home, he holds Claudia's hand across the gearstick.

'We could sue them, darling,' he says. 'That buffoon virtually handed it to me on a plate.'

'What a good idea,' Claudia says. 'Shall we?'

He squeezes her fingers. He makes a vow, to be good.

# XX

She is planting a hydrangea in the shady bed behind the house. It is morning. The village lies stunned in its newborn quiet. The grass is silvered with dew. The soil is black, and riddled with life.

Just after ten her husband comes out; she hears his feet approaching on the gravel. They stop an arm's length away.

'I'll say goodbye now,' he says.

She rises, pain in her knees. Her hands are caked in soil. He puts out his own clean hand, palm up like a policeman to stop her.

'No need to get up. I can say goodbye here.'

But she is already up, as he can see. She chaffs her hands to get the dirt off. Even so he winces, in his brushed blazer and clean shirt.

'Am I not allowed to touch you?' she says, advancing on him so that he stiffens with discomfort. 'You do look smart.'

'Best not.'

'But I want to touch you!'

He smiles coldly. The day stands around him, pale grey, windless. Suddenly she feels a loss of weight, of density; she is being abandoned. She is being sealed up, in a place where there can be no touching.

'I'll be back at five o'clock,' he says. After all, he is only going to the Bridge Society annual lunch in Tunbridge Wells.

She puckers her lips and leans forward, her dirty hands clasped behind her back. She receives his dry kiss. She could never touch her mother's clothes, nor her father's. They kissed her thus, across the chasm of departure. There is darkness down there, fathomless. She knows she mustn't fall in. But the scented, smart atmosphere of people who are leaving tempts her. She wants to hurl herself towards them, dirty fingers clutching and clawing at their clean pressed garments. Yet she knows the chasm is there.

'Goodbye,' she says.

'Goodbye.'

He is gone: she kneels down again in the earth. She picks up her trowel and digs a hole, as she used to dig in her sandpit as a child. She watches her fingers moving in the soil. She is surprised to see that her hands are old. She digs a hole for the hydrangea, and plants it, and carefully beds it in.

A jackdaw has got into the greenhouse and broken two of the panes. She opens the door to let it out but it continues to fly in slow circles above her head, round and round, never alighting anywhere. She goes back to the house and returns with a blanket. The bird has destroyed a whole tray of seedlings. Her plants are lying on their sides in little spills of earth. She is afraid of birds, an old fear: her father, a bad shot, the birds never dead but denatured, roiling in the grass, mad with disorganisation. This one, so black, so evilly circling, is like something she herself has caused. Her fear roams out in the world, causative. It is the loss of identity that she fears. The jackdaw, circling in its captivity, is programmatic. She grips the blanket, and at the right moment she springs up and catches it in the folds, and clasps its hooded form in her arms. It struggles: its beak pecks and pecks at her arm through the wool. She goes out into the garden and releases it.

Thomas is there, standing on the lawn.

'What are you doing?' he says.

She is not certain he is real. She gazes at him, confused. Yet she is speaking.

'Oh, you're here – I wonder why I didn't hear the car?'

He walks across the grass towards her. She had forgotten he was so old. She folds the blanket while he kisses her cheek.

'I rang twice but you didn't answer. I was late leaving the house.'

'Never mind,' she says. 'You're here now.'

'I was worried you'd start moving the boxes without me.'

'I haven't touched them. I've been terribly sensible.'

She hears her own voice; what it says is perfectly true. She knows that she spoke to her son two days ago about the boxes. He offered to help her bring them down. This morning she cleared the upstairs landing to provide easier access to the attic. She does not doubt the reality of these things; it's just that she hasn't, in the strictest sense, experienced them. They have happened to someone she knows well, who is sometimes with her and sometimes not. She has always been aware of this being; even as a child she knew that someone lived in her, someone who wasn't herself. But more and more often now, this person goes away. She has come to dread her departure, yet when it occurs she doesn't notice that she's gone. It is when she returns that the absence is made clear.

Thomas takes her arm and they walk around the herbaceous borders.

'Look, the oak tree's got a face,' she says gaily, pointing.

It's strange that she hasn't noticed it before, a long face with a big chin and sad eyes. It looks like a monk's face, in its cowl of bark. She knows most of the other faces in the garden. But this one she hasn't seen before. It stares at her from its prison in the trunk.

'So it has,' Thomas says. He stops to examine it. He is always a little too eager, too responsive; when he was a child she wondered whether he might not be something of a simpleton. Her dogs were the same, quivering like compasses around her, so that her husband could never get them to do a thing. She notices that Thomas has put on weight. He has pouches under his chin. His hand is hurting her arm. There are red marks on the skin where the jackdaw pecked her. She shudders at the recollection of what she did. She makes a note to tell her father, though he is dead, and the world he lived in is dead too.

'Shall we go in?' she says. 'We may as well get these silly boxes over and done with.'

They turn towards the house. It is Charles who says the boxes have to go. He has them in his sights, though they have sat discreetly beneath the roof for years. Something gave him the idea of them and now he wants them gone. They are the last hidden part of her and he has found them out.

'What's in them, anyway?' Thomas says.

'Oh, just a lot of old rubbish really. Daddy says they ought to go, and I expect he's right.'

In fact she has fought him over the boxes, and this struggle has been so bitter that it has invoked her deepest capacity for submission. He has made her see them, see them clear as day: thirty or so large boxes with her name written on, that she hasn't opened – he forced her to admit it – since the day they first went up to the attic, where they occupy so much space that there is no longer any room to store necessities. And in the end she agreed that the situation could not continue. Truly, she felt that it couldn't. She wept and was grateful to him. So she is surprised to see that when Thomas has brought down the boxes and retracted the ladder into the roof, there are only six of them.

'Is that all?'

'That's all. I double-checked.'

She remembers Charles leaving the house. Was it only this morning? He has gone to Tunbridge Wells and won't be back until teatime.

'I thought there were dozens,' she says, helplessly. She sits down on the landing carpet.

Thomas opens one of the boxes and looks inside. He takes out her crumpled christening gown, her old almanac, a doll with a tartan tam-o'-shanter who she recalls – oh, the dreadful surge of memory! – is named Clarissa.

'Daddy wants it all to go to a charity shop!' she bursts out. 'I can't bear it! Don't let him send my things away!'

Thomas looks stricken. He kneels down beside her.

'Of course he can't give them away,' he says. 'They're your things. It's up to you what happens to them.'

'But I promised – I promised that by the time he came back they'd be gone!'

'Oh, for heaven's sake,' Thomas mutters.

He is angry. But not with her. He picks up Clarissa, turns her stiff body in his hands.

'I suppose Alexa might like to look at some of these things,' he says.

Her voice is meek. 'I dare say she might.'

He sighs. 'What else is there?'

'Not much – some books, a few mementoes. It's a silly thing: they mean so much to me, but they'd mean nothing to a complete stranger.'

The truth is that she can't remember what is inside the boxes. He is silent.

'We've got less space than you do, you know,' he says presently. 'It seems ridiculous.'

She pouts and looks at the carpet. 'Then I suppose Daddy's right. It'll all have to go.'

He sighs again, tormented. This is an old alliance, older than Thomas himself, for its source is her own first loneliness, when her dolls – Clarissa, she recalls, was one such – befriended her and offered her their pliant hearts. Thomas, as a baby, had something of this pliancy, this bright expectant blankness; and after Howard – greedy little brute, always thumping her with his fat fists – she rather doted on Thomas, whose round eyes followed her with such astonished love. He used to cry whenever she moved out of his line of vision.

'All right, then,' he says finally. 'We'll fit them in somewhere. Though God knows what Tonie's going to say.'

At the mention of Tonie's name she feels the shiver of compunction that normally only her husband can elicit. She recalls taking Tonie blackberrying once in the hedges along the road outside the village; recalls the way Tonie persisted at each bush until she had stripped it of every last one of its fruits. Her own method is to cover more ground, grazing whatever falls to her hand.

'Oh dear – I don't want to cause any trouble.'

'No, it's all right. It's fine.'

She beams at him. She finds that she wants him to go, now that he has taken her burden of submission from her. In the end his availability grates on her. It was sweet in a child, but people cannot be children all their lives. These days she finds that after all she prefers Howard.

'Oh, you *are* kind,' she says. 'Shall we take them down to the car? I expect you have to rush off.'

He smiles, a peculiar smile she hasn't seen before.

'I thought I might stay for lunch,' he says.

'Oh!' she says. 'Well, of course, you're very welcome, if you haven't anything else to do.'

But even after lunch he doesn't seem inclined to go.

'Doesn't someone have to fetch Alexa from school?' she asks.

He smiles again. 'She's going to a friend's.'

'Well, I was only going to take the dog for a walk. Don't feel you have to come.'

He says, 'Would you like me to come?'

It strikes her as a very impolite thing to say.

'Yes,' she says coldly. 'Of course. That would be very nice.'

They take Flossie up the lane, and in a ditch full of reeds and brambles they find a tiny deer, dead.

'How sad!' she says. 'A car must have hit it.'

She gazes at the little shrivelled muzzle buzzing with flies, the closed eyes, the tangled infant legs in their cold bed of winter grasses. It can only have happened a day or two ago. She looks up and to her surprise sees the doe, standing motionless in the shadowy lane ahead of them. She grips Thomas's arm.

'Look – it's the mother. See how unafraid she is. She's looking for her child. She knows it's here somewhere and she's waiting for it to come back. Oh, how sad!'

The doe lifts her head. Her large almond-shaped eyes are pools of blackness. They wear a frightful expression. Flossie barks. For a while the doe doesn't move, but at last she goes heavily back into the trees.

'Oh, how touching.' She unclips Flossie's lead. Beside her Thomas gives a sort of gasp. She turns and sees to her astonishment that he is crying.

'Whatever's the matter?' she says.

# XXI

Something has changed. Or not changed: been lost. Tonie realises it with a jump, a start, the way she might feel around her throat for a necklace and realise it was no longer there.

They are walking with Alexa to Beacon Park, where there are swings, where they have taken her a hundred times since she was born, and not one of those times has Tonie felt that something was missing in the way that she feels it now. It is Saturday. Alexa is wearing new shoes, red, the leather plump and glossy and unmarked. Thomas bought them for her. They were very expensive. Tonie would never have bought Alexa such expensive shoes, beautiful Italian shoes with white kid insoles. She can't decide whether it is the beauty or the expense that troubles her more.

The day is cold, bright, a diamond-hard February day, and Tonie walks ahead of the others on the pavement with her hands stuffed into her pockets. At the gate she stands silently back, to let them pass through. Alexa goes first, then Thomas. Tonie notices her daughter's small, delicate shoulders as she passes, the head turning like a flower on the fragile neck, the dark, glossy ponytail tumbling down her back. She would like to touch it. Just then, Thomas puts his own hand out and touches the ponytail, fingering its ends. That's when Tonie realises that something has been lost. She has lost his attention.

In the afternoon she decides to make spaghetti Bolognese. She gets out the saucepans, clanging and clattering. She fills the kitchen with the fumes of cooking onions and meat. She chops things and hurls them into the pot. She is frenzied, transfixed; she is engulfed in the preparation of this red sauce which bubbles, thick and volcanic, at her fingertips. She doesn't know what will happen when the sauce is finished. She doesn't know what she'll do.

Occasionally Thomas comes into the kitchen, searches around, leaves again. Tonie, at her cauldron, brews up her red anger, her face damp with steam. She wants to scream, to throw things. Every time Thomas appears, blank-faced and diffident, searching for something, she has the desire to shock him with violence. She wants him to be brought into line. She wants him to be punished. For the first time, she wishes he were back at work. She wants him held and constricted, fenced round with regulations; she wants him corrected. Now he has the look of someone who has got away with something. He can withdraw his attention, with no fear of reprisal.

'What are you actually looking for?' she says coldly, when he has come in for the third or fourth time.

'What?' He looks up, notices her. 'Oh, nothing.'

When she goes upstairs she finds Thomas and Alexa, all quiet and companionable, in the sitting room. She stands in the doorway but neither of them looks up. She doesn't go back to her red sauce, which is still bubbling on the cooker. She leaves it, abandons it, goes to her bedroom. She lies on the bed. Later, Thomas puts his head in.

'I think your sauce is done,' he says. 'Shall I turn it off?'

'If you want,' Tonie says.

He goes away again. The house is full of the red rich smell of what she has created. The room is getting dark. She can hear music playing downstairs. She lies still. She doesn't turn on the lights.

# XXII

Claudia suggests giving Lottie an allowance. Now that Lottie is fourteen, Claudia says, she should have some money of her own. She says this to Howard, who is a little remote and businesslike, as though he were being informed of some minor by-law that is about to come into force. He stands there in his suit and goes through the post.

'She ought to open a bank account,' he says. 'We should open bank accounts for all of them.'

Claudia looks astonished.

'Why does Martha need a bank account? She's only six.'

'Everyone should have a bank account.'

'What, a six-year-old child should have a chequebook and pay bank charges, and get letters pouring through the door about personal loans!'

Howard opens an envelope and reads what is inside. Claudia watches his eyes moving from left to right. When he has finished he says,

'I'm only saying that if Lottie's going to have an allowance we should pay the money into a bank account.'

Claudia is silent: she wants to give the impression that she is thinking this proposal through. It isn't that Howard is wrong exactly. It is that the idea of opening a bank account takes away what is pleasurable in the prospect of giving Lottie money.

'It's too complicated,' she says, after a while. 'All Lottie actually *needs* is some spending money of her own.'

'It's not as complicated as all that,' Howard says.

'I think it's too soon. She's too young.'

'It's the easiest thing in the world, Claude. Then she can begin to save.'

'What does she need to save for?'

'All of them should learn to save,' Howard says sententiously.

Claudia feels that Howard is missing the point. What she wants to know is how much he thinks they should give her. That is what she imagined them discussing. She has already decided that Lottie's allowance should be twenty-five pounds a month.

'What do you think we should start her on?' she says.

Howard muses, considering the ceiling.

'Fifty?' he says.

'A month? You must be joking.'

'Too little?'

'Too much – I thought twenty-five.'

Howard seems surprised. He is wearing his reading glasses and he looks at her over the top of them.

'She won't get far on twenty-five pounds,' he says. 'That's only six or seven pounds a week, Claude. Hardly enough for a stick of gum.'

'It's plenty for a fourteen-year-old girl.'

Claudia doesn't remember anyone ever giving her money, though they presumably did.

'And that's to cover clothes too? Shoes?'

Claudia reconsiders. 'All right, thirty. And I'll buy her shoes.'

Claudia informs Lottie that, effective from the first day of the coming month, she is to receive a regular personal allowance of thirty pounds.

'Okay then,' Lottie says.

'Not "okay then,"' Claudia corrects her. '"Okay then" is for when I ask *you* to do something for *me*.' Lottie looks at her dumbly. 'It isn't for when I offer to give you something.'

Lottie is silent. Claudia says,

'I'll still pay for your shoes, and anything you need for school.'

'Oka – all right.'

'Your allowance is for you to do what you want with. It's *your* money. If you want to save it, you can. If you blow the whole lot in the first week, then you'll have to manage till the end of the month without any more.'

'I know,' Lottie says.

'There's no point coming to me halfway through the month and saying you haven't got any money. The purpose of the exercise is to teach you how to budget.'

'I know.' Lottie looks bored.

'You're obviously an expert,' Claudia says. She recalls that she expected to enjoy this conversation. When she thought about it earlier in the day, it was with a warm feeling of pressure in her chest, as though there were something in there, something waiting to be lifted out and given, like a bouquet of flowers.

'I'm not an expert,' Lottie says. 'I didn't say I was.'

'You didn't say thank you, either.'

Lottie is silent. She looks to one side of her with downcast eyes.

'Does anyone else at school get an allowance yet?' Claudia asks brightly, after a pause.

'Most people do.'

'I shouldn't think it's *most*,' Claudia says. 'I should think it's *some*.'

A week later, on the first of the month, Claudia hands

Lottie thirty pounds in ten-pound notes. During the week she has experienced a kind of regression in her attitude to Lottie. She wonders whether she has spent so much time trying to see what Lottie is becoming that she has failed to notice what she actually is. In the afternoons, when Lottie comes home from school, she goes straight to the kitchen and stands there eating slices of bread lathered so thickly with jam that her teeth leave an impression in it when she takes a bite. Claudia seems fated to enter the kitchen at the decisive moment of this ceremony, to see Lottie hunched over the counter, her hair hanging over her face, her mouth clamping around the red and white slab and coming away engorged. Lottie makes strange little groans as she eats. Her body in its school uni-form seems afflicted and uncomfortable. As a baby Lottie seemed uncomfortable, and afflicted by her own helplessness. Yet Claudia can feel no sympathy for her now. To pity Lottie would be to pity herself.

'Great,' Lottie says, when Claudia gives her the money.

On Saturday, Lottie tells Howard and Claudia that she is spending the day in town with Justine and Emily.

'What about lunch?' Claudia says.

'I don't know. We might get something there.'

'Your money will be gone in one day if you start spending it on eating out.'

Immediately Lottie looks evasive. She stares off to the side, at something just above the level of the floor.

'We're not giving you an allowance just so you can sit in McDonald's all afternoon,' Claudia says.

Lottie rolls her eyes. She makes a little snorting sound, like a pony. She is like one of those short, round, bad-tempered Shetlands who flare their nostrils and toss their matted waterfalls of hair. Lottie has the same spirit of animal vigour about her, the same disproportion of flesh to rationality.

'Is it just you three girls on your own?' Howard asks her.

'There might be some other people.'

'Oh, good,' Howard says.

Lottie returns from town at half past four. She did not take her coat. Claudia found it still hanging on its peg in the hall. All afternoon she has been aware of it. Several times, walking past, she has caressed it: she has run her hand down the unresponsive fabric all the way from the shoulder to the hem. She has watched the weather out of the window. It is gusty and grey, and sometimes the wind blows the trees wildly this way and that and then for no reason stops again. Lottie's coat hanging on its peg is like a version of Lottie herself, a discarded stage in her evolution that Claudia has been allowed to keep. She thinks that she loves this Lottie, the coat Lottie, better than the real one. The coat hangs by its hood: from a distance it looks like a little head.

Howard has spent the day making a bonfire in the garden with Lewis. Martha is upstairs with her friend Sadie. Occasionally Claudia passes the door to Martha's room and sees the two children sitting together on the carpet surrounded by Martha's toys. Once when she looks they have made long headdresses for themselves out of sheets, which they have secured on their heads with the braided loops that hold back Martha's curtains. They sit cross-legged in their white veils, locked in endless low-voiced discussion, like two important delegates from distant, miniature countries. When Claudia goes downstairs she can smell the smoke from the bonfire, which has slowly penetrated the house.

Lottie is in the kitchen. Claudia comes in behind her.

'How did it go?' she says brightly.

Lottie looks startled.

'It was just – normal,' she says.

'You forgot to take your coat. I found it hanging in the hall. I worried that you'd be cold.'

'I wasn't cold.'

'You might not have *felt* cold,' Claudia says. 'But if you're not properly dressed you're more liable to catch things, and then everyone else in the house gets it as well.'

The kitchen is gloomy and untidy. Claudia switches the lights on. She begins putting everything away. She puts away all the pots and pans that stand on the drainer. She puts away everything lying on the counters. The aluminium pans clatter when she sets them on their shelves. She opens the cupboard doors and bangs them shut again. The glasses chatter against one another; the cups rattle in their saucers. She opens the fridge, sweeps a whole armful of things from inside, kicks it shut behind her. She stamps on the lever that opens the bin and the lid crashes like a pair of cymbals as it hits the wall behind. One after another Claudia flings in empty milk cartons, rotten bits of food, old plastic containers. *Thud! thud! thud!* they go, disappearing into its rustling depths. Claudia feels possessed by a mad kind of genius. She is filled with sound: she is a composer creating a crazy, dissonant symphony. She bangs the cupboard doors again. She takes out the cutlery drawer and spills its contents over the kitchen table in a bright shrieking cascade of steel. *Ting! ting! ting!* go the knives and forks and spoons as she drops them back in their proper compartments.

At each sound, Lottie flinches.

'What's that smell?' she says finally.

Claudia stops what she is doing. She stands, alert, in the silence. A feeling of great weariness, almost of despondency, passes over her.

'It's a sort of burning smell,' Lottie said.

It is the bonfire. Claudia can smell it too.

She says, 'Daddy's been having a bonfire out in the garden.'

Lottie's expression brightens.

'Really?' she says.

The next time Claudia looks, she sees them all out in the garden in the gathering dusk. She stands at the kitchen window. Howard rakes up leaves and Lewis throws them on the fire in big armfuls. Lottie has a long stick in her hand. She is tending the smouldering heap, forcing the new leaves into its hot centre, compacting the top. With her stick she rounds up stray bits of paper and twigs and rams them back into the fire. Claudia can hear Lottie and Lewis and Howard talking. She can't hear what they say, just the sound they make saying it. The smoke comes out in big grey rolling waves, one after another. Sometimes they roll towards the window where Claudia stands. Then, suddenly, the smoke changes direction and is drawn helplessly upwards into the sky.

In the evening, Howard and Claudia are going out.

Claudia stays upstairs getting ready while the children eat their supper. She puts on black trousers and a black jersey. She puts on the necklace Howard gave her. It is silver, a paper-thin silver leaf on a silver chain. She sits down in front of the mirror and draws her hair back from her face. She is surprised by how finished she looks, how completed. It is as though there is nothing more for her to do. It is as though the mirror has told her that she has come to the end of some long and complicated task, that all is done that needs to be done.

How funny it is not to want anything, not to need! She thinks of the banknotes she gave Lottie. When she imagined this money, it was as the material proof of a developmental stage, like the first spoonfuls of food she put into Lottie's mouth as a baby. She always does these things a little too soon. She hurries her on. She has wanted to teach Lottie how to want, to need. She supposes it is her way of trying to simplify things between them, for if Lottie needs something, then Claudia has the task of providing it. Lottie would want something and she, Claudia, would be able to give it to her. That is how she has always imagined it, anyway. Lottie never *asked* for money. It was just that by giving her some, Claudia thought she would align Lottie with herself. They would both be facing the same way, side by side, looking out at the things they wanted. But now it seems that Claudia doesn't want anything. She doesn't need anything at all.

Howard comes in. He puts his face into the crook of her neck where she sprayed her perfume.

'Do you think Lottie enjoyed herself today?' Claudia asks him.

He raises his head and they look at themselves in the mirror.

'I don't suppose it matters one way or the other, does it?' he says.

Downstairs, the two younger children are watching television. Claudia goes into the kitchen to see if Lottie is there, and then stands at the bottom of the stairs and calls her to come down. Lottie is babysitting. Claudia sits at the kitchen table and writes down the telephone number and address of the place they are going. She hears someone coming down the stairs.

'I'm in here!' she calls.

After a while, she goes out and looks in the hall. Then she looks in the sitting room. Lottie is sitting there with Lewis and Martha. The television feels her motionless face with its blue lights. Claudia sees she is wearing a new skirt.

'Lottie!' she says softly. 'Can you just come out for a minute? I want to give you some numbers and things.'

She turns and goes back to the kitchen. There is a pause, and then Lottie comes in.

'We're only going to the Carters',' Claudia says. The Carters live on the other side of Laurier Drive.

She gives Lottie her instructions. Claudia can hear herself speaking, but she can barely concentrate on what she is saying. She tries to keep her eyes on Lottie's face but they keep straying – magnetised, astonished – down to her skirt.

'Did you get that today?' she says finally.

Lottie looks down at herself, as though to check they are talking about the same thing.

'Yes,' she says.

'Where did you get it?'

'A shop.'

It is a pink skirt with a ruffle around the hem. It comes down to Lottie's knees. The pink is a candyfloss pink. The ruffle has been badly stitched. It is both too big for Lottie and too small, sagging around the hips and straining at the stomach. The material is so cheap that Claudia can see Lottie's underwear through it. It is a child's skirt, the kind of skirt Claudia might have bought a version of for Martha, but on Lottie it is without doubt the least flattering item of clothing Claudia has ever seen. She wears it with her usual hooded sweatshirt.

'It's lovely,' Claudia says. 'Well done.'

Lottie seems pleased. 'I thought you'd like it,' she says.

Later, one Saturday, Claudia has to go into town. She leaves Howard and the children and goes on her own. The streets are thick with people. They roam the pavements like unquiet souls, like hundreds of homeless spirits come to find all the things they have lost. They carry bags, boxes, great plastic sacks wrapped around bulky objects. Some of them can barely hold the quantity of things they have bought. She sees a man carrying a pair of garden shears, a man carrying a plastic lounger, a woman with a child's bicycle in a giant plastic bag. Its handlebars stick out, each one tied with a tinselly tassel that trembles like a little girl's ponytails as the woman walks along.

The day is bright and windy. Overhead the sky streams blue. Claudia picks up speed. She strides along the littered pavement, glancing in the windows, glancing at the faces as they pass her. She begins to forget herself, to feel a kind of exhilaration. It is good, after all, to be away from what is yours: from home, where everything either belongs to you or speaks of you or reflects you, until it becomes a kind of consuming sickness, the need to exist, to dominate. Yet here she is, free! Why does she care what people buy, where they go, how they spend their time? What does it have to do with her? She isn't responsible for them – they are free, like her. It is responsibility that sets its pins and screws in your nature, that warps and gnarls you and makes you ugly to yourself. She strides along, the wind whipping in her hair. Ahead of her she sees a group of teenaged girls coming out of a shop. They come up the pavement, all clutching each other and laughing. They are like a laughing, many-tentacled creature, their arms and their legs and their smiles all jumbled together. They have bags and bangles and earrings, and hair that the wind blows all around them in ribbons, so that you can't see which hair is connected to which head. One of them catches her attention. She looks at this girl for a long time before realising that it is Lottie.

# XXIII

There is a woman Thomas sees in the school playground. She is often early, like him. She sits on a bench at the edge of the tarmac, reading a book.

He doesn't really know why he has noticed her, but now that it's happened he finds himself forming an ethereal kind of relationship with her. When he arrives he searches the playground for her brown-haired form, bent over its book. It comforts him to see her, as it comforts him to see lights on at the windows of strangers' houses, knowing someone is there. Once he notices her in town, crossing the road towards him. She is with another woman, talking, and when she happens to glance his way he smiles. Momentarily her eyes widen, confused, and then she is gone. Occasionally she isn't there in the playground and he feels irritable. He imagines himself leaving this place, taking action: he has the urge to do something that will rinse this passivity from his brain. He feels formless, like a lump of dough in which anyone who chooses can leave an impression. But then, the next day, there she is again, and the dent she has created is filled in.

One afternoon Alexa comes out clutching the hand of another girl. She is the brown-haired woman's daughter. Thomas knows: he has seen them together.

'This is my friend Clara,' she says.

'Hello, Clara.' He smiles. He thinks of Clara Schumann. He wants to ask the child whether she is named after her. He considers how he could put the question. 'That's a lovely name,' he says.

Suddenly the woman is there. Close up she is smaller than he expected. Everything about her is brown, her large eyes, her coat, the hair that falls in flossy-seeming wisps over her shoulders. He is embarrassed. He realises that he has carried this woman's image around with him, as people used to carry around little painted miniatures. He feels as though he has stolen something from her without her knowing.

'I was just saying what a lovely name your daughter has.'

She smiles, slightly surprised. 'Thank you.'

'I don't think we've met before.'

She cocks her brown head, quizzical. 'Haven't we? I do know your – is she your wife?'

'Yes. Yes, she is.'

'I was thinking the other day that I hadn't seen her for a while.'

He is already used to this discourse of the playground, with its strange elisions and old-world delicacies, its sudden, startling thrusts of frankness. This is not the first time he has had to explain Tonie's disappearance to an imperative female audience. At least now he doesn't mistake their curiosity for friendliness towards himself.

'She's working full-time now,' he says.

She nods philosophically. 'I thought it might be that,' she says, as though it might equally well have been something else, death perhaps, or imprisonment.

'Yes, they offered her a promotion and she just couldn't turn it down.'

'That's wonderful,' the woman says. She does, genuinely, seem to find it wonderful. She is smiling, her cheeks lifted, the skin crinkling beneath her large chocolate-coloured eyes. He notices that her lips have little fluting curves in the corners, like quavers.

'Yes, I suppose it is,' he says.

There is a silence. Thomas wants to go away. He wants to go home and play Bach. He is not enjoying this conversation after all.

'Daddy, can Clara come back to our house?' Alexa is still gripping the other child's hand. 'Please can she?'

'Not today,' he says. 'Another time.'

Alexa persists. 'Tomorrow?'

He glances at the woman. She smiles again and he grimaces awkwardly in return.

'We'll see,' he says. 'We'll talk about it when we get home.'

He takes Alexa's arm and leads her firmly out of the playground and into the street. All the way home he has a sour sense of disappointment, but in the evening, when Tonie is there, he finds himself thinking about the brown-haired woman again. Her image is once more in its frame. Tonie is moving around the kitchen, pale-faced, distracted. For a moment he forgets the nature of their bond: she has a kind of detailed neutrality about her, a compendiousness, as though he could ask her anything, this sturdy friend of his life.

'Do you know the mother of a child named Clara?' he says.

'Who?'

'Clara.'

She pauses beside the sink. He sees her mind ticking over, locating the details. She is wearing a mauve-coloured sweater that looks thick and itchy. Vaguely it appears to him as a symbol of affliction, this garment with its heavy knitted cables and constricting neck, its impenetrable fastnesses of wool. It is as though she has put it on as a warning to the world, to keep away from her.

'I think the mother's called Helen,' she says presently.

'I met her in the playground today. She said she knew you.'

'Did she?'

'Alexa seems pretty keen on the daughter.'

'On Clara?' Tonie turns on the taps. 'That's new. She and Clara have never had all that much to say to each other.'

She speaks with a certain finality. She is telling Thomas that whatever his impressions of the situation might be, her own knowledge is superior. She is reminding him that in the world he now inhabits there is nothing new for him to discover. There is nothing to know that she has not known already.

'Well, they seemed pretty friendly today.'

'Did they? These things come and go. Alexa probably fell out with Maisie and brought in Clara as a sop.'

Thomas laughs, though he finds her remark faintly irritating.

'I wouldn't have suspected her of that degree of cynicism,' he says.

Tonie raises her eyebrows. She does not reply.

'Actually,' he persists, 'I thought it was rather touching, the way they were holding hands together. It all seemed perfectly innocent to me.'

Her expression is inscrutable. 'That's fine,' she says, as though he'd asked her permission for something. After a pause, she adds: 'You should make friends with Helen. She's nice. It would do you good to have a friend at the school.'

'Thanks,' he says flatly.

'Oh, you know what I mean,' she says. 'I just think you'd get on well with her, that's all. She's a musician, you know.'

'Is she?'

'She plays the violin. You should ask her about it.'

Thomas goes upstairs to say goodnight to Alexa. He feels enveloped, vaguely suffocated, as though Tonie has spun another mauve-coloured sweater around him to match her own. Before he turns out the light, he says:

'Shall we see if Clara wants to come round tomorrow?'

Alexa's face is blank. She shrugs. 'All right,' she says.

He is vexed. 'Don't you want her to come?'

She thinks about it. 'I don't mind. I suppose so.'

But he doesn't see her the next day, nor the next. Alexa says that Clara is ill.

'What's wrong with her?'

'I don't know. She's always ill,' Alexa says, balefully.

Then, one day, the mother is there again, sitting on her bench. He realises that he has forgotten her. She was a habit his mind had formed, that's all. He can't remember now what the particulars of the habit were.

'Hello,' he says.

His shadow falls across her. She looks up. She seems pleased.

'Oh, hello,' she says.

'I haven't seen you here for a while.'

It becomes apparent that she is not going to stand, and nor does she make any accommodating gesture for him to sit. This is the adult physicality of the playground, this non-directive bodily stance. She can neither welcome him nor send him away. He sits anyway, beside her on the bench.

'It's spring,' he says, for he has only in that moment realised it. It is March. The sun is lapping weakly at his white face and hands, and there are hard green buds on the naked branches of the trees that stand here and there in their concrete moorings. He wonders how it can possibly be enough, this timid force, to renew all that has to be renewed. He hums a few phrases from the 'Spring' Sonata.

'I don't know your name,' she says.

His eyes are closed, feeling the sun. 'Thomas,' he says.

'I'm Ellen.'

'Ellen?'

He opens his eyes. She is offering her hand. He is coldly amused by Tonie's mistake. It makes him like the woman better. After all, there *is* something for him to find out.

'You're a musician,' he says.

She is surprised. 'How did you know that?'

He considers tormenting her. 'I thought everybody knew. You're famous, aren't you?'

'No, not at all.' She isn't upset. She looks confused.

He closes his eyes again. 'My wife told me that you played the violin.'

'Actually,' she says, 'it's the viola.'

He smiles to himself. He does not think that Tonie would care for the difference between a violin and a viola.

'I'd like to have been a musician,' he says.

The bell shrills; the children come out. The playground fills. Suddenly Clara is there, clambering on to her mother's lap. The woman kisses the top of her head, and it is then that Thomas realises that she is beautiful, as though her daughter's arrival has unveiled her. He thinks of the woman-shaped viola, tawny and glimmering, the child like a bow in her lap. He realises that he cannot look at something beautiful without wanting to comprehend it completely. He looks around for Alexa, suddenly embarrassed to be sitting so close to them, as though these thoughts were public acts he might be made to stand by for life. He remembers the way he used to look at her from far off, the sense of ownership he had over her form. He doesn't understand himself. He rises, pushes forwards into the crowd.

One day Clara comes to the house. She is a mute and fragile child, tremulous as a bead of water, so insubstantial as to be exhausting. Thomas was expecting a child like a prelude, a flowing, melodious thing; he realises that it is from her mother that this expectation has come. But without her, Clara is formless. Or at least, he has failed to decipher what her form might be. He finds himself looking frequently at his watch. Again and again Alexa leads her upstairs to her bedroom and each time, after a few minutes, Clara reappears alone, descending the stairs slowly one by one, seeking him out. He finds himself becoming irritated by her small, hovering form. He knows that it is not him she really wants.

At five o'clock he opens a bottle of wine.

'Would *you* like something to drink?' he asks Clara, who is standing silently at his heels, an orphaned expression on her face.

She nods. He gives her orange squash in a plastic cup. It is strange, serving this unfamiliar child. He experiences a kind of intimacy with her mother, inhabiting the vacuum where Ellen ought to be. Forgetting how small she is he sets the cup slightly out of her reach, and when she tries to grasp it she knocks it over and the orange liquid pours across the table and down the front of her white shirt. She looks down at the orange stain silently.

'Oh dear,' Thomas says.

He takes her upstairs to Alexa's room to get a clean shirt, holding her by her tiny hand. Alexa is lying on her bed, reading.

'Yuk,' she says, when she sees the stain. She reminds him, in that instant, of Tonie. It is as though the two of them are lying on the bed, spectating on the curious mess Thomas has got himself into, on this strange little child he has been determined to acquire and is caring for so badly.

He sits Clara on the end of the bed and tentatively removes her shirt. She is entirely passive, letting him undo the buttons with her arms hanging limp at her sides. He opens the front, and though his heart stalls momentarily at the sight of the raw red surgical scars that score the length and breadth of her quail's chest his demeanour remains perfectly calm. He finds a clean shirt and does up the buttons with feather-like fingers.

# XXIV

A professor comes to give a talk on the poets of the First World War.

The department advertised the talk, but in the lecture hall only a few of the front seats are occupied. Tonie is embarrassed. She had half-hoped to get out of coming herself, but everyone else is ill or away, and the professor is on her hands. She waits in Reception. He arrives, coming through the glass doors out of the dark street, where the traffic stands end to end in the rain. He is much younger than she expected. She glances at the printed flyer, to remind herself of his name.

They walk briskly along the grey neon-lit corridors to the lecture hall. Tonie tries to slow him down: she doesn't want him in a mood of urgency. She tries to impart the attitude of casual acceptance that is the hallmark of her English department. She hopes that by the time they get there more people will have arrived.

'Don't expect a crowd,' she says at the door. 'They're not very good at evenings. They go back to their burrows once darkness falls.'

He laughs politely. She sees that he is very smartly dressed. He is wearing a suit and tie, cufflinks, polished shoes.

'Never mind,' he says.

She opens the doors. If anything, there are fewer people inside than there were before. She introduces him – his name is Max Desch, from the University of York – and there is a faint sound of clapping as she leaves the podium. She sits a few rows back, alone. She watches him adjust the microphone, lay out his notes. For a long time he doesn't speak. He gets various books out of his briefcase and lays them out too. Then he shakes his head, puts some of them back and gets out others. People start to turn around in their seats, looking back at her. They sense that something is wrong. They expect her to act, but what can she do? In a way, she admires him. She admires people who don't do what they're supposed to.

He is silent for so long that when he finally speaks into the microphone, everybody jumps.

'Why don't you all come up here?' he says.

Everyone troops up on to the podium. They don't even complain about it: they're too unnerved. Tonie comes last. There are a few chairs up there and she sits on one. Other people sit on the floor. The professor sits on a chair.

'The best thing about poetry,' he says, 'is reading it. Don't you think? I'll just read one now.'

He reads a poem by Wilfred Owen. Everyone listens. He has an unusual style of reading. He declares each line flatly and leaves long pauses between the lines. He is not at all self-conscious, in his impeccable suit. One or two of the students laugh. But after a while everyone is quiet.

'Who wants to go next?' he says, when he is finished.

To Tonie's surprise, a few hands go up. He points to a girl and passes her the book. It is Julie Bowes: Tonie often sees her on the bus, whispering into her phone and staring wanly out of the dirty window. She reads a poem by Rupert Brooke, the famous one. It is hard to think of something less associated with Julie Bowes than this poem. She reads it softly, falteringly, with her south London accent. Tonie's neck and shoulders begin to ache. When Julie Bowes asks, 'And is there honey still for tea?' Tonie's whole being cringes. She feels angry with the professor, with his suit and his cut-glass accent. She herself makes every exception for these students, who look so exhausted by life before they've even begun. She is angry that they should be made to read the patriotic words of public schoolboys. Yet they don't seem particularly to mind.

The professor motions Julie to pass the book along. She gives it to Nile, a big silent boy in tracksuit and gold chains, trainers like showboats, his muscled legs uncomfortably crossed in front of him. He leafs slowly through the pages. Then he starts to read, Siegfried Sassoon. His voice is strong and beautiful, simple as a beam. It is as though he has never used it before; as though the poem has hewn it out of the substance of what he is. Slowly, Tonie gives in. She listens to the sound of them saying what they do not normally say. She sees how innocent they are, how unformed, how transitive. They pass easily into the vessel of the poem. For an instant, they become it. Her consternation and embarrassment fade. She is amused, impressed, and in the end she forgets to be anything at all. The hour passes easily. A feeling of comfort, almost of love envelops her. For the first time in a long time, she loves this place.

'What about you?' he says. 'Will you read something?'

They are all looking at her. They want her to become human, like them. They want her to emerge from her authority, her fixed life, a small figure emerging from a large building. They want to see what she really is.

'All right,' she says.

Suddenly the book is in her hands. She reads where the page is open, Wilfred Owen again, 'Insensibility'; a poem she remembers, though she hasn't read it in years, hasn't even thought about it. His voice speaking through hers surprises her. Like the others, she does not often say beautiful things. Yet the words seem to be her own – they feel like what she would have invented, if only she knew how to. They seem to delineate an unlived passion, a dark form, like a second, nameless body inside her own. When she reads the lines,

. . . whatever moans in man
Before the last sea and the hapless stars

her voice trembles. The book is old, with yellowed pages. It is older than her, and Wilfred Owen is dead. She feels sad, sorry, as though he represented a missed opportunity; as though he has left her to go on alone, full of stillborn passion. When she has finished, she returns the book to the professor. Their eyes meet.

'Goodbye, then,' he says to the students.

He starts putting his books and papers back in his brief-case. They stand, hover uncertainly, trail towards the doors. They don't want to leave: they want to be looked after. He has made them feel secure, and now they want to surrender responsibility for themselves.

Tonie remains behind, to see him out.

'Is there somewhere near here we can get a drink?' he says.

They go to the pub that is the traditional refuge of the English department, where Tonie half-hopes she'll meet someone she knows. She doesn't know what she'll find to say to him. She watches him while he gets the drinks. Now that it is over, she isn't sure what his talk really amounted to.

'It was nice, hearing them read,' she says, when he returns.

He puts the drinks on the table. His is something clear, gin or vodka.

'Was it?' He drinks from his glass, apparently indifferent.

'Generally they don't talk all that much.'

'Talk is a snare,' he says.

She glances at him, surprised. He is looking at her steadily. He smiles, a smile that is much less polite than the rest of him.

'I wanted to hear *you* read,' he says.

156

She holds his eyes for a second. 'Well,' she says, 'you did.'

He says, 'I hate to tell you, but your voice gives you away.'

She reminds herself of his name. Max Desch.

'I thought talk was a snare,' she says brightly.

He tilts his head, strums his fingers against his glass. 'There are different kinds of snare,' he says. 'This is quite a pleasant one. It reeled me in firmly but gently.'

There is a silence. Tonie does not want silence. To be silent suggests that she is willing for him to take control of things.

'You seem very young to be a professor,' she says.

He looks surprised. 'I'm thirty-three.'

Tonie laughs, relieved, and vaguely disappointed. He is even younger than she thought. She had imagined he was flirting with her. It is a bad sign, to believe that young men are flirting with you.

'That's young,' she says. Yet she cannot quite believe that she is so much older, almost a different generation. She has clung to youth, she realises. She has no idea what she will do when it is entirely gone.

'Is it?' he says.

'To me it is. I just turned forty.'

He waves this away with his hand. 'What does that matter?'

'I don't know what it matters. It just does.'

He leans forward, rests his elbows on the table. She sees his cufflinks, little polished silver discs in the stiff cloth. She imagines him putting them in. His fingers are broad and pale and clean.

'Why? You're still young. And beautiful,' he adds, lifting his glass to his lips.

Tonie laughs. 'Stop it.'

'I'd like to go to bed with you, that's all,' says Max Desch.

Tonie's cheeks grow red. How strange, that when she was

younger and more free, she reserved all her scorn for a remark such as that; and yet now it has all the mystery for her
that the idea of love had for her then.

'You can't say that,' she says.

'Can't I?' He swirls his drink around. 'Why not?'

She wonders whether he is going all the way back to York
tonight, whether he will sit on the train and feel the particular weight of his visit, as the fisherman returning home feels
the particular bodies of the fish he has caught. There is no
reason, in fact, why he can't say whatever he wants to her. It
is too late – isn't it? – for loyalty, for compunction, for guilt.
The time for these things is past. There is only any point in
saying what is true.

'No reason,' she says. She composes herself. 'So what's
your interest in Wilfred Owen? Where does that come
from?'

'I was in the army.'

She smiles. Vaguely, she doesn't believe him. 'That too.'

'I joined when I was still at school. It was a way of getting
sent to university.'

She is surprised. He has fooled her. She mistook him for a
typical eccentric, of the academic type. But in fact, none of
the academics she knows are anything like him at all.

'And then – what – you didn't go back?'

'I had to go back for a while. I was sent to the Middle
East. After that I was discharged.'

'Oh,' she says. 'And what was it like? The army.'

He looks at her coolly. 'It was all right.'

She imagines him with other men, a male-only place,
something clarifying about it; a disentangling from women
that might bring with it a capacity to see them whole.

'Did you like the other men?'

'Yes.'

'Did you learn how to shoot a gun?'

He smiles his slow, mocking smile. 'Of course. Do you find that exciting?'

She smiles back. 'Not particularly.'

They sit and look at each other. After a while he reaches out his hand and touches the rim of her glass.

'Would you like another?'

She shakes her head, slowly. 'I have to get home.'

He looks so disappointed that she almost laughs. His sincerity is a kind of event. She wants to tell someone about it, but he is the only person there.

'What a pity,' he says. 'Do you really?'

It is clear that he is completely unfamiliar with the idea of home as a set of responsibilities, a scheduled place, like work. Yet there is something about him that makes her feel secure. She is reluctant to leave, as the students were reluctant to leave the lecture hall. He appears to have no other ties. He seems to exist only for her. She has his full attention.

'I do,' she says. 'I'm sorry.'

Outside in the dark street he stops and turns to her. He puts out his large white hand and rests it flat against her clavicle.

'You're very delicate,' he says. 'I want to know what it would be like to overpower you.'

'I'm not easily overpowered,' she says.

'Aren't you?'

He presses with his hand. With his other hand he covers her eyes. He walks her backwards across the pavement until she feels a wall behind her. His hands are very warm. Through the slits in his fingers she can see him. He bends and kisses her throat.

'I can't do this,' she says. 'Someone might see me.'

He kisses her mouth, the skin beneath her ear, her throat again. She laughs. His hand is firm on her chest, fixing her to the wall.

'Just a minute more,' he says. She feels his teeth biting gently at her neck.

'Don't you dare,' she says, laughing, blindfolded.

She feels him smile. His lips brush hers, moth-like. She takes his wrist and moves his hand from her eyes. She frees herself from him, moving out into the pavement.

'I have to go home,' she says.

A taxi rounds the corner and she hails it. It swerves to the kerb and he opens the door for her and she gets in.

'I'm going to the station,' she says. 'Do you want a lift?'

He shakes his head. He raises his hand to her in farewell. She looks back at him through the window. He is striding away down the pavement. She glimpses his face under a street light, chiselled, eternal, like a face in a church, a face on a silver coin.

The house smells of decay. Tonie goes through the rooms, sniffing. It is stale-sweet, nauseating, like the smell of the care home her grandmother lives in, like the smell of the dead men's suits that hang in the charity shops on the High Street. She only smells it when she isn't expecting to. It confronts her among her possessions and then it vanishes, nowhere to be found.

Lately she has been troubled by horrible dreams. They soil her all day with the feeling of dirtiness and unease. They are the dreams of a lunatic. What is it, this black river that runs like a sewer through her sleep? Mostly she dreams about animals. She probes their dumb panic, their cheapness of life and death. Last night she dreamt of a man spearing birds with a garden fork. He wore a park-keeper's uniform. He was putting twigs and debris into a municipal wheelbarrow. He was so lumbering and methodical, walking around the silent park. He speared an owl that was sitting on the grass, then a bird with a long neck and beak like a cormorant. He carried each one to his wheelbarrow on the tines of his fork while they looked around with bright, bewildered eyes.

In the mornings she stands at the window, looks into the street. She wants to see concrete things, continuation, people getting in their cars to go to work, the blue or grey of today's sky. She sees a man at the window opposite, bare-chested, leaning his tattooed arms on the sill to smoke a cigarette into the new day. Down below, the big, distracted lady bursts out of her front door, as she always does at this time, and charges off up the pavement with her arms full of bags. One after another her children come out behind her, following in her wake like ducklings following their mother upstream.

Tonie opens and closes her drawers, looking for clothes. The smell comes out of the third drawer. Formaldehyde, hospitals, rotting bandages. Years ago, the smell of the dirty-grey plaster cast when they took it off her arm. She remembers it, the dead-looking arm underneath, both her and not-her; the realisation that her body was separate from herself, that it could die. And afterwards the faltering sense of space, a rift in the air, something not there that had been there before.

She dresses, like an actor assembling a costume. Head of Department: tailoring for responsibility, black for rebelliousness. She gives thought to this, to her appearance, her part. Today she wears unconventional shoes, a Jimi Hendrix T-shirt under her jacket. She lets her hair go frizzy and wild. She puts things into her satchel, looks at her watch. At this hour of the day each minute is an entity, solid. They cross her consciousness like stepping stones cross a river. She has to be careful not to lose her footing. Upstairs she creeps into Alexa's darkened room to kiss her sleeping form goodbye. When she does this, it is as though her parents are watching her. They observe her movements with the same upright bafflement as they might watch a foreign art-house film. The smell rises from Alexa's bed. Later, when Tonie opens the airing cupboard, it billows out at her from the clean sheets and pillowcases. She smells it on her coat; sometimes she smells it on her food. She tries to give it a name: futility, mortality, meaninglessness. It represents the loss of illusion. Down in the kitchen she says to Thomas,

'Have you noticed a strange smell?'

He thinks about it. 'What of?'

Death, she thinks. Wasted time. Rotting beliefs, sending out their stench.

He is reading *Kobbe's Complete Opera*. He turns one of its thousand pages, wafer-thin, like the pages of the Bible. 'There *was* a smell, but I traced it.'

She lifts her brows in amazement. She imagines him alone here during the day, moving stealthily through the rooms like an Indian in a western. She imagines him kneeling, his nose to the floor.

'Where to?' she asks.

'The cupboard in the hall. It smelt awful. It was full of old shoes.'

'Oh.'

She is in charge here now. She is alone, at the head of her life, subject only to craziness like a king in Shakespeare. It is what she has wanted, to free herself from authority. She has put so much behind her that she is a little frightened of what is to come. She will go to work each day, that's all. She will do her job. What else is there for kings to do?

# XXV

All sorts of things were forecast: weather systems with long, lashing tails spiked with blue or red, winds bearing ferocious hails of arrows, rods of sunlight showing like lances around a shield of cloud that shed blue droplets in the shape of tears.

Leo needs a coat. He looks in the shops on West Hill Road, where big dirty buses thunder past the lit-up window displays, and the pavements are crowded, even on a Tuesday morning. West Hill Road is where the big chains are, and the pound shops, and the junk-food places you can smell from a hundred yards away. It is where people who spend money go, as opposed to people who make it.

'What happened to the coat you wore last year?' Susie said, when he told her that morning where he was going.

Leo shrugged. 'I don't know.'

'What coat *did* you wear last year?'

She seemed confused, as though it was not just the coat but the year itself that had been mislaid.

'I don't know.'

'No, really,' she pleaded, touching his arm. 'What was it like?'

But Leo couldn't remember either. He and Susie clutched each other shakily and laughed, glancing in each other's red-rimmed eyes. Justin and Madeleine sat stiffly at the breakfast table watching their parents.

'You must remember your own *coat*,' Madeleine said, disbelieving.

'I don't!' Leo protested. 'I must have lost it.'

'He probably left it somewhere,' said Justin. 'He probably got drunk at some party and forgot it.'

Leo has not gone to Temple Street, as Susie advised him to – Temple Street with its faux-Victorian street lamps and planters full of shrubs, its little boutiques like silvered webs with a black-clad assistant waiting inside like a charming spider. A saxophonist plays atmospheric jazz on the swept pavements in Temple Street. But he has not gone there. He has come to West Hill Road, where men and women with colourless hair and shapeless bodies carry giant bags stuffed full of clothes and shoes from China or Taiwan, as cheap and unflattering as the ones they already have on. From the top of the bus Leo watches them coming and going through the big electric doors. They come out and stand for a moment in the ferment of the threshold, where the shop's air conditioning meets the gusty grey air of outside. The turbulence ruffles their hair and makes their clothes balloon and shrink against their bodies. It is as though they are being momentarily handled by some careless god. He sees the way they brace themselves against the frisking wind, their look of determination. They cling on to their purchases, glancing to left and right.

There is a coat Leo wants. It is a long coat in a dark colour. He looks for it in the men's departments as impatiently as if it is an actual coat he possesses and has mistakenly left somewhere. And it does appear to him as a sort of soulmate, this coat: as something home-like and familiar, like Susie. It is strange, to be searching these huge stores, in which all the world's randomness seems constantly to be being incarnated in these millions of orphaned garments, for a piece of home, a piece of his soul. It is as though he is looking for himself. And the longer he looks, and fails to find something he recognises, the more strange he feels himself to be: yes, this is what distinguishes him from the others, who rake through rail after rail of jackets and jeans and sweatshirts with a thoroughness that he would almost call professional, were it not so obsessive and so debased.

Most of the men he knows are at work at this time of day. Even Susie is at work, at eleven o'clock on a Tuesday morning. It is only Leo who can feel cold at that hour and have the freedom to go and buy himself a coat. In Marks & Spencer he tries on three or four. He is shy, and slightly disgusted. It can feel like a kind of prostitution, the first cold forays into a shop. His needs are so private, so over-fashioned by his imagination, and the shops so concrete and matter-of-fact: it takes a while for him to warm up, and reshape his desires to match what is actually on offer. This is why people like Susie do their shopping in Temple Street. They don't cast themselves out into the world when they need to buy a coat. They go to places that specialise in what they want.

There are two other people in the men's department, a couple, shopping together. The woman goes into raptures about whatever unexceptional garment her eye happens to fall on.

'Oh, isn't *this* nice!' she keeps saying to her husband.

In each coat he puts on Leo looks like a different person. He is surprised: he wouldn't have thought it was possible. On the hangers these coats have a vague look of uselessness, but when he puts them on they are startlingly powerful and complete. There is a navy blue one with square shoulders and a tapered body that particularly disturbs him. It is the coat men of his age wear over their city suits, or have hanging from a peg in their company cars: men Leo knew at school, as boys, who still seem frozen in childhood in spite of their paunches and their balding heads. Wearing that coat, there seems to be no difference between himself and them. This is the son his parents wanted, this red-faced man in the mirror with a coat that suggests a job in banking: he knows it beyond any doubt. He takes it off and puts on a horrible black tailored cashmere that turns him into an undertaker.

'Oh, that's *lovely*. Isn't that just *lovely*,' the woman says.

She speaks so sombrely, so profoundly, that he has to turn his head. He sees her, a nondescript person with cropped, rigid hair, holding up a tan-coloured anorak. Her husband is a tall silent hunk of grey flesh who stands behind her with his giant hands hanging lifelessly at his sides.

'I just think that's really lovely,' she repeats.

He takes off the black coat and drops it in a bundle over the rack. Momentarily he catches the woman's eye. She is looking to see what he has discarded. Her face wears a gleam of predatory interest. He stares back at her reprovingly. Doesn't she see how ugly she is, how repellent? She reaches past him and picks up the coat where he has let it fall. She seems to have no awareness of him at all. She looks at the label and runs her hand over the heavy black cloth. To Leo it is as if she is running her hand over death itself, blindly stroking its nullity, its soft evil.

'That's nice too,' she says to her husband.

'Excuse me,' Leo says loudly.

They are standing so close to him that they are blocking his way out. He has to force himself sideways through the space between them, and even then he remains invisible. The woman's padded jacket makes a rasping sound all down Leo's back as he pushes past her and stalks away towards the escalators.

Susie would laugh at a woman like that. She would get

her exactly, the way she touched everything, the way she said, *That's nice too.* She would neutralise her: she could neutralise the devil himself. Susie could make even the most horrible things seem harmless simply by retaining her ability to comment on them. Leo sometimes wonders what becomes of the fact that some of these things are not harmless at all. The other day he read something out to her from the newspaper, about a man who had been attacked in the street – stabbed nine times in broad daylight by some mental case and left there to bleed to death. No one had stopped to help that man. No one had knelt down beside him and held his head, held his hand. He said – because he'd survived and recovered to write the article that Leo was reading – he said that he remembered seeing people huddled at a distance calling an ambulance on a mobile phone, but that no one had spoken to him or come near him. Leo was very upset by that. He read the whole thing to Susie.

'That's horrible, isn't it?' she said, exactly as she would have said it about something they were eating that didn't taste very nice.

'No one even *spoke* to him!' exclaimed Leo, stricken. 'For all they knew he was about to die!'

This idea, that the world could triumph in its coldness, could triumph even over one man in its despicable bleakness, was abhorrent to him.

'I expect they were frightened,' Susie said; so that their being frightened became normal, became understandable even. There were people who were mad and there were people who were unlucky enough to be stabbed by them, and then there were people who were frightened. The only abnormal thing, in Susie's view, seemed to be Leo himself. 'Why does it get to you so much?' she said. 'At least they called the ambulance. You couldn't expect them to do more than that.'

If he could only leave it all to her; if he could simply be incorporated into her beliefs, the way people are absorbed into religion: Susie never worries that she and Leo always seem to be reaching and reaching for something they can't quite touch, striving for a satisfaction that eludes them. She doesn't think about it like that. She lives in the moment as though moments are all there are. She swabs away the past and the future from the shining instant. She deals efficiently, hygienically, with its rich waste-product of guilt and shame and apprehension. She laughs at the children, and the way Madeleine says, 'Not *again*,' in the mornings, with a puckered little face like a raisin. She makes it seem as though all these things are one thing, one entity neither good nor bad.

Leo wonders if he has been too easily defeated in the men's department. There was a coat he didn't try on. He left it there, out of the rack, hanging over the others. He had it all arranged. That woman and her husband have driven him off before he was finished, like hyenas from the kill. The escalator carries him fatefully downwards. His eyes fill with electric light. Above his head are strange geometric distances and perspectives, a labyrinth of grilles and air vents and sections of false ceiling that seem to travel upwards and upwards towards some unseen core, strung with cables like giant nerves. A dazzling yellow haze stands just over him. It makes his eyes water: it is almost alive. It seems to have no source other than the building itself, as though a monstrous god or spirit has struggled into being somewhere up in that grey labyrinth. The escalator carries him past a blown-up photograph of a woman standing in a doorway in her underwear. Her hand rests on the doorknob and she looks at the camera with a beckoning expression. Her lips are parted to show a glimpse of her teeth and tongue. The underwear is intricate and white, but somehow little-girlish on that obstinately self-regarding body. What does she think she is doing, standing there? It is the door to a hotel room, he realises. A sign reading 'Do Not Disturb' hangs from the doorknob. Leo lets out a strange bark of laughter. At the bottom of the escalator he turns around and goes up again on the other side. She reminds him unexpectedly of his sister-in-law, Tonie. She has curly brown hair and a tight little midriff. She has a body so buffed and groomed that it vitiates her nakedness. It seems a form of clothing in itself. But it is her eyes that he can't stomach. That fake, play-acting expression, as she goes about her fake hotel tryst above the endlessly revolving escalator on West Hill Road – she makes it seem as if there is nothing lovely or true in the whole world.

Someone has returned the coat to its place on the rack. He takes it off the hanger again and puts it on. The woman and her silent husband have moved away to the shoe section. He can see them in the distance, together, like little figurines. In the mirror he strikes himself as extraordinarily flawed. His skin looks rough and red and his hair goes everywhere in painful-looking spikes, and he seems riven through with wearying variation and texture, with pores and veins and cracks, with moles and bumps and broken fingernails. By contrast the coat is amazingly bland and smooth. It is like something that has been cut out and pasted on to him, like a felt coat from Madeleine's Fuzzy Felt kit. It is brown and big. It envelops his strange particular contours like a large brown generalisation. His soft belly, the little breast-like mounds of flesh on his chest, his white, womanly haunches: those are all now as private as thoughts, unseen behind the brown shield of the coat. It is not exactly the coat he has imagined – that coat actually transformed his defects rather than simply obliterated them – but all the same it has the feeling of a good idea. Already he is getting used to it. What a relief it is, what a blessing, to be completely covered up. It is the same sensation he sometimes feels getting into bed at night and drawing the covers over himself, a feeling of being returned to an original innocence; as though his years of life drift away once his body is hidden from view. When he and Susie have sex, it is spoilt for Leo by the sight of their abundant mottled bodies all grizzled with pubic hair. He never looks the way he feels, any more than Susie looks like that girl in the poster. But in the dark all of that moves away from him, that dirty, densely wrought revulsion.

At the till he has to take the coat off to pay for it, but as soon as the woman has his credit card he lifts it from the counter and tears the price tag off with his teeth.

'Do you want a bag for it?' she says.

'No. I'm wearing it.'

'Do you want a bag for what you were wearing before?' she says, as though every second person who comes into her department does precisely what Leo has just done.

'Oh. I suppose so.'

'Hanger?' She waves it in the air, a plastic shape.

'No, thank you.'

Leo feels deflated. Somehow, in the course of that exchange with the woman at the till, the desirability of the brown coat has peaked, has reached the summit of what it is or ever could be. The woman hands him the plastic bag containing his rumpled grey jacket. She has folded it carefully: she has smoothed the exhausted fabric with her long, brilliantly varnished nails. She seems to take pity on it, this discarded piece of his life. She seems to feel for it, for all unwanted things, for everything that is old and abandoned: he feels that by her folding and smoothing she has criticised the world for its inhumanity.

'Very nice,' she says, when Leo puts the new coat on.

She gives him a little approving smile. He looks at his watch. It is a quarter past ten. He takes his card and his receipt and stuffs them in his coat pocket. The pocket's silky lining, cold and unfamiliar, closes around his hand.

# XXVI

Her mother has different faces. Sometimes she has a face like a witch. It is on the back of her head, not the front. Alexa sees it when she walks up the stairs behind her.

In the mornings, when Tonie comes into her bedroom, Alexa pretends to be asleep. Often she *is* asleep. It is the presence in the room that wakes her up: she feels it through her closed eyes, something warm and soft and attentive, though at first she doesn't remember what it is. She keeps her eyes shut. She lies still. She thinks her mother will love her better that way. She feels beautiful, lying completely still in her nightdress. She is like a doll. She imagines her mother looking at her and loving her. But at the same time she knows she is pretending.

'Are you awake?' Tonie whispers.

There is the tiniest smile on Alexa's lips. Her mouth wants to twitch at the corners, feeling it. But she stays totally still. She wants her mother to think that she is a girl who smiles in her sleep. The bedclothes rustle beside her. The mattress creaks. Her mother's hair tickles her face. She kisses Alexa's cheek. Sometimes Alexa will pretend to wake up then, like a princess waking from her enchantment. She will yawn and stretch her arms, and say, 'You woke me up,' in a pretend-sleepy voice.

But sometimes she remains still, smiling, with her eyes shut. She wants to bring her idea, her pretence, to perfection. She wants to fool her mother entirely. There is something she senses she will gain if she succeeds. She waits to receive the kiss. It comes out of the infinite blind distances beyond her eyelids. She never knows quite when it will come. Afterwards she hears her mother softly leave the room. She hears the door close.

When she opens the curtains the day is already in motion, alive, waiting for her to get up. She stands at the window in her nightdress. The sun bursts and bursts again against the glass. The wind is tickling the bare branches of the trees, jiggling them up and down, up and down. A dead leaf twirls past, spinning through space. Alexa watches a tiny airplane stitching a white line across the blue sky overhead. She watches a bird springing amidst the waving branches, alighting and then springing again.

Her father walks with her to school. His feet are next to hers, going along the pavement. His shoes have big frowning creases in them. They wink and frown at her as they walk. They are old and angry and brown, with drooping laces.

'You need new shoes, Daddy,' she says.

'Do I?' He stops and looks down at them. 'These are all right, aren't they?'

'They're old. And the laces are too long. They're dirty.'

'They can still take me where I need to go,' he says.

She laughs. She imagines the shoes walking all by themselves, all around the world; something you could hitch a ride on, like a bus.

'You could attach little rockets to them,' she says. 'And wheels.'

'Rocket-powered shoes,' he says, and she laughs again.

They reach the road, where the cars come like waves out of the horizon, building and rising and breaking, going over with a roar. They cross to the other side.

'I can go on my own from here,' she says.

'Don't you want me to come?'

She shakes her head. He bends down and there is his face, in front of hers, the lips puckered in a kiss-shape. Close up his face is complicated. His eyes have tiny paths in them, and there are little valleys all around his mouth and hairs like miniature trees, and the skin is bumpy, detailed, like the surface of the globe in Mrs Flack's classroom. He kisses her. He lays his hand on the top of her head. She has to turn away from her knowledge of him. She takes a few steps and when she looks back he is smaller. She knows his shape but it is less complicated. He is standing on the pavement. He waves.

Mrs Flack has given out their French exercise books. Alexa turns the pages. She sees her own writing. She sees things she has coloured in. The colouring is a bright little memory; the writing is a message from herself. She loves her exercise books. She loves to see what she has done, what she is. But this book, the French book, gives her a slightly sad feeling. It is the words that are sad. She wrote them and yet they are strangers: they seem to bear some hostility towards the words she knows. They are like mistakes. They make the pictures unfriendly, like certain things in dreams.

She is sitting at a table with Katie. Usually she sits with Maisie or Francesca, but today she came in late from the playground and there was no empty chair except the one next to Katie. Mrs Flack is handing out worksheets now. She goes all around the classroom, sometimes far away, sometimes close. She has yellow hair and her body is made of balls and circles, like the man in the picture made completely of car tyres. Every part of her is completely round. Her face is bright with make-up. She has a nice smell, and when she is nearby Alexa can hear her clothes whispering and hushing, like there are tiny magic voices in the folds. It takes a long time for Mrs Flack to give out the worksheets. Alexa waits. Finally her turn comes. Mrs Flack's hand with its painted fingernails appears before her eyes and places the worksheet on the table. Alexa twists round, smiles. She wants Mrs Flack to see how good she is, how patient.

'Thank you,' she says.

There is a picture of a girl on the worksheet, drawn with black lines, like a cut-out girl. She is wearing a hat, a triangle-shaped skirt, a pair of shoes. She is beautiful, in a way, in her incompleteness. There are black lines sticking out of her body like arrows. On the other side of the page there is a boy.

'Look at him,' Katie says next to her. She jabs her finger at the paper boy. 'He looks gay.'

Mrs Flack is writing words with her marker on the board. They are meant to be attaching the words to the arrows. There are windows all along one wall of the classroom and for a moment Alexa stares out of them, at the day passing outside. Katie has snagged her attention. She drifts around it, the snag, like a balloon drifting on its string tether. She stares at the day, behind glass. Then she glances at Katie out of the corners of her eyes.

'You aren't meant to say that,' she says.

'Aren't I?'

'No,' Alexa says. 'Mr Simpson says you're not.'

Alexa's knowledge of Katie is awakening: she remembers that she has sat next to her before. Katie is like a story she has read and then forgotten, the details stored but not often revisited. Now she is unfolding again, her particular shape and atmosphere, her scuffed shoes, her lazy hair pegged back with a clip, her mouth that goes all the way across her face when she grins, her pale, insolent eyes.

'I like saying it,' Katie says. 'I say it all the time. It's fun.'

'What's fun about it?' Alexa says scornfully.

Katie shrugs, and twists her pencil in her stubby fingers. There is something attractive about her, something magnetising that Alexa feels guilty about. She gives Alexa the feeling that she has forgotten something important. She makes it seem as though it may not have been important after all.

Mrs Flack is calling out the words and people are putting their hands up. On the other side of the room, Maisie and Francesca put their hands up. Alexa would like to put her hand up, but she has not been listening. Because of Katie, she does not know the answers. The French words fall on her ears and die away, uncomprehended. This is Katie's power, the power of ignorance. For a moment Alexa thinks she likes it, this huge, unspecified freedom that lies darkly all around the fussing, probing point of knowledge. Other people are writing things down. Alexa does not know what she is meant to be writing. She is lost. The drawings and the arrows and the words don't fit together. It is as though she has lost sight of Mrs Flack and the others; as though one minute she was following them and the next they had turned a corner and disappeared. Mrs Flack turns and writes something on the board. Her round body jiggles as she writes. Katie nudges Alexa in the ribs and Alexa looks. Katie is half-standing in her chair, wobbling like a belly dancer. She is being Mrs Flack, wobbling and writing in the air. Petrified, Alexa pulls her back into her seat.

'Stop it!' she says in a whisper.

Katie laughs, a raspberry sound that bursts noisily through her lips and coats them with a sheen of spit. There is spit on the table too. Mrs Flack stops writing. She turns around, cocks her head, scans the silent classroom. Alexa stares straight ahead. Her cheeks are hot. She has forgotten that the lesson will end: she has lost the chain-like sequence of the day, the prospect of morning break and lunch, the light-filled distances of the afternoon. There is only this ever-enlarging present, extending outwards into the darkness of ignorance. Mrs Flack returns her attention to the board. When Alexa looks down at her worksheet, she sees that the paper girl and boy have changed. The girl has a dark scribble of hair in the middle of her skirt and big round bosoms on her shirtfront, and the boy has a carrot-shaped penis drooping obscenely between his legs. For a moment Alexa thinks that she has drawn these things herself. It is as though some shameful desire of her own has been mysteriously enacted. Mrs Flack will collect the worksheets at the end of the lesson. This one has Alexa's name on it. Alexa is like the paper boy and girl, violated. Katie's face beside her is white and grinning, her eyes large, her hand with its pencil comically twirling a strand of hair by her ear. At the sight of her face Alexa laughs, a laugh that struggles frantically in her stomach, that convulses her whole body and finally escapes, pealing, from her mouth.

Mrs Flack snaps round, outraged.

'Alexa Bradshaw!'

Her voice is shrill and angry. Alexa sees the glaring face, the body briefly lit up with fury, the transformation of Mrs Flack from one thing into another. It is Alexa who has transformed her. The class is silent.

'Alexa Bradshaw, will you be quiet!'

The sound of her own name is a kind of death. Then, unexpectedly, Mrs Flack is herself again. She picks up her marker; she returns to the lesson. She does not appear surprised, or disappointed. She does not say that Alexa has let her down. She does not comment on Alexa's violated goodness, on the white record of her conduct that has now been stained. It is

Mrs Flack, in a way, who has stained it. She has treated Alexa as she treats everyone. She does not love Alexa; she has never, Alexa sees, loved her. Yet Alexa feels guilty, as though Mrs Flack's indifference, too, were her own fault.

She sits rigid and silent until the bell goes. She does not hand in her worksheet. Instead she folds it up tightly and puts it in her pocket. It has become possible to deceive Mrs Flack. The stain has made it possible. At break time she tears it into pieces and hides them under the rubbish in the bin.

On Saturday her mother is taking her to the city museum. Alexa stands in the kitchen in her coat while her mother puts things into her handbag.

Her father says, 'Shall I come along and keep you company?'

There is a little underwater silence, a kind of blank.

Tonie says, 'Don't you have stuff you need to do?'

'Not really.'

Alexa listens. The way her parents speak has changed. Their conversations used to travel towards agreement, the way in snap the cards keep turning until two identical ones come up. But now it is the differences Alexa notices. It is as though their talks stop before the end: the identical card is never found. They walk away unresolved, two people who don't match.

'I thought it would be nice to go together, that's all,' her father says.

Tonie purses her lips, forages about in her bag.

'Really, I'm happy to take her,' she says. 'I've hardly seen her this week.'

Alexa doesn't hear the end of that conversation, if it had an end. The scene in the kitchen has a ragged edge. The next thing she knows, she's out on the pavement with her mother, walking downhill. She is holding her mother's hand. They are flying over the cracks between the paving stones, over the dead leaves and empty sweet wrappers, flying away from the house, where her father remains.

'Isn't Daddy coming?' she says.

'No.' Her mother sounds surprised. 'Did you want him to come?'

She doesn't know the answer to that question. Her mother squeezes her fingers.

'I wanted it to be just us,' she says.

'Me too,' says Alexa. Instantly she feels unhappy. She touches a lamp-post, for luck. 'Can we have hot chocolate in the café?'

'If you want.'

'Can we have it first? Before we go in?'

Her mother is silent. They pass a lady standing on the pavement. She is talking on her phone, laughing. She is wearing a black coat. She is laughing and laughing, standing there.

'Can we?'

'No. We'll have it afterwards.'

'Why can't we have it before?'

'Because I say so.'

'But why?'

'Hey. Stop asking for things.'

Her mother has stopped and is looking around, to right and left. For a moment Alexa thinks she is looking for someone to tell, about Alexa's behaviour. But they are only crossing the road.

'Stop asking for things,' she repeats, when they reach the other side. 'We've only just left the house and you're already asking for things.'

'Sorry,' Alexa says.

Her mother halts again. She bends down and puts her arms around Alexa, so that the street disappears and Alexa is lost in her hair and the folds of her clothes.

'No, I'm the one who's sorry,' she says, into her ear. 'I'm just tired. I need to get used to you again.'

Alexa wonders what this means. It gives her the feeling that she is in some way extraordinary. She wonders whether it means they will have hot chocolate first. They reach the main road and wait at the bus stop. Her mother seems smaller here, in the noise and the traffic. She is wearing a red jacket.

'Where's the bus?' Tonie says. 'Can you see it? Your eyes are better than mine.'

Alexa looks down the milling grey stretch. She looks for the form of the bus. She knows what she is looking for, yet she is anxious. It seems possible that she might not recognise the bus, or that it might not come. She looks at the shapes of cars and vans and lorries, wondering each time whether they are the bus.

'I think I see it,' she says. There is something big and blue in the distance. Are buses blue? She thinks they might be.

Tonie peers. 'That's not a bus,' she says, laughing.

Alexa frowns, looks at her shoes. She looks at the grimy pavement.

'Here it is,' Tonie says. 'This is it.'

The bus is coming towards them, a double-decker, dark red and cream. Alexa recognises it, the cartoon face with round headlight eyes, the tall flat front winking in the sun, the people looking out of the dusty upper-storey windows. It surges out of nothingness, all colourful and alive. She feels relieved. It comes in its certainty, its reality, and her doubt disappears.

'Can we sit at the top?' she says.

There is a man up there with a little dog. The dog sits on the man's lap, looking at Alexa. Alexa looks back through the gap in the seats. It has a twitching little nose and funny brown eyes. She looks at the man and then back at the dog.

'It's all right,' he says. 'She won't hurt you.'

'What's she called?' Alexa says.

'She's called Jill,' says the man.

Alexa puts her hand through the gap and strokes Jill's coarse little head. The head moves eagerly beneath her fingers. The stubby tail wags. The brown eyes are willing.

'She likes that,' the man says.

Alexa turns to her mother.

'Look, she likes me,' she says.

'I can see that,' her mother says. She is smiling. Alexa imagines her feeling glad, that the dog likes Alexa. Yet her eyes are not as willing as Jill's. Her smile has something secret in it, something private and sealed.

'Can we get a dog?' Alexa says. 'Can we?'

Her mother's face closes shut. She turns and looks out of the window.

The museum is big inside, like a church. It glimmers brownly, as detailed as a forest, little scenes everywhere behind glass. People's footsteps echo when they walk. They go upstairs, to Alexa's favourite room. The room is full of gemstones, crystals, rocks, all lying on their black plinths. Each one is lit up. The light is white and limited, precious in the surrounding blackness. It glitters like frost on the crystals and the rubies, the aconite, the amethyst. The crystals are strange, slightly frightening. They seem to have a mind and purpose of their own. They look like things that could take over the world, with their startling thrust-like growths. Alexa imagines a crystal world, growing and advancing out of the dark earth, obliterating language. Her favourite stone is the purple amethyst. It is like a flower. Its ladylike colour pleases her.

'These are so weird,' Tonie says, moving along the glass cases.

'Which one do you like?' Alexa asks her. She wants her to like something.

'I like that one. The opal.'

She points. The opal is pale and milky. It is not a colour. It is vague, like a cloud. Alexa looks at it. She waits for it to tell her something, but it seems to lie beyond her comprehension. It is secretive. She wonders why her mother likes it. She wonders why she doesn't choose the flowerlike amethyst.

'Look at that,' Tonie says, pointing at a spiked hunk of black quartz, flecked with light. 'That's like something out of a horror film.'

Alexa laughs. She imagines the black rock, rampaging through outer space. She makes her fingers into spikes and growls like a monster. Tonie smiles.

'Let's keep going,' she says.

They walk through silent rooms filled with animals. Tonie seems to like these rooms. She stops and looks and reads the names of things aloud from the little cards. The animals are all dead. Alexa wonders whether Tonie is being respectful, stopping at each one and reading out its name; whether she feels sorry for the animal, having to die. There is a polecat crouched on a fake branch, looking at Alexa with yellow eyes. Suddenly she is afraid. She wishes she hadn't noticed its eyes. Now, all the animals seem to be looking at her, the fierce eyes of exotic birds, the strange hooded downward glance of a bear standing on its hind legs, the narrowed eyes of things that are baring their teeth: they are all motionless yet poised, as though awaiting their opportunity. But she knows they are dead.

'Who does that remind you of?' Tonie says, pointing at the porcupine, with its fussy little face and extravagant rigid plumage of quills.

Alexa doesn't know who it reminds her of. She wonders if Tonie is saying that it reminds her of Alexa.

'Daddy?' she says.

Tonie laughs. 'Not Daddy. Grandma.'

'Why is it like Grandma?'

Tonie laughs again. It seems she doesn't feel sorry for the animals after all. They remind her of things that are alive. Alexa thinks it is dangerous, to connect the living with the dead. She worries that her mother is endangering people.

'Oh, no reason really,' Tonie says.

'Can we go and see Grandma?'

'Not right now we can't.'

'When can we see her?'

'I don't know,' Tonie says. 'I don't know the answer to that.'

She stares into the glass case with the porcupine.

'Can we go to the shell room now?' Alexa says.

'If you want. Don't you like the animals?'

'I don't like their eyes,' she says, reluctantly. She thinks her mother ought to know about their eyes. She thinks she should know, to be more careful.

They go back out into the main hall, with its dim commotion, its underwater light and strange echoing sounds. Alexa can't remember where the shell room is. They look around, peering into rooms full of old pots and china plates, rooms bristling with swords and lances, rooms with plaster people in old-fashioned clothes. Today Alexa doesn't want to look at human things. They seem dowdy and sad, compared with the spangled eternal crystals, the miniature perfection of shells. But she cannot remember how to find the shells.

'Maybe there isn't a shell room,' her mother says.

'There is. I remember it.'

'Are you sure? Maybe you remember it from a different museum.'

'I remember the one *here*,' Alexa says, though her mother's words have unnerved her. This can happen, she knows it can. You can remember something, and you can fail to ever find it again, no matter how hard you look. The perfect shells, so pink and miraculous, so blank and yet so intricate, might never again be found.

'Well,' Tonie says, 'I'm pretty sure it isn't here now.'

'It is!' Alexa cries. 'It *is* here!'

Her mother stops, looks at her. Then she says,

'I'll go and ask at the information desk.'

She leaves Alexa on a bench in the hall. When she returns her face is different. She holds out her hand.

'They've moved them,' she says. 'They're in Coasts and Rivers. It's all changed since the last time I was here.'

'So I *wasn't* wrong,' Alexa says.

'You weren't wrong. You were right. We were both right.'

Coasts and Rivers is new. It is dark and glamorous around the lit-up displays. There are recorded voices speaking, and buttons you can push that turn on little chains of lights. Alexa finds the shells, but they are not as she remembered them. They are different. The display is full of sand, and there are dirty-looking nets with plastic starfish in the tangles. The shells lie on the sand carelessly, as though someone just dropped them there. Somehow, they have become ordinary. She turns away, goes to find her mother. She walks through the darkness and the voices, through the unfamiliar carpeted spaces. At last she sees her, at the far end of the room. She is standing in a labyrinth of shadows. She is looking through glass, a greenish light on her face. Alexa approaches and stands beside her. In front of her is a river scene, with jewelled dragonflies in the reeds and a plaster swan sitting on the painted blue water. This is what her mother is looking at. The river twists and turns between its green banks, meanders away amid trees into painted distances. There is a kingfisher, and little animals on the banks, and a duck with her ducklings. There are flowers, and a bird's nest full of tiny eggs. But it is the swan that is beautiful, central, in its splendour of white. Alexa stands beside her mother at the glass. She has never seen something so lovely as this place. She wishes she could walk into it, sit on the enchanted banks beside the river and feed the swan, walk and walk among the trees until she was out of sight. She aches to enter its reality. She feels it, the ecstasy of the imaginary becoming real.

'Look at the ducklings,' she says to her mother. 'Look at the little eggs in the nest.'

Her mother is silent. She is staring at the river, at the swan. She stares and stares.

'Look at the dragonfly,' Alexa says.

The dragonfly hovers, blue and glinting. The bulrushes are tall and straight, perfectly brown and rounded at their ends. The kingfisher plunges. The swan curves her white neck like a ballerina. The painted river sparkles.

# XXVII

Olga has met a man. He is a porter at the hospital. His name is Stefan. One day, in the tearoom, he asked her where she came from and when she told him the name of her home town he leaped in the air and shouted, 'My God!' so that she thought he must come from there too. But he is only Lithuanian. She still doesn't know why he got so excited. He is six-and-a-half feet tall. It is important, when a man that tall throws himself in the air.

The supervisor has moved Olga to the place where women come to have their babies. Before, she cleaned in the old people's wards, the big quiet rooms far inside the maze of the building where the windows don't look out at anything, just brick walls or stairwells or the vents and pipes of the hospital heating system, as though someone decided that these old people didn't need to see the world any more because they were about to leave it anyway. The old ladies would lie in their beds, all white and tiny and soft, like wrinkled little fairies. They were no trouble to anyone. They lay there like babies in their cots under the bright overhead lights, with just a few trinkets beside them: a photograph in a frame, a card, a magazine. They had so little, less than people take with them in their handbags when they go out to the shops. The white lights interrogated them, clarified them in their poverty, rinsing and rinsing each object of its significance until the photograph and the card seemed to have hardly any right to be there, impeding the encroaching whiteness. Olga would dust their trinkets for them, set them square and triumphant on the bedside tables again, smooth the covers of the magazines.

The maternity place isn't like that at all. The women here have giant, lurid bunches of flowers and bowls of exotic fruit, and presents, always more presents, new items the mothers carelessly husk of their packaging, discarding it for Olga to pick up. She picks up the torn shapes of brightly coloured paper, the gold ribbons, the tags and labels, the rustling plastic shrouds in which the new things came encased. She takes these things, so recent and yet so superfluous, and she crams them into her black rubbish sack. Next to the beds the babies writhe like naked grubs in their perspex boxes. At the end of her shift the rubbish sack is full, full of weightless crackling wastage, chemical-fresh and nameless. There are no words for the kinds of rubbish Olga picks up. It is strange, that new life should come into the world garlanded in nameless rubbish.

The corridors outside the labour rooms echo with terrible screams. Olga pushes her mop there, at the closed doors. Inside, the women bellow like animals. Stefan works in these corridors: he wheels the patients on trolleys in and out. This is how she sees him, pushing the suffering ladies towards their destiny, their release; and then retrieving them, limp and tangled and silent, the baby clamped like a grub to their breast. His tall, upright form seems to preside over their suffering, almost to describe it, as the artist's brush describes the image it is painting: impassive in himself, he nonetheless finds himself there, at the fulcrum of creation, guided by an unseen hand. He distributes its shapes and properties; he passes in and out of the birthing chamber, besmirched by creation.

But in the pub, showered and changed out of his hospital

uniform, his functionality clears like mist; his authority is restored, the clean authority of the brush, the tool. He says,

'This is a bad country.'

Over the weeks Olga has unravelled her woes to Stefan, her loneliness and bewilderment, her exhaustion and superstition, the feeling she has that in this place she is drawing evil towards herself, attracting it as blindly as a magnet attracts steel; the whole tale lies at his feet, undone.

'Why should it be worse than other countries?' she says.

He nods, raises his hand: he has already considered this.

'It is our position here that brings out the bad. Like the mouse brings out the bad in the cat.'

Olga is frightened. She wants to hear that her problems will disappear. She does not want to think of them as inalienable, like the mouse and the cat. And she dislikes mice: at home she has a beautiful cat, Mino, who catches mice and eats them whole. She has watched, disgusted and fascinated, the toothpick legs and tail wriggling madly at Mino's lips even as the head was already down his throat. Afterwards he would wind himself around her legs, purring; he would gaze at her with his clear, calm, staring eyes. He was referring his superiority to her; he was claiming kinship, the kinship of superior beings.

'It takes time,' Olga says. 'Maybe a long time.'

Stefan is shaking his head. 'We can be here a hundred years and we still won't belong,' he says.

'Maybe we don't need to belong. Maybe we just want to live.'

All at once he has reminded her: of the limited town, the grey colours that seeped into her brain and stained it, the feeling everywhere of defacement, of everything being known and defaced, herself spoilt and defaced by others' knowledge of her. And the terrible certainty of repetition, her grandmother and mother and sister, replicas of one another, using and reusing the same grey rag of life. Lately, a feeling of yearning has stolen over her, for her home town and her family. It has been stealthily painting out the greyness, this feeling; it has been going over her memories and painting them in rainbow colours. In Poland, she used to imagine in these same rainbow colours what her life would be like elsewhere. Now she is here, imagining again.

'As servants,' Stefan says. 'As outsiders. But as equals, never.' He points at her with his long, strong finger. 'You, a qualified teacher in Poland, a university degree, high social status, and what do they let you do here? They let you wash the floors.'

'I earn more here in one week than in one month at home,' Olga says. 'And anyway, they treated me like a servant before. In Poland, a teacher is less than a cleaner. Less!'

On this point Olga retains a foothold in reality, when all the rest has become bodiless, rainbow-coloured myth. She does not want Stefan to succumb here, where the danger is greatest. She does not want him to slip away into illusion and leave her all alone with her one bitter certainty.

'But as a teacher you have dignity,' he says. 'You have self-respect.'

'I had no respect. The parents did not respect me and neither did their children. I hated them!'

He raises his eyebrows, purses his lips.

'Even if I go back to Poland, I will never again be a teacher,' she says.

And as she says it, her foothold crumbles imperceptibly away. She is released, into the memory of crisp snow on winter streets, of her grandmother's warm kitchen, of the hot flat days of summer, of familiar sounds and smells; of herself moving, acknowledged, through the landscape, being seen and known, her friends and family crowding round her at every turn, calling her name. Olga! Olga! Suddenly it seems clear what the problem was, the blockage. If she goes back to Poland she will get a job in a bank, and everything will be different. She sees herself sitting behind the cashier's window, in a tailored suit and high-heeled shoes. She sees herself smiling, showing her straightened teeth.

Stefan reaches out and takes her hand between his own. They are large and white, peaked with knuckles like mountains.

'Here we have the intimacy of outsiders,' he says. 'It is us against them. We are a little nation, fighting the world.'

'It's true,' she says, smiling wearily. She is tired. The effort of resisting illusion has exhausted her. And still it pricks her, through her sleepy surrender: the feeling of panic, the terrible feeling that drove her out of her home, that drove her here. It was the feeling you have when you break something. You break it, and there is nothing for you to do but run away.

'I want to have the normal life of a man and a woman,' he says. 'I don't want us to have the false intimacy of people on a little island. I want us to belong somewhere, to be a normal man and woman.'

She thinks of the women in the maternity ward, steeped in refuse; the fruit rotting in its bowls, the flowers drooping and browning. She hears the bellows and screams, sees the baby clamped grub-like to the breast. Really, she preferred the old ladies. She preferred their daintiness, their dispossession.

'But in Poland you don't belong either,' she says.

'I belong more. I belong enough.'

She strokes his fingers, her eyes grazing her surroundings, unseeing.

'My mother will be happy to see me fail,' she says. 'And my

sister even more. She will be happy for the rest of her life if I come home, because it means I have failed.'

'Let them be happy,' he says gently. 'Give them their happiness.'

She ponders it. In the evenings when her shift is over she often goes to Stefan's flat, a small flat on a busy street near the hospital. She sleeps in his bed, beside his body that is like a long white root, firm and forked. He sucks her large breasts in the darkness, while cars roar along the road outside. Is it normality they lack? For her these nights are abstract and solitary, tiny, like a seed from which something great and branching might grow. The seed gives no sign of what that thing will be. It is silent in itself. It has no connection to anything else, just the silent mystery of its future locked inside it.

But Stefan is right, in a way. It is hard to be sure that it is each other they really want.

'The people I live with look perfectly normal. But they are not normal,' she says. 'They are not a normal family. Maybe it isn't so easy to be normal.'

'Why?' he says. He is curious. 'How are they not normal?'

'I've told you about them,' she says. It is true that her conversations with Stefan are repetitious. Perhaps this is what happens when you live on an island. 'All I'm saying is that just to be a normal man and woman isn't so easy.'

Lately, she has been watching Thomas and Tonie. It is her relationship with Stefan that has caused her to become aware of them: now that she has love, she is more interested in the sorts of love other people have. Before, she could find no frame of reference for Thomas and Tonie. They seemed both polymorphous and somehow null. Sometimes they were like brother and sister, at other times like old people imitating young ones. There was something iconic about them,

191

something representative and wooden in the way they kissed or touched. But now she sees that they are real. She sees that they are serving the form of love as people used to serve their gods. She sees that love is as rigid and as invisible as a god, to whom over time people grow wooden and automatic in their obeisances. Yet it does not occur to them to deny it, this god of love. She wonders whether that constricted, invisible life is what Stefan means by normality.

'I will support you,' Stefan says, folding his arms across his chest magnificently. 'If you want to have a child, that is all right. I will support you.'

'I don't ever want to have a child,' Olga says.

She has had a child already. It was baptised before she gave it away: her mother insisted. Her sister's boyfriend was the father. They all came to the baptism and stood around the font in smart clothes.

'I guess it's easier that way,' Stefan admits.

'Maybe we will always be outsiders,' Olga says. 'Maybe that won't change.'

She thinks Stefan should know, that this safety can turn to imprisonment. When she hears Thomas playing the piano she thinks of a bird singing in its cage, lamenting in its safety. Yet she herself would like a cage. She would like a way of keeping the others out.

She looks at her watch. 'We should go home,' she says.

He rises. Already he has become her home. It doesn't matter which room they are in, which country. Out in the street he lays his arm around her shoulders. They walk towards his flat. She thinks of her little room in Montague Street, the nights she spent alone there, innocent in her single bed. She has begun to think of those nights fondly. She recreates them in her mind. She remembers them, with rainbow-coloured nostalgia.

# XXVIII

HOWARD [*upstairs*]: Claude! Claude, are you there?

CLAUDIA [*downstairs*]: What?

HOWARD: Claude!

CLAUDIA: What *is* it?

HOWARD: Claude, where are my deck shoes? They're not in the place they normally are.

CLAUDIA: I'm on the phone.

HOWARD: They're where?

CLAUDIA: I said I'm on the *phone*! I'm on the phone to Juliet. [*To Juliet*] Sorry.

JULIET: That's all right.

CLAUDIA: It's just Howard wanting his deck shoes. You know what it's like when he starts looking for something. He starts taking everything out of the cupboards. We're like the regional office, being visited by the chief executive. I feel I'm being audited.

JULIET: Why does he want his deck shoes? Are you going away somewhere?

CLAUDIA: Just Cornwall for the weekend.

JULIET: What, now?

CLAUDIA [*surprised*]: Yes.

JULIET: But it's ten o'clock at night!

CLAUDIA: Is it?

JULIET: Ten *past* ten.

CLAUDIA: It can't be! Ten o'clock? That's ridiculous – the children ought to be in bed!

JULIET: You're not taking them with you, are you?

CLAUDIA: Of course we are – we can't put them into kennels, like the dog! They're doing a weekend sailing course.

JULIET: But you won't get there until two in the morning! How are you going to get them up to do a sailing course?

[*Silence*]

CLAUDIA: Well, I suppose they'll sleep a bit in the car.

[*Silence*]

JULIET: I ought to let you go, in that case.

CLAUDIA: But I feel I haven't heard anything about *you*!

JULIET: Oh well. Another time.

CLAUDIA: *Soon*, I promise.

JULIET: Bye then.

CLAUDIA: Bye. Howard?

HOWARD: Did you find them?

CLAUDIA: Howard, it's ten o'clock! It's far too late to go. The children ought to be in bed!

HOWARD: But I only got back from work at nine, Claude.

CLAUDIA: I thought you were going to come back early so that we could go!

HOWARD: I got back at nine. I came back as soon as I could.

CLAUDIA: Well, you could have told me.

HOWARD: I thought you knew. You usually know what time it is.

CLAUDIA: The children should be asleep. They probably *are* asleep. Have you checked?

LOTTIE: We're not asleep.

CLAUDIA: This is ridiculous! Absolutely ridiculous! You should have heard Juliet on the phone when I said we were setting off tonight. She obviously thought we were *completely* mad!

HOWARD: Your sister thinks everyone is completely mad, darling. With the notable exception of herself.

CLAUDIA: Don't be horrible, Howard.

HOWARD: Of course Juliet thinks ten o'clock is late. She's in bed at ten o'clock. She's in bed in her wimple, like a nun.

CLAUDIA: She wasn't in bed. She was talking to me.

LEWIS [*from his room*]: She can be in bed and talk to you at the same time. She could even be asleep and talk to you. She might actually have been hypnotised.

CLAUDIA: She obviously thinks it's *me* who's driving everyone into the ground and forgetting I've got a family, including a child of six whose growth will be restricted because nobody could be organised enough to put her to bed –

LOTTIE: Sometimes I think I'd like to be a nun.

CLAUDIA: – and I can't say, look, it isn't me, can I? I can't tell her it's because some people are completely selfish and think only of themselves. It's a sort of joke [*laughs*], a joke, when I could have spent all day in my studio working, all day and all evening too, and still have been in *exactly* the same position as I am now!

HOWARD: Well, you could have, Claude. That's a true statement of the position, isn't it?

CLAUDIA: What is?

HOWARD: That you could have spent the day working, without any loss to the family.

[*Silence*]

CLAUDIA: Just like you do.

HOWARD: I suppose so. I don't know. I'm only repeating what you said yourself.

CLAUDIA: You, who come home and find that the beds have miraculously been made and the house tidied, and the food bought and the children picked up from school –

HOWARD: I'm just thinking of you, Claude. Your happiness.

CLAUDIA: – you, who have a slave, an actual slave, an unpaid person whose time you own!

HOWARD: Lucia's not a slave. We pay her, don't we? We can

195

pay her more. She can pick up Martha, she can do the shopping –

CLAUDIA: I'm not talking about Lucia. I'm talking about me.

HOWARD: You don't have to do anything. You can have all day.

CLAUDIA: You can't pay Lucia to be your wife.

HOWARD: All day, if you want it.

CLAUDIA: It isn't a day – it's a hand-me-down, it's a thing made out of other people's leftover time. You can't be creative between nine and five, Monday to Friday except bank holidays!

HOWARD: Can't you?

CLAUDIA: You don't understand creativity! You don't understand what an artist loses by being responsible for other people!

LOTTIE: Are we going?

HOWARD: No!

[*Silence*]

HOWARD: Look Claude, let's forget it. Let's forget the weekend. Let's stay here.

CLAUDIA: We can't. You've booked the sailing course.

HOWARD: I'll un-book it.

CLAUDIA: And the children have been looking forward to it. We can't.

HOWARD: Then I'll take them. You can stay here. You can have all tomorrow and all the next day on your own.

CLAUDIA [*pause*]: Now I feel like I'm being punished.

HOWARD: But you just said –

CLAUDIA: I feel like you're saying, all right then, if you want more time we'll all go off to Cornwall and have fun without you. You can have your time, but only at a cost. Only at the expense of fun.

HOWARD [*bemused*]: Then come.

196

CLAUDIA: All right.

HOWARD: Though perhaps we'd better go in the morning. It's nearly eleven.

CLAUDIA: But then you'll miss half the day! There's no point in going if you miss half the day.

HOWARD: It doesn't matter all that much.

CLAUDIA: We're better off going now. There won't be any traffic.

HOWARD: What about Martha's growth problem?

CLAUDIA: She can sleep in the car. I'll put some blankets and pillows in the back.

HOWARD: Oh, Claude, it's crazy. We won't get there till two. Wouldn't you rather just relax and go in the morning?

CLAUDIA: It's fine. I can't bear the thought of crawling across England on a Saturday morning with everyone and their grandmother. It'll be fun, *rushing* through the night, don't you think?

HOWARD: Oh, Claude. Oh, darling. I do love you.

[*They kiss*]

LOTTIE: Are we actually going or aren't we?

HOWARD/CLAUDIA: Yes!

# XXIX

Tonie goes to a party at Janine's flat in Battersea. It is a warm evening and everyone is out on the terrace. Tonie looks around, not recognising anyone in the indistinct light. Then she sees Janine, a dark shape with pale accents, her bare arms and glittering dress picking her out from the others. But the terrace is crowded and Janine is far away. Tonie gets a drink. She wonders why everyone here is so formless and anonymous. Their bodies look lumpy in the dusk, their faces featureless and indifferent as stones. The lack of excitement almost frightens her. Only Janine, in the glamour of her party-giving, is distinct. The others, half-hidden in the shadows, don't seem to belong to the same reality as Tonie. Either they are unreal or she herself is.

She sees Lawrence Metcalf, too late to pretend that she hasn't. He doesn't move, but his eyes take on a devouring expression that obliges her to approach him.

'How are you?' she says.

He is tall, so that she has to look up to talk to him. He wears a gold hoop in one ear, like a pirate.

'I'm very well, actually,' he says, his eyes already moving around above her head. 'I've just been in Stockholm for a few days, which was fantastic.'

'You got your funding,' Tonie says, resigning herself to the conversation.

'Oh, absolutely. There was never really any question. The board put it straight through.'

'That's great.' She tries to remember what his funding was for. Something to do with Vikings.

'Stockholm is just a different world. Beautiful place, beautiful people, everything so clean and well organised – do you know it?'

Tonie does not know Stockholm.

'They're just light years ahead of us in every conceivable way. We're like a Third World country by comparison, in terms of educational provision. And the quality of life is just staggering.' His eyes dart around. 'The women are pretty staggering too. Every other girl that passes you in the street is like a bloody goddess.'

'Really,' says Tonie.

'And they're pretty liberated, you know, I don't mean in terms of the – ah – cliché about the Swedes, which they all seem to find quite funny, but in terms of their attitudes. You don't get that female resentment you have here. Wouldn't you say that's true, Dieter?'

For the first time Tonie notices that there is another man there. He is much smaller than Lawrence. In the darkness Tonie can see only the bland oval of his face, and the watery shapes of his glasses.

'I'm not sure I know what you mean,' he says.

Lawrence throws back his head and laughs. The other man smiles slightly and looks at him inquisitively.

'You see?' Lawrence says to Tonie. 'He doesn't even know what I'm talking about. Resentment, Dieter. It's what gives English women all those little lines around their mouths.'

'I know what resentment is,' the man says. 'It is the ubiquitous consequence of sexual inequality. Swedish women are better protected by the law, that's all. But it has to be enforced.'

Lawrence looks slightly sulky. Tonie ponders his big, fleshy face, his darting eyes, his luxuriant hair that he wears slightly long, curling around his gold earring. He is the sort of man that makes Tonie feel invisible. His interest seems to go in every direction but hers. She consciously dislikes him – why, then, does it trouble her that he has no interest in her? Why does she feel negated by the restless eyes of men like Lawrence Metcalf?

The small man turns to her.

'I take it English men don't have wrinkles.'

'Only around their hearts,' Tonie says.

He laughs warmly and his eyes glow at her behind his glasses. 'That is much more off-putting.'

'Dieter,' Lawrence says, 'come on, I must introduce you to our hostess. The fabulous Janine.'

Tonie is left alone again. Then she spends a long time talking to a junior lecturer whose name she can't remember. The sky is black and smoky and starless overhead, and the commotion on the terrace remains formless and indistinct. She can't seem to make a connection anywhere. She can't seem to see people's faces, to understand their motives, to penetrate their reality. She sees her boss Christopher and for a while she watches him, watches the way he talks and listens and laughs, watches his Adam's apple moving in his narrow throat. He is not questioning the reality of Janine's party. He is absolutely concrete, just as Lawrence Metcalf is concrete. She realises that most of the people here are men. In her life before, she was almost always in the company of women and children; she remembers the feeling of perennial afternoon and of something growing, growing and growing unimpeded, her unopposed sense of self expanding into empty space. She did not resent men, in those days. She forgot, quite simply, that they existed. It was as though she had become a child again herself, her knowledge of the male obliterated and replaced by a perennial female afternoon. When Thomas came home in the evenings, he seemed to have risen straight out of the swamp of creation, a recent invention, or else an obsolete one. It was his masculinity she could never remember. He seemed to stand at the door with it in his hands, an implement whose uses she couldn't quite determine.

But then, slowly, over the years, she came to crave something else. She began to remember how variegated life used to be, how full of contrast: it would come over her suddenly, the realisation that existence was not single-stranded, univalent, but dual. Each thing had its necessary opposite – this is what she had forgotten, in the torpor of unending afternoon. She had forgotten that she would die. And suddenly she craved it, her opposite, masculinity. She craved it not of Thomas nor of any other man, but of herself. She wanted her own duality. She did not want to grow and grow, a branching tree of femininity: she wanted her own conflict of female and male, her own synthesis.

But now, this evening, she wonders whether she has failed to find what she wanted. And the world of men, perhaps, will not satisfy her after all. They, too, lack the knowledge of contrast; they too have lapsed away into a single-stranded existence, in which the feminine has been utterly forgotten. Did she come all this way merely to bump up against their stiffness and self-importance, their barren fantasies? It is passion she wants, the passion of synthesis. But she isn't going to find it here.

She notices that Christopher has gone. It is the behaviour of a professional: she, too, should go, and get home while it is still early. Except that when she thinks about it, she realises that she doesn't want to be at home.

She feels a hand on her arm and she turns. It is the small man, Lawrence's friend. Though now that he isn't standing next to Lawrence, she sees that he isn't small after all.

'We were interrupted,' he says. 'I was sorry.'

'The fabulous Janine,' Tonie says.

'The perfectly nice Janine,' he says.

Tonie laughs. He presses his fingers lightly on her sleeve.

'Would you like me to take you somewhere else?' he says.

He is German, not Swedish, though he has lived in Stockholm all his life. He is a doctor. He is here on a three-month secondment to a London hospital. At dinner he takes off his glasses and folds them into his pocket.

'Tell me about your home,' he says.

She tells him about Thomas and Alexa, explains the events of the past year, going over its conflicts and difficulties, touching even on the green shoot of feeling that has struggled up through it all, her own desire to experience life, to live fully in her own body. She cannot believe she has told him so much, so quickly; and just as she thinks it, she sees him close his eyes. She laughs, troubled.

'I'm boring you,' she says.

He shakes his head slowly. He smiles. He doesn't open his eyes.

'I just want to hear you speak,' he says. 'It's better with my eyes shut.'

And in fact it is what she needs, though it feels a little strange; this witnessing of her voice, which leaves her body innocent and unimplicated. He is older than her, perhaps fifty. She watches his face while she talks. It is a small, strong, highly modelled face, with narrow cheeks and a prominent brow and mouth, like a face from profoundest antiquity. It is not a face she has any previous knowledge of. Yet she seems to recognise it.

When she has finished he opens his eyes again. She is intensely moved by their warm brown colour.

'I want attention,' she says. 'I don't know why.'

'That is the tragedy of most people,' he says.

'What about you? Is it your tragedy?'

'I had a good mother.'

She smiles. 'Does it have to be the mother?'

'No. But mine was what was available.'

'What about your father?'

'My father was what you call standard issue. Cold and critical.'

She thinks about Thomas, who has given his attention to Alexa. In a way, then, he has liberated Tonie. But here she is, giving her attention to another man.

'There isn't enough attention to go around,' she says, laughing.

She sees that she will go home after all, that she will abandon her quest for attention, for passion. This man is too old, too unfamiliar. He is too formed in himself: she can't see what his intentions are.

'That sounds like the end of the conversation,' he says softly.

'This is a tragedy, remember,' she says.

He reaches across the table and grasps her fingers.

Outside in the street Tonie waits beside him while he looks for a taxi to take her to the station. In the darkness the traffic seems full of abstract patterns and strange revolving lights. She has surrendered to his authority: she is not required to make sense of what she sees or does. Yet she knows that this authority is ephemeral, in so far as it relates to him. Rather, it is a place in herself, a kind of hollow. A complete stranger can come and fit the shape of his authority into that hollow. He can cause her to succumb, to obey him. In a few minutes she will be alone in a taxi, on her way to the station. It is fortunate that there are such things as taxis and trains and places she needs to be at particular times. Otherwise he could make her do anything, anything at all.

But there are no taxis. Exasperated, he turns and rests his hands on her shoulders. She is beginning to understand that this man has power. When he touches her she is paralysed by his authority. It is fortunate that there are practicalities to bear her away.

'We're not going to find one here,' he says. 'But I live very close. We can get my car and I'll drive you.'

'That seems ridiculous,' Tonie says. 'I'll wait. Something will come along.'

'Please,' he says. 'It would make me unhappy to leave you here.'

They walk away from the main road, into the deserted quiet of residential streets. Tonie begins to feel uneasy, moving away from the general into the sordidness of the specific. She imagines a spartan rented flat, strewn with the sad detritus of solitary living. She imagines herself confronted not by power but by failure. In fact he lives in a house, not a flat. It would have shamed her, somehow, to go up to a flat. But the door is there on the street, correct.

'Come in,' he says. 'I need to find my car keys.'

Inside it is home-like, beautiful. There are books and paintings. He goes around switching on the lamps.

'Do you want anything?' he says.

She is looking at his things, his antiques and rugs, the books on his shelves. She is filled with strange yearning, as though she has no home of her own, no possession, no place where she belongs.

'This feels so – permanent,' she says.

He laughs. 'I'm too old to be anything except permanent,' he says.

He has told her that he is amicably separated from his wife, that his children are grown-up, that his work has become increasingly vocational, like that of a priest; and it seems to her now that this is the true accomplishment, this informed solitude, this independence. Is it not sad, then, to be alone? Is it, after all, truer, more honourable? She imagines herself and Thomas, old. She imagines their lives so entangled that they could never be extricated. It would be horrible to die tangled up with another person, not to know precisely what it was that was dying.

He is standing in front of her. The door to the street is open. She looks at his face but she can only see his eyes. They are so warm, so possessive. They leave no part of her out.

'How is it possible?' she says. 'I feel like I know you.'

It is because he is already formed: there is no entanglement, no blurring of self. She supposes he can be petty, boring, demanding. But it would have nothing to do with her.

'Tell me what you want,' he says, touching her face.

She laughs. 'I want to know the nature of your relationship with Lawrence Metcalf.'

His hands are in her hair. He is kissing her, kissing her throat and mouth, and speaking while he kisses.

'Lawrence Metcalf is a friend of my cousin,' he murmurs, against her lips. 'I thought he was a bore but I was wrong.'

'Were you?' she laughs, while he puts his fingers under her jacket and slides it from her shoulders.

'He is a – what's the expression? A good bloke. I will

always care for him. Always,' he says, kneeling, unbuttoning her shirt, kissing her navel. Then he stands and goes to shut the door. He picks up her jacket. She watches him fold it carefully and lay it over a chair. He holds out his hand to her. 'Come upstairs,' he says.

He drives her all the way home. It is past midnight and the roads are empty. His car is clean and fast, expensive. She wonders what she will do. She does not feel anxious. It is his authority, the authority of his age and his decisiveness, of his knowledge and his fast car that allays her anxiety. It is as though he has authority not only over herself but over Thomas too. Just as he has dispensed with the fiddliness of her arrangements, scattered the train timetable to the winds in his fast, efficient car, so the tangle of her bonds and loyalties seems to fall away and dissolve in the darkness of the swiftly running roadside. She feels powerful and calm, sitting beside him. She feels free. But as the familiar outskirts of home appear, she is suddenly riven by thrusts of fear. She feels that he is going to abandon her. He is going to leave her here, stripped of the integrity of her own life, her arrangements all destroyed. Whatever he has dispensed with, he gives no sign that he intends to replace it with something else. He assumes she knew what she was doing, that she did what she meant to do. It is up to her what she does. She realises that she is not powerful after all. The power is his: it has enclosed her for a few hours, as his car now encloses her; it has moved her from one place to another.

He puts out his hand and touches her. The other hand is on the steering wheel. She feels again how formed he is, how complete. But now it is something she is on the outside of. She is shut out, yearning to be let back in.

'This is difficult,' he says.

She wonders what he means. Is he referring to a generic difficulty, the difficulty of returning a married woman to her home after a sexual encounter?

'It's okay,' she says, staring through the dark windscreen at the familiar streets. They have stopped at some traffic lights. He is watching her. He is watching her staring at the things she has broken, as an adult watches a child staring at a broken toy. He is sympathetic, but he is not a member of her world.

'It's not okay,' he says. 'Do you want to go back to my house?'

She shakes her head. But he has made her pain go away. She feels better. She feels powerful again. Only this time, she is suspicious of the feeling.

'You turn left here,' she says.

Yes, it is bewildering, unfathomable, to find that love and loss and despair and hope are cellular, partitive; that in the fragment of each the structure of the whole is present, like the specimens scientists examine under microscopes; the whole structure and character of her life present in these moments of terror and elation. How can she love a man she only met a few hours ago? How can she feel abandoned by someone who this morning she didn't know was alive? Yet she does. Her love and her terror lie beyond her scope, at cell-level. They existed before she herself knew what existence was.

This is what the call of her body has been, the very cells asking for assuagement.

'It's just here,' she says, at the top of Montague Street.

'I feel that something is wrong,' Dieter says. He pulls into the darkness at the side of her road.

And she will never afterwards know what exactly he meant, though it will seem to her as though he was in that moment mysteriously gifted with a special insight, with new forms of knowledge; she will never know exactly what he intended to say. She will only marvel at how quickly and glidingly it happened, the fusion of impulses, so that she snatched her phone from her bag and remembered that she had switched it off, hours ago. She thinks of it often afterwards. She thinks of the way she felt during that drive with Dieter, of her realisation that her fate was inscribed in the smallest particles of her being, inextricable; that she would always love and despair and struggle and succeed without knowing quite why she did. She thinks of the passion she experienced with Dieter, a passion of the cells, of the smallest particles. This, she believes, is why no logical explanation can be found for what he said. And it died the instant it was born, this chance of proceeding without logic, without reason, without explanation. For a beautiful, catastrophic moment she glimpsed the possibility of a relationship of pure instinct.

The phone pulses and bleeps, pulses and bleeps, spewing out messages. Thomas has called more than twenty times in four hours. He is at the hospital. Dieter turns the car around and drives her straight there.

# XXX

Thomas is reading a story by Tolstoy called 'The Kreutzer Sonata.' It is about a man who is driven by his wife's piano playing to murder her. It is not clear whether this is entirely the fault of the music. As well as being what it is, the music has a symbolic function in the story. What it symbolises is sexual desire. When the lady plays Beethoven's *Kreutzer Sonata* with a dashing gentleman violinist, it is as though they are conducting an affair before the husband's eyes. He is driven mad with jealousy and murders her most horribly, having chased the violinist away. There should be no music, the man – his name is Pozdnyshev – says. It is too arousing; it facilitates immorality, removing the power of individual thought, as sexual feelings remove the proper inhibitions.

It was the title of the story that attracted Thomas, so he is surprised by its curious message. But there is one part of it that particularly startles him, in which Pozdnyshev argues quite persuasively that love does not exist. Love is only an aspect of sexual desire: like music, it is a culturally sanctioned disguise for the state of arousal. But sexual desire – love – destroys the moral being. When a man loses his virginity, Pozdnyshev says, he should consider himself married for life to that woman – a prostitute, in Pozdnyshev's own case. Thomas thinks about sixteen-year-old Emily Griffiths, who seemed so cool and composed in the days when he first attracted her attention, and fell dismayingly to pieces a year later, when he ended their relationship. He was going to university, and cheerfully thought it was for the best. But Emily would not accept it. She bellowed and shrieked, like the piano-playing wife when Pozdnyshev stuck his knife in her ribs. Truly, it was as if he were murdering her. And he went off to university a murderer, for Emily never spoke to him again. Perhaps she did consider them to be married for life, so that the life she lived afterwards was a kind of death. When he came home for the holidays, his mother told him that Emily had had a nervous breakdown. She seemed to think it was a good thing Thomas had got rid of her.

'You don't want to be saddled at your age with a girl who's a nervous wreck,' she said.

Yes, it was Emily's grief, her extraordinary distress, that was Thomas's formative experience, far more than the handful of times they had shared a bed. They talked and laughed while they made love: who was to know that these were the fatal moments? Ever since, Thomas has recognised that he could be undone by an unhappy woman. And yet thinking about it now, he wonders whether the unhappiness is precisely what he has looked for; whether it is there that his interest picks up and his feelings are engaged. Emily unhappy seemed far more real to him than Emily happy. Watching her, he felt in himself the male inexorability he had always witnessed in his father, lashing his mother into storms of emotion. For years he had allied himself with his mother, defended her, suffered on her behalf. But looking at Emily he realised that he, too, was a man.

It is half past eight in the morning. Breakfast is all laid out on the table. He looks up from his book: Alexa is nowhere to be seen.

He climbs the stairs, calling her. There is no reply. When he pushes open the door he sees that the curtains are still closed. She is lying in her bed.

'What's the matter?' he says. 'Are you ill?'

She looks at him. She nods her head.

'All right, then,' he says. 'Stay where you are. You can have the day off school today. And no, I won't forget to ring them and tell them.'

He walks around the room, picking things up off the floor. When he looks at her again he sees that she has gone to sleep.

At half past ten, Tonie calls.

'Did you remember that I'm going to Janine's tonight? I forgot to remind you this morning.'

'Oh,' he says. He is disappointed. 'No, I didn't remember.'

'Do you mind?'

'No.'

'You sound like you mind,' she says.

He is silent. 'No, I was just thinking maybe I'd see if I could get a babysitter and come too.'

'Really?' she says. She appears to find this proposal somewhat outlandish.

'Actually,' he says, 'on second thoughts I'd better not. Alexa's ill.'

He realises that he has completely forgotten about Alexa. She has been so silent. He has forgotten that she is not at school.

'What's wrong with her?' Tonie says, with the hard sound in her voice that she uses to lever him out of the way and get at certain information.

'I don't know. She's asleep. She's been asleep all morning.'

'Oh. Oh well. She's probably just tired.'

'Probably.'

'But yes, I suppose we'd better not risk a babysitter.'

He can tell she is relieved.

When he goes upstairs, Alexa is still asleep. He sits on the landing outside her room with his book. He feels lonely.

He wants her to wake up. He thinks that this is so that he can comfort her, but in fact it is the other way around. He wants her to console him for his conversation with Tonie. He wouldn't actually tell her about the conversation; he wouldn't mention Tonie at all. He would merely soothe himself with her acceptance of him. She is so innocent, so small; she trusts him so completely, more than he trusts himself. It is this that makes him feel lonely. When she is present, he realises how little he can ask of her. In the end, there can be no equality between them. He has to conceal himself so that her feelings for him can be revealed. He can never ask her for them directly. Yet he knows, at least, that they are there.

At midday he goes in. She is still asleep. He smiles, as though at her eccentricity. He remembers coming home once from work and Tonie telling him that Alexa had slept all day. She was ill, and had slept off her illness, a miracle of self-correction. In fact it is quite pleasant, he thinks, to have her here and not-here, correcting herself, making herself well. He wonders whether Tonie enjoyed such days, whether these were part of her secret; the life he doesn't seem to have heard enough about, now that he is living it himself. He goes downstairs and eats a sandwich. At two o'clock he goes back up. This time he is surprised to find her still asleep. He sits beside her on the bed. He lays his hand across her forehead. Instantly she screams, a horrible, maniacal scream. For a second he is more irritated than shocked. He thinks she must be pretending, screaming like that just to frighten him. He thinks he has brought it on himself. He has spent his day revering her for her sweetness and sympathy, and she has been lying up here plotting to upset him.

'What is it?' he says. 'Tell me what the matter is.'

Her eyes are still closed. She does not reply. He cannot get it out of his head that she is deceiving him. He is aware of a great deal of heat in the room, and slowly he realises that its source is Alexa. He touches her arms, her chest, her neck. She is burning. He goes and gets a thermometer.

'Try to sit up,' he says. 'I need to take your temperature.'

He lifts her up by her arms and her head lolls forward. He sees that there is vomit on her pillow. He removes the pillow and lays her down again. He gets a wet cloth and wipes the traces of vomit from around her mouth. He sits beside her on the bed. He wonders what to do. After a while he rises and goes downstairs, but when he gets there he can't remember what his intention was. He goes back up. She is lying in just the same place. A strand of her long hair is webbed across her face. He tries to lift her up again by her arms but she is so limp that he can't hold her. He puts her down, and then scoops her up from underneath. Her head rolls on his arm and she opens her eyes briefly. The whites are completely yellow. He is frightened. All at once, she has become a stranger.

Downstairs he staggers around, holding her, looking for his keys. Her head bangs against his shoulder and she screams again. He edges her through the front door. Outside the day is grey and warm. He has got her out. It seemed important, to get her out, but now that he has done it he isn't sure it was right. Surely she should be indoors, in bed? She moans and puts her hands over her eyes, like a prophetess. He struggles with her to the car and lays her clumsily across the back seat. He spends a long time trying to secure her with the seat belt. The car is untidy and dirty-smelling. It doesn't seem right that she should be there. Finally he gets in and starts the engine. He was planning on driving her to the doctor's surgery, but when he gets there he can't find anywhere to park, so he goes on, the car strangely gliding, the people on the pavements looking alienating and unreal. Alexa moans and cries on the back seat. He talks to her as he drives, staring straight ahead.

'It's all right, my love,' he says. 'It's all right, my pet.'

He drives to the hospital. When he opens the back door of the car, he sees that Alexa has vomited again. She is lying sprawled across the seat. He wants to cry out, to surrender her. He imagines how angry Tonie would be, if she saw what he had done. He is certain she would have done something else, would have called on some knowledge he doesn't possess. He picks Alexa up and carries her into Casualty. Her head is jolting up and down on his arm. There is vomit on her face, in her hair. He goes to the woman, sitting behind her glass screen.

'I think she's got a bit of a temperature,' he says.

He expects her to castigate him and send him home, but instead she picks up the telephone beside her and dials a number, her eyes holding his. Her eyes are brown. She inclines her head towards him, never looking away. She speaks, and then she holds her hand over the receiver.

'The doctor's coming,' she says.

Some hours pass, five o'clock, six o'clock, seven. Alexa has meningitis. They have put her in a room on her own. Thomas sits beside her, while the doctors come and go, while the nurses put a drip in her arm and secure it with a white bandage. At six o'clock he goes out into the car park and calls Tonie.

He has been told that Alexa might die. He should have brought her in earlier. They don't say it, but he knows. They give him information, printed brochures, like brochures for an evening class, or a holiday. He reads them, reads about his situation, its special features and perils. It is stupid to be given these brochures after the event. The brochures all agree that early detection, though difficult, is paramount. They disclose his failure, his failure in this difficult test. Yet he cannot see precisely where the difficulty lay. There was never any possibility of his bringing Alexa here, this morning, when she was asleep. To have passed this test he would have to have been a different person.

'Is there anyone you can call?' the nurse asks him.

She is suspicious of him, he can tell. She is wondering where Alexa's mother is.

'I can't get through at the moment,' he says.

Apparently there is nothing anyone can do. There is only waiting. Thomas, in the car park, rings Tonie again. There is a boulder of guilt in his chest. His fingers shake as he presses the numbers. He expects the terror of her voice at any moment. But as the hours pass he grows accustomed to her silence, her absence. His guilt transfers itself, becomes anger, is transformed yet again into peace, the pure peace of responsibility. He remembers waiting in this hospital for Alexa to be born. His concern was all for Tonie then, for her pain. Now, in a sense, the pain is his. He is being broken, broken at last. He does not believe that Alexa will die. But for her to live he has to be broken, as Tonie was once broken. He has to offer it up, finally: the way he was, the way he will never again be.

Towards midnight the door to the little white room opens. It is Olga.

'Hello, Olga,' Thomas says. He is only moderately surprised. He has forgotten that he is not in the kitchen at home.

'I am here,' Olga says.

'Yes,' Thomas says. 'Thank you for coming.'

She sits down beside him, her hands clasped in her lap.

'This is a terrible thing,' she says.

Thomas nods. The doctor has told him there is a possibility that Alexa's hearing will be damaged. And a silence has descended on him, thick and blank, like snow. He sits shaking in his chair, enveloped in suffocating silence. There is no thread of sound to pull him out. He finds himself thinking about 'The Kreutzer Sonata.' He visualises the words on the page, like black little armies marching across the whiteness. The book is still in his pocket.

'I forgot,' Thomas says, 'that you work here.'

'Yes,' Olga says. 'Tonight, for no reason, they put me on this ward. It was lucky.'

The silence comes again, so heavy and blank.

'I was reading a book earlier today,' Thomas says, 'about a man who kills his wife for playing the piano.'

His voice is scratchy and faint. He can barely force it out of his throat. Alexa's eyes are open. She is looking at him out of her ghastly face, as though she is listening. But he can see she doesn't recognise him.

'The man blames it all on the music,' he continues. 'He says that under the influence of music, people feel things that are not their true feelings. They think they understand something when in fact they don't understand it at all. It's all a sort of illusion, like love.'

Olga stares at him.

'That is a bad book,' she says finally.

'Yes,' he says. If he hadn't been reading it, he might have taken more notice of Alexa. He might have been aware that he was being tested. Suddenly he can't bear to have the book in his pocket any longer. He takes it out and throws it into the bin. Then he sits down again.

'You should read happy books,' says Olga. 'Why make life more difficult?'

'I don't know,' he says.

What is art? It is, perhaps, a distillation of the difficulty, like the hospital brochure – a kind of knowledge after the fact, a description of what cannot be known until it is lived, by which time it is too late to know it. When he plays the piano he is not living. He is describing what it lies beyond his own capacity to redeem.

'I don't know why,' he says. 'I've never really thought about it. Do you read happy books?'

It is midnight. There is total blackness at the windows. He sees his own reflection in the glass. It is fractured, splintered, a composition of a million separate lines.

'I read magazines,' Olga says.

# XXXI

The Bradshaws are going away. Ma and Dads are taking the dog.

It is always an ordeal, going on their summer holiday: it is the same every year. All the Bradshaws' problems seem to rise up and confront them, almost to surround them, like a menacing crowd they have to pass through before they can be on their way. There is a strange feeling of the dust sheets being taken off the furniture, when of course it should be the other way around. As if life itself – or their living of it – were a set of blinkers, a blind: that is how it always feels, in the days before they leave for France or Spain, with the three children stuffed into the back seat and the bags crammed so tightly in the boot that the laden car seems about to explode for either fury or joy.

Yes, it is an ordeal: not just the cleaning and packing, the organising and arranging, but also the unpicking of a kind of estrangement that seems to have knitted itself among them over the course of the year. There is a stiffness at the start of their preparations, a constriction to their relationships. Usually, by the time they leave, it has gone: by the time Howard and Claudia have argued about the state of the house and the children, about the fact that there is less money and more things that need to be done with it than they'd thought, about the fact that Howard has worked too much and Claudia too little – let alone started on the grievances, the real injustices that have remained outstanding not just for a week or month but for years, some dating back to the time before the children were born, even to the very first evening Howard and Claudia spent together almost twenty years earlier. Though they don't always get to that. Those are in a sense the leap years of their marriage, the times when, mysteriously gifted with an extra reach into the past, they can, as they pack, quarrel over the fact that Howard spent their first important hours in The Freemason's Arms in Camberwell talking about how much he loved Angelina Croft, who had recently abandoned him. Some years he flatly denies it. Others he claims that this was a tactic by which he hoped to demonstrate his sincerity, for Claudia's benefit. One awful year he was suddenly unrepentant. So what? Who cared what he'd said? Why was Claudia always trying to get her claws into everything?

Sometimes it is more than a clearing of the air, this business of going away. It is a death and rebirth for them all. The problem is that the holiday, when it comes, sometimes feels like it is happening to someone else.

The morning sun shines down on Laurier Drive, presses itself, as if through a latticework or grille, through its countless details of human habitation: through the syncopated absences in fancy brickwork and Spanish-style wrought-iron balustrades, through spear-topped ranks of electronic security gates and pergolas of tannalised pine. Here and there the planted borders cast lacy shadows on the pavements, and all along the roadside the breeze moves the heavy summer boughs of the chestnut trees, so that they seem almost to be stiffly dancing in swirling skirts of light and shade.

'Howard's making a meal of that roof rack,' Dads observes, standing at the kitchen window with folded arms. 'He'll mark the paintwork if he isn't careful.'

Ma sits in a chair at the table, yawning. Howard's mother goes in for dramatic displays of exhaustion whenever she visits. There she sits, with her grey frizzy hair and her drooping face, releasing larger and larger yawns until it seems that she might deflate entirely. Often she goes to sleep in her chair, a faint snore whistling in her filigree elderly nose. It is strange: in her own house she is alert and beady-eyed, moving briskly around her chilly domain. It is as though she cannot tolerate the warmer climate of Howard and Claudia's world, the humidity of its passions and its tolerance, its lush atmosphere of emotion. Out of her element, she grows soporific; she is plunged into the torpor of deracination.

Skittle is scratching at the door with his hard little claws. Now and then he lets out a high, piercing yelp.

'He's forgotten that he's still got to reverse it out of the garage,' Dads remarks. 'It would have been more sensible to get the car out first, *then* attach the roof rack.'

'I suppose I really ought to help.' Ma comes to her senses and looks around blankly. 'Isn't there something I can do to help?'

Claudia, cleaning inside the fridge, withdraws for a second and shouts:

'Skittle! Quiet!'

Skittle hesitates. A look of torment passes across his bulging yellow eyes. The catflap is broken: the door is no longer permeable. His troubled narrow face and asymmetric ears tremble. His hindquarters writhe. His small sausage-shaped body is beset by the strange contortions whose cause the Bradshaws have been unable to fathom.

'Yes, *what*'s that awful noise?' says Ma. 'I hope we aren't going to have our hands full with *you* this week.'

The dog flings himself once more against the door and

rebounds sprawling on the tiled floor, where he scrabbles frantically to his feet, emitting nervous little squirts of golden urine. This is the first time they have left Skittle. Ma and Dads are taking him home with them to Little Wickham. Sometimes Claudia perceives that the spirit of delinquency has entered their house in the body of this animal. It has come as it were by the back door, on four legs.

'Do you know,' yawns Ma, 'I don't think I even know where it is you're going.'

'Oh, it's just France,' Claudia says. She can hear Howard calling her from outside. 'The usual thing. Sorry, do you think you could let the dog out?'

Yes, it has got in, disaffection, discontent – she doesn't really know what to call it. She knows only that she has always made great efforts to ward it off: with the birth of each child, the passing of each year, the passing, even, of every night she spends with Howard – she has stayed vigilant through it all, through the turning of one day to another, has adhered to her belief, which is in the importance of wanting what you have. It is this belief that makes her life real to her: more than that, it is, in a mysterious sense, what gives it its worth.

'Oh!' Ma flings back her head rhapsodically, as though Claudia has said they are going to the South Pacific. 'France! I had no idea! Did *you* know they were going to France?' she enquires of her husband.

'I don't recall their making a particular secret of it,' Dads replies.

'I would *so* love to go to France!' she says disconsolately, so that Claudia feels they are directly preventing her from doing so, by the fact of going there themselves.

'Why don't you go, then?' she says from inside the fridge. She has been up since six o'clock and has not yet started on the upstairs rooms. 'It's not very far. It's not as though it's Timbuktu.'

Howard's faint, infuriating shouts of 'Claude!' are like a pair of spurs applied to her sides as she works. It was Howard who brought Skittle home in the first place. Skittle was his idea. That is the trouble: she has not found a way to want him herself. If she had only concentrated, taken the time – if she had only remembered the point, the central tenet of her belief, which was the avoidance of *not* wanting what you had!

'Your father-in-law would sooner go to Timbuktu than cross the Channel,' Ma says. Her expression is morose.

Dads, smiling menacingly, continues his scrutiny of Howard from the window.

'Why should I go and spend my money there?' he says presently. '*They* don't come *here*.'

'I don't think you can say they don't *come* here! That's an utter generalisation!'

'It doesn't matter what you call it.' Dads continues to smile. 'It's a fact, that's all.'

Yes, it is a terrible thing, not to want what you have. Claudia would suffer – has, she felt, suffered – every abasement to avoid it. One after another she takes things out of the fridge. Inside, a mythic struggle has apparently taken place. The collapsed, decomposing forms of old vegetables and waxy remains of butter and bacon and hard rinds of cheese like pieces of dead skin, seem to Claudia to be a kind of representation, a portrait, of the passage of time. With what brutality these things have been made to surrender their shape and essence – how coldly and mechanically they have been broken down, curdled, liquidised!

'You say it's a fact –' Ma blinks. 'But where did you actually *get* it from? You're always saying things are facts, but I sometimes think you're a little guilty of confusing a fact with an opinion.'

'That's an illogical statement,' Dads replies. Behind him Skittle is still scratching at the door, then crouching and shrinking in an attitude of persecution. 'A fact and an opinion are not mutually contradictory. At least, not in the minds of most of us. *You* might find them so because you aren't observant. You don't notice things.'

Claudia, rising to her feet, sees her father-in-law, gilded in the light of the bay window. His bank of white hair is as smooth as a snowdrift, and he wears a spotted cravat tucked into the neck of his shirt. Sometimes Claudia is unable to believe that Howard is the offspring of this man. He is so opaque to her, and Howard so transparent. Yet when they are together, it is Howard who doesn't entirely make sense. He seems less real, more self-constructed. She finds herself beginning to doubt him, as though his father's presence proves that Howard is in some way artificial.

'I suppose I'd better go and see what Howard wants,' she says.

She opens the door and Skittle bolts out of the kitchen. He shoots into the hall and goes careering off down the corridor, banging crazily against the skirting boards and stumbling every now and then over his own frantic little legs. Claudia goes out after him.

'Lottie!' she shouts at the bottom of the stairs. 'Lottie! Lewis! Martha!'

Only Martha replies, a faint squeak in the distances of the house. Claudia goes out of the front door and round to the side, where Howard is standing in the open mouth of the garage doing something to the roof rack with a screwdriver clenched between his teeth. His balding head is dark red and streaked with perspiration. Skittle runs in neurotic circles around his feet.

'Your father thinks you won't be able to get the car out of the garage,' Claudia says.

'Let him watch,' says Howard gamely, around the screwdriver.

'I suppose there's no real reason to put it on in here, though, is there?' Claudia persists. 'You might just as well do it outside, like you usually do.'

Howard does not reply. His head grows redder. He tightens the straps of the roof rack so vigorously that the thick muscled flesh of his arms shakes and the car rocks from side to side.

'Is there?' Claudia says.

Finally Howard takes the screwdriver out of his mouth.

'It's just how I decided to do it, Claude,' he says reproachfully.

Claudia folds her arms and faces away from him, towards the dappled spectacle of Laurier Drive. She notices that number twenty-two have put a pair of white plaster unicorns on their pillared porch.

'I don't see why I should be the one having to manage your parents, on top of everything else,' she observes.

'You're very good,' says Howard.

'It's horrible, the way they're at each other's throats. And the children just sit in their rooms like ministers of the doge.'

'I'll speak to them,' says Howard. 'Send them to me.'

'I'm a sort of *slave*,' says Claudia disgustedly. Every year it is the same. 'There I am, cleaning on my hands and knees, with your mother thinking I'm the idle rich because I'm going camping for two weeks in the Auvergne, when the only thing I'm looking forward to is getting away from the dog!'

Really, it makes her want to cry. 'And to think I could be in my – in my . . .'

Howard has already abandoned the roof rack. Never has Claudia's mention of her studio failed to summon his immediate attention. Yet all at once she understands that this attention is a pallid substitute for the satisfaction she might have got from actually painting something there. It was once a derelict shed, full of spiders and evilly rusted old tools. When they arrived in Laurier Drive, fourteen years ago, with Lottie a babe in arms and Claudia already pregnant again, she set eyes on the tumbledown place at the bottom of the garden and saw in it the reflection of a part of herself. It seemed to stand poised between existence and annihilation, just as she in that moment felt herself to hover, a dissolving image, at the very brink of identity. In its abandonment it had become theoretical, like the mysterious region of herself that life could seem to find no use for, the series of urges to which she gave the name of creativity. And the work was done, the heat and light installed, the walls re-plastered, the roof repaired. The fading image was brought back into focus, hauled back from the edge of dissolution. But Claudia's baby miscarried. After all, the structure is powerless to hold it, the mystery of creation. Claudia willed the baby not to come out, but though her body housed it, it seemed she could not dictate its comings and goings. It had an ultimate freedom.

And in much the same way her studio has stood at the bottom of the garden, year after year, completed. It no longer bears any relationship to her theoretical urges. Though she hasn't told anyone of it, they too have slipped away.

'Poor Claude,' he says, gripping the tops of her arms and looking beseechingly at her with his small round eyes. 'Poor thing. *Poor* Claude.' He waits for a few moments, searching her face, then he says: 'Do you think you could just help me with something? There's a thing with the strap that it takes two to do. I tried to do it earlier, but I couldn't seem to find you. It'll only take a minute, I promise.'

On her way back through the house she passes the kitchen door with Skittle at her heels, and hears her parents-in-law's excited voices.

'That's simply *not* true!' Ma shrieks.

'So you say.'

'But it's not!'

'So you say. *So* you say.'

Claudia puts her hands over her ears. His voice is so stiff and repetitive. It sweeps hers out of the way, like a stiff broom sweeping random brittle fallen leaves out of its path. Upstairs, the children are sitting in Lottie's room beside their suitcases in pensive attitudes. Lewis has headphones on. Only Martha looks up when Claudia comes in. She has noticed before how they stay upstairs when Ma and Dads come. It is the coldness that drives them up here, the coldness of these people with their snowy hair and eyes like chips of ice. The sight of them makes her pity her husband. She feels she is looking down a strange tunnel of time towards Howard and his brothers, is seeing the whole arc and motion of their lives, their struggle to migrate to where it is warm.

'Are you all right?' Martha asks.

Martha is only six, and knows better than the others what her mother wants. Lewis, the headphones clamped around his ears, is making big eyes at Claudia and dramatically semaphoring. Finally he takes the headphones off.

'Look!' he shouts, pointing at the floor behind her. 'Skittle's being sick!'

They all look at Skittle, who with trembling haunches is disgorging a stiff pile of vomit on to the carpet.

'That's it!' cries Claudia tearfully. 'That's it! I've had enough! Your father can clear it up! He was the one who wanted a dog in the first place! I never did – never! And who's done everything? Where was he, when the work had to be done? Who's fed him and taken him for walks, taken him out in wind and rain because there was nobody else here, not a soul, and he wouldn't stop scratching at the bloody door –'

'*Mum,*' Lottie shudders. 'Look! He's *eating* it.'

It is true. Quivering all over as though in an ecstasy of perversion, Skittle bends above the steaming pile, his jaws moving wolfishly. They all watch, fascinated, as every trace of the vomit disappears back down the dog's throat.

Lottie screams. Lewis rolls around on the bed in disgust. Martha says:

'Well, at least now you don't have to clean it up.'

With trembling legs, Claudia stands in the doorway.

'Bring your cases down, all of you,' she says in a shrivelled whisper. 'We're leaving.'

The car is still in the garage when they get outside with their bags. Howard has half-filled the boot. Luggage bulges between the straps of the roof rack.

'You'll never get it out,' Claudia says, with bleak finality. 'We're going to miss the boat.'

Howard comes out into the sunlight and stands beside her with narrowed eyes, measuring up the car and the doorway it has to reverse through.

'I think it'll go,' he says.

'Never,' says Claudia.

'If everyone gets in it will.'

Claudia sees her parents-in-law come out of the house.

Dads is walking ahead along the path, and Ma is coming like a fury behind him. While he seems to plant each step with agonising precision and care, she appears to fly, her skirts billowing out after her, her arm curiously upraised, as though she were giving the signal to advance. It takes Claudia a moment to realise what it is she is witnessing. She sees Ma gaining ground on the path, sees Dads walking on, unaware even as her raised arm comes down and lands a blow on the top of his head. He sinks a little at the knees, his expression momentarily shattered by surprise. Then he walks on.

'Everyone in!' Claudia shouts, startled, so that the children run to Howard, who is once more in the garage. They open the back doors of the car and pile in.

'All fatties welcome!' Howard calls. 'All elephants cordially invited!'

None of them have seen, except Claudia; and she finds she cannot go after them and get in the car, even though Howard needs her weight to reverse it under the frame. She has to stay where she is, a child immobilised by the breakdown of authority; by the recognition of authority itself as childlike. It is only in this recognition that her own authority becomes apparent to her, so that she can't cast Howard's parents off. They are too infantile, too helpless: is this what Howard feels? Is this what explains the feeling she has, that he never really gives himself to her and the children? That though he wants more and more he is never really there, there at the root; but rather, like next-door's cherry tree, whose boughs reach over into the Bradshaws' garden while its trunk stands on the other side of the fence, maintains a perpetual presence among them from which the fundamental comfort of belonging is forever denied? When the cherries fall on the Bradshaws' lawn, the Bradshaws are never sure who they actually belong to – perhaps after all it is nice for Howard, to be so ambiguous, so free; to feel that he is not entirely owned by anyone. He starts the engine and at once a black plume of smoke streams from the exhaust.

'Claude!' he calls. 'Are you there, Claude?'

'Yes!' she shouts back.

Howard's parents stand a short distance away. The sound of the engine has caught their attention. Their faces are perfectly composed. She realises that they are used to it, used to whatever it was she witnessed on the path. It was not, as she thought, an emergency. What she saw was much worse: it was intimacy.

'Claude! I need you to guide me out!'

Lewis rolls down the window and puts his head out. 'Dad's let the air out of the tyres!' he cries, delirious with excitement.

Slowly the car begins to reverse out of the garage. Claudia watches as it clears the doorjamb by the slenderest of margins. She feels it, its impossible passage, as she seems to have felt so many things in her life with Howard. It is all, very nearly, impossible. She shakes helplessly with strange, silent laughter.

'Careful!' she calls in a strangled voice, when the lamed wheels meet the slight rise of the concrete floor where it gives out on to the driveway.

The car judders a little and rolls back. Howard puts his foot harder on the accelerator. On the periphery of her vision Claudia sees the white darting shape of Skittle. He tears down the path towards the car, his body making its strange contortions as he runs. In an instant he is there behind the wheels. While she watches, he plunges his nose into the exhaust pipe and shudders ecstatically, inhaling the black fumes.

'Howard!' Claudia shrieks.

She sees the dog fall unconscious on to his side. A moment later, the revving engine forces the wheels over the concrete rise and the car comes in one movement out of the garage, thudding over Skittle and rolling him stiffly into the darkness beneath its belly. There is a pause, and then another thud as the front wheel goes over the body.

'Oh, mind the dog!' calls Ma. 'Do mind the dog, Howard!'

The car shakes to a halt. Howard leaps out. He runs around to the front and kneels over Skittle's body where it lies in the dirt, a thread of blood at the corner of the mouth.

'Poor boy,' Howard says, shaking his head. 'Poor old fellow.'

One by one the children emerge from the back of the car. Lottie is crying. Lewis looks white and stricken.

'There were two bumps,' Martha says significantly to her mother. 'First there was one bump. Then, a little while later, there was another bump.'

'Is he dead?' Lewis says.

'I'm afraid so,' says Howard tenderly.

'*Two* bumps,' Martha repeats, to herself. 'First one bump, then the other.'

Howard grips Claudia's hand. She sees that his eyes are red with tears. Ma and Dads approach the family where they stand in a circle.

'Oh dear,' Dads says, looking down at the small body. 'That was a shame.'

'It'll make life easier for you, at least, over the next couple of weeks,' Howard says grimly.

'I suppose it will,' Dads says.

'I was looking *forward* to him coming!' Ma says. 'You make it sound as if it were nothing but a nuisance! But I was looking forward to it!'

Lottie starts to cry again.

'Well,' Dads says presently. 'If there's nothing else we can do, we may as well be on our way.'

Howard stands and faces his parents. The dog lies on the ground between them. His body imparts a finality to it, to Howard as he faces them in their coldness. It is as though, with this offering of death, he is freeing himself of his obligation to them, freeing himself from the curse of their sterility.

'Goodbye,' he says, embracing first his father, then his mother. 'See you soon, I expect. Goodbye.'

Howard and Claudia bury Skittle in the back garden. They agree the dog was too much for them. They agree that they were, in this case, overstretching the mark. For all the work of a dog, Claudia observes, they might as well have had another baby.

Then they get the children in the car and drive like the wind, hoping to make the boat.

# XXXII

On the train, Thomas thinks about money. He has always had enough of it, enough money. Then, for a year, he earned nothing at all. Now the money is flowing again. What is money?

'Excuse me, is this seat free?'

He looks up. A girl is standing there. She wants to sit down, but his briefcase is in the way.

'I'm sorry,' he says, putting the briefcase down by his feet.

'That's all right,' she says. She is extremely serious, forgiving him. She sits down and gets out sheaves of papers, a laptop computer. She begins to type rapidly with her varnished fingernails.

Money is a representation – strictly speaking, it has no authenticity. It may be that the value of a thing decreases in proportion to the power of money to represent it. The girl beside him is wearing a diamond ring on her wedding finger, in a big gold setting. The diamond is worth a lot of money. Yet it has less value than almost anything Thomas can think of. If that girl lost her finger, it would upset her far more than losing her diamond. But her finger isn't worth anything at all.

All the same, there is danger in a life that is of high value but little worth. There is a vulnerability that comes with the absence of representation. That girl's ring represents the fact that she is loved. But the things that Thomas has lost he has no proof of. He has nothing to show for himself, for the days that left no money-trace behind them but simply vanished, like the days of an unrecorded civilisation. He looks out of the window at the passing countryside. He wonders whether Tonie felt this once; whether she sat on this train, a year ago, and pondered the life that had vanished like smoke behind her, its love and its hours, its uncommemorated emotions. And then coming back to find Thomas in the space where she used to be, like returning to a childhood home and finding new people living there. Thus he returns to Tonie at the day's end, and finds her intimate with what no longer belongs to him. He has noticed that Tonie tidies around the piano with particular care, dusting the closed lid, making tiny adjustments to the already orderly stacks of music books. He does not play the piano any more. Sometimes she puts flowers in a vase on the top. He sees them and laughs. It is ghoulishly touching, like the sight of a well-tended grave.

On the evening train he falls asleep, his cheek pressed against the glass. It is September, and still light. He walks home from the station. He thinks of what will happen when he gets there. Usually Tonie is solicitous of him in the evenings. She fusses around him and talks animatedly. In the mornings she is more silent, slightly rigid. It is as though she has to make it up in its entirety every day, the story of her love for him. In the morning the page is blank. He sees her watching Alexa with red-rimmed eyes that nonetheless are dry, her manner devotional and slightly shrill. Tonie has never asked him to account for what he did the day Alexa got ill, just as he has never asked her where she was that evening. There has been an exchange of territories, ratified by a treaty of silence. She did not return to work, not even for a day. She donned the plain garment of motherhood, there in the hospital. She was alone when they told her that Alexa had lost the hearing in her right ear. She had sent Thomas home to sleep, to make arrangements, to be male again. Perhaps she has forgotten that he was ever there at all.

Sometimes, in the evenings, they look at one another with eyes that seem to Thomas to be full of guilt. These looks are accidental: their roaming eyes meet, surprised, and for an instant something new discloses itself, a new separation between them, as though they are strangers whose eyes are meeting for the first time. The guilt is the guilt of experience, which only strangers admit to one another. Yet quite what they are guilty of they will never say.

Montague Street is quiet, almost silent. He walks up the pavement with his briefcase in one hand and his keys in the other. The road is silted with fallen leaves. The air is still. There is no movement, no sound. He himself has become soundless, his feet weightless on the pavement, his breath paused, the keys mute in his hand. The silence swells and swells, thick and blank. He stops and waits. At last it comes, the trill of a bird joyously piercing it, trilling and trilling, garlanding the still air with a ribbon of song.